Sampson's Ring

Trish Gomez

Key-Holder Publishing

Nashville, TN

This book is a work of fiction. The characters, circumstances, and events are solely the creation of the author's imagination. Any resemblance to actual events or persons, living or dead is entirely coincidental.

Copyright © 2013 Trish Gomez All rights reserved.
ISBN: 0615769969
ISBN-13: 978-0615769967

www.sampsonsring.com

Thank you to Derri Smith with End Slavery Tennessee for your support, encouragement and information, to Nina and John McCormick, and Michael Gomez for believing in me.

One

AS THE SWEAT poured down her legs, it formed a glue that bonded her jeans to her thighs. The saltwater beads falling from her brow ran her make-up. And the humidity turned her perfectly straightened hair into a frizzy mess. The hot, wet air was so oppressive at 7:00 am that Stephanie felt as if her breath was being sucked out of her. The man on TV said that the "feels like" temperature was 95 degrees this Monday morning and was expected to reach 110 degrees by late afternoon. For Stephanie Miller, the walk to the bus stop on her first day of high school was the fitting beginning of her journey to hell.

The day had started out well. Stephanie was up and showered by 5:30 am. She looked great in her new outfit, and her new mascara lengthened and plumped just as promised on the package. She had practiced her smile a million times in the mirror and decided she was ready. *If* she were lucky, she thought, as she walked down the stairs to the front door, she just might blend in.

"It's gonna be a good day, Steph. I know it." Her mother tried to console her with a kiss as she headed for the door.

She pulled away from her mother's grasp.

"Mom, just leave me alone." And with that, Stephanie left her house and ventured off on her first day at her new school in her new town.

But the day had been ruined before it had even started. Stephanie would argue that her life had been ruined the day her parents had made the decision to move the family 1,000 miles from their home and plant themselves in the middle of nowhere. 'Who's even heard of Franklin, TN?' Stephanie thought. 'It's a stuck-up suburb of Country Music USA. YeHaw!' Stephanie hated country music. She hated Franklin, TN. And she hated her parents for ripping her away from her life in Philadelphia at the beginning of her freshman year of high school.

There were three other kids at the bus stop. She hadn't met any of them yet. The two girls at the corner watched Stephanie approach and averted their eyes as she came within talking distance.

'Whatever' Stephanie thought. She expected as much from the stuck-up suburbs.

The boy stood on the other side of the street, and watched her as well. He was tall and thin, with red hair, freckles, and a lot of acne. He was wearing black basketball shorts and a red compression shirt which accentuated his lanky frame and brought out the orange in his hair. 'Red is definitely not his color', she thought, as she walked towards him.

"Hi." Stephanie had nothing to lose.

"Hi, my name is Donald. Donald Strickland. I live in the yellow house right there." Donald pointed to a ranch house with yellow siding, white trim, and a pretty rose garden surrounding a fountain in the front yard.

"Where's your picket fence?" Stephanie mocked, but Donald didn't notice.

"Oh, well, my mom voted for it, but my dad said no. We just did the floors in our entire house, and dad says that it cost him an arm and a leg. Mom says it was just his right arm and his left toe." Donald began to snort with laughter.

He continued to share with Stephanie the details of his parents renovations beginning with the kitchen, which included granite countertops, glass tile back splash, and a pot filler sink. His father thought the pot filler sink was a little over the top. Donald's incessant rambling continued for what seemed like hours, despite Stephanie's obvious lack of interest. She was about to feign heat stroke when her ride appeared.

It was a baby blue convertible 1957 Chevy. Stephanie had never seen anything like its long fins, real chrome, and white leather interior. The car was beautiful, the driver amazing. He was tall; at least he looked tall sitting in the driver's side of the pristine antique car. He had brown hair, a strong, prominent jawline, bright green eyes, and a tan that looked Caribbean. He also had a friend, just as good looking. They pulled up right beside Stephanie, and gave her a nod. She nodded back.

"Hey." The driver looked right into Stephanie's eyes.

"Hey." She was even more aware of the sweat-glue on her thighs.

"You're new, aren't you?"

The driver was looking her up and down. She should be used to this kind of attention. At only 14 years old, Stephanie Miller was already 5'10" tall, with wavy blond hair, blue eyes, and naturally red lips. Her friends back home were jealous of her model looks, but here, at this point in time, Stephanie felt conspicuously gawky and out of place.

"Yeah." She tried her best to appear confident.

The driver leaned towards her and motioned her to do the same. Stephanie leaned her head closer to him, and smelled his cologne. It was clean and fresh. She liked it.

"Why don't you ditch the snobs and the dork and come on with us. I'll give you a ride."

"You're going to West Franklin High?" Stephanie was looking for a way to back out, she was nervous about getting in the car with boys she didn't know.

"Where else? C'mon, hop in."

'Screw my parents', she thought. It's their fault she was here. Why should she care what they thought?

"Why not."

The driver's friend got out of the car and held the door open for Stephanie. He winked at her as she smiled at him and climbed into the back seat.

"I'm Stephanie." She said to the two as they pulled away from the curb.

"We know." The driver replied.

Two

JULES SPALDING had an uneasy feeling as she traveled down Highway 96. She couldn't help but sense that someone was following her. She told herself to stop being paranoid. But as she rounded the corner and headed into the Five Points district, the tan Mercedes SUV continued, two cars behind. It wasn't hard to miss. It was the same SUV she had seen as she left her neighborhood in Bellevue, 10 miles back. Coincidence? As she pulled into the 4th street parking garage the Mercedes continued south. Maybe, but Jules wasn't convinced.

"Jules, you look like you've just seen a ghost, are you ok?" Monica Perry was Jules' best friend. The two had grown up together, roomed together in college, and planned to grow old together. Monica was the one constant in Jules' life.

"I saw another car today, Mon, this time a Mercedes SUV. It followed me from my neighborhood all the way downtown. I'm really starting to think he's stalking me!"

"He" is Richard Sampson, the former business partner of Jules' husband, Mitch Spalding. Mitch and Sampson had had an ugly falling out just over a year ago that ended with vicious threats and lawsuits. The ultimate fate of ownership was in the hands of the Davidson County Circuit Court. Jules was convinced Sampson would stop at nothing to win.

"Jules, I really think you're overreacting, I mean, this is all sounding too much like a made-for-tv-movie!"

That was funny, Jules thought, because Monica was usually the one full of drama. Jules had always been the practical one, the sensible one, and the rational one. Monica on the other hand, became hysterical at the sight of a spider, was continually suspicious her husband was a cheater, and was voted 'The One Most Likely to Chew Out a Waiter for Screwing Up Her Order' in high school.

Monica was so angry at the yearbook committee for printing that superlative that she ransacked the yearbook office and spray painted "Fascist Propaganda!" all over the walls. Ironically, her reputation saved her in the end. In past years, Northern Virginia Senior High had dealt with end of the year vandals by delaying graduation and sending them through summer school. But by this time, the principal and administrators of NVSH had had enough of Monica Atwood, and overlooked the infraction.

The story always made Jules laugh. Her best friend was a piece of work. Jules always felt that Monica needed Jules to stay close to the ground. But today, the tables were turned.

Jules took off her coat and scarf, placed them on the back of the chair, and sat down at the table across from Monica in their favorite coffee shop, The Grind. The two met every Wednesday at 9 am. It was the highlight of Jules' week and she often marked Wednesday mornings on her calendar as 'group therapy'.

"Monica, this is the third time this week. Yesterday there was a red minivan parked across the street from the house for two hours. I called Wendy at work and she had no idea who it might be. She and Jack didn't know anyone with a red minivan. Just as I was about to call the police, the car moved. I couldn't see who was driving, the windows were tinted dark. And Sunday I noticed the same tan SUV I saw today, following us home from church. From church!!!"

"Jules, I'm sure these are just coincidences. You know how many people from your neighborhood go to your church.

And the minivan? How do you know the driver wasn't visiting Meg and the kids next door? Have you checked with her?"

"No, I hadn't thought about that actually. But Mon, I just have this feeling, an intuition."

"Intuition? Ok. Like your intuition that Beanie Babies were good investments, or that Brian Hopper liked me in the 10th grade?"

"Shut up!" But finally Jules laughed. For a moment she was back in high school, reliving the hysterical times she had with Monica. It felt good to laugh for a minute, but the reality of this morning was still present. She was afraid of Richard Sampson.

"You sound like Mitch", Jules said bitterly. Her husband Mitch thought she was crazy and was ready to send her out for real therapy.

He had chided her many times. "Sampson's bark is much bigger than his bite, Jules. He thinks he's a tough guy, but really he's just a coward, hiding behind empty threats and lots of money. He's harmless and you're making a much bigger deal out of this than is necessary. I'm telling you, you need to let this go or you're going to have a nervous break-down!"

Perhaps Mitch and Monica were both right, but today, she had a terribly uneasy feeling. And it was getting old. For the past year, the anger and frustration had become an ugly distraction. Then the threats started. An email, a voice mail, and then the stalker. Jules would love to believe they were harmless and empty- Sampson's last ditch efforts to remain the alpha. But what she wanted most was to shake this new feeling of disappointment in the human race.

Jules had always been an optimist. She preferred to look at the sunny side of life chose to believe the best in people. She had been accused of being naive, but Jules knew the power of expectations. When she looked at another person with anticipation of good, they never failed her. Until now. And her outlook was fading fast.

Monica changed the subject. "I think you just need a vacation. Eight months in that house and you really need to get out of town for a while. Why don't you and Mitch spend a weekend at the lake, my treat? I'll even take the kids for you."

Now that was a proposition Jules could not resist. Monica and Douglas' retreat house on Old Hickory Lake was a vacation destination. Yes, she did need some time off, and so did Mitch. Her weekly therapy session was already starting to work.

THE SCREAMS woke him. He was disoriented. It was dark. The air was hot and stale. The voices were in Spanish, but he could not understand. They were muffled and frantic. He couldn't tell how long it continued. There were no clocks, no windows in the room to let in light. He did not know if it was night or day. He only heard screams. And they seemed to go on endlessly.

When the door opened, a flood of light invaded the tiny space. As his eyes adjusted, Richard Sampson saw that he was in a small room, about 8 feet by 10 feet, on a military cot. There was a table by the bed with a lamp. Otherwise, the room was bare. A young girl, in her early teens maybe, was waiting in the doorway.

"It's time for breakfast, come."

Richard stood on shaky legs and followed the girl out into a lit hallway. He was led down a long corridor, then up a flight of steep stairs. And then he remembered.

"Richard?"

Jenny's voice woke him. He had fallen asleep in the recliner with a newspaper in his lap and a beer can wedged between his leg and the arm of the chair.

"Richard, you were talking in your sleep. You were calling her name again. Do you want your medicine?"

"No Jenny, just dreaming. Did you need something?" Richard Sampson abruptly changed the subject.

"This came for you today." Jenny Sampson handed her husband a large envelope.

He sighed as he looked at the return address, Davidson County Circuit Court. Richard Sampson got out of his chair and threw the envelope in the trash on his way out of the room.

ELIANA HAD studied hard for her math test. She would be the first in her family to finish school and get a job outside of Santa Lucía Cotzumalguapa. Farming was hard work for her mother, who earned around five dollars a day, and the food shortage left her baby brother bloated and lethargic. Eliana sustained herself on the bits of sugar cane her mother smuggled home from the fields in her aprons and scraps of old bread she found in the dumpster behind the local bakery. She needed her energy for her studies.

Eliana sat under a tree during her recreation period. She thought she did well on her test, but reflected on each question one by one.

"Excuse me young lady..." Eliana opened her eyes to find two well dressed women standing over her.

"Yes?" Eliana was polite.

"My name is Anna Sophia, and this is Mariana. We are from Guatemala City. We have business opportunities for promising young women, and your teacher, Señora Reyes recommended you personally. We'd like to talk with you about a job."

Eliana's eyes grew wide. She was cautiously curious. "A job?"

"Yes, we are working with an American business interested in helping young Latin American women like yourself. We start you in an entry level position and help you work towards owning your own business."

"What kind of business?" Eliana tried to contain her excitement, not wanting to appear too eager, but this seemed like the opportunity she'd been waiting for.

"We specialize in hospitality. Hotels, restaurants, and nightclubs. We send our trainees all over the United States, from Houston, to Detroit, to Nashville."

"Nashville, TN?" Eliana's father used to talk to her about Nashville, about the country music legends like Little Jimmy Dickens, Bill Anderson, and Johnny Cash. When he would return from the fields, Eliana loved to watch him play his records and dance with her mama to the sounds of steel guitar and southern twang. That was before the accident.

"That's right, Eliana. You could be earning enough money to support your entire family, in Nashville, TN, before you know it. We would love for you to join us." Mariana was smiling at her. Eliana thought she looked like an angel. Her guardian angel.

Three

THE DRIVE out to the lake was just over an hour. It had been a long time since Jules and Mitch had had some real quality time alone together. They had spent the last eight months living in the top apartment of his mother's home. After the business split, the Spaldings were broke. They had put every penny into the business. It had been Mitch's dream. Jules was reflecting on the events of the last couple of years as Mitch drove in silence.

For 15 years, Mitch Spalding had been a successful real estate broker, one of the best in his district, and he and Jules had grown accustomed to the good life. Five years ago they found a 15 acre piece of land right in the heart of their own community. Franklin, TN was a swiftly growing suburb of Nashville, but amidst the subdivisions lied pockets of land still untouched by developers. The Spalding's 5,000 square foot custom built home sat in the heart of one of these rural islands, a mile from the river, surrounded by horse farms, yet less than five miles from the civilization of the suburbs.

Shortly after, the real estate bubble burst, and with that the good life devolved into a daily struggle to stay afloat. Amidst mounting debt and late mortgage payments, Jules decided to go to work.

Jules began her own personal training business the fall of 2009. This was something she'd dreamt of doing since college. Almost two decades and four kids later, she decided it was now or never. It was a slow beginning, but she knew that if she put the energy back into her passion it would eventually pay off. Not in time, unfortunately, to save their home.

Losing everything gave Mitch a new perspective in life. Humility, empathy, and a feeling of connectedness with others changed him. Mitch's heart for the troubled and helpless grew the months following his foreclosure. After experiencing a seventy-five percent cut in his income, Mitch understood the fear, uncertainty, and stress of trying to care for a family in troubled times. He was thinking about this one winter day as he was making the rounds.

'Making the rounds' was his weekly practice of scouring the city for abandoned warehouses, old manufacturing plants, and dilapidated business offices. He was a wiz at connecting entrepreneurs with the right location for their businesses, and ten years ago he obtained his commercial real estate license. Ten years ago, investors and venture capitalists lined the blocks looking for opportunities. Today, the average small business owner had a better chance of being struck by lightning than finding financing.

His idea for The Office came that cold day. He was driving through the industrial area when he noticed a group of homeless men working together to construct a shelter in an abandoned parking lot. He pulled over and watched in awe as these men helped each other help themselves. Community- a group of individuals, all helping each other to meet their needs. Mitch marveled at the concept, as old a Jesus Christ, but seldom seen in today's business world. And that day, the concept for The Office was born.

"I've gone over the numbers five times, Jules. Once we fill all of the offices, account for overhead expenses, marketing, and legal fee, we should be able to establish a base profit of $50,000 a year in the first quarter."

Mitch had made a replica of the building out of a shoe box, toothpicks, and extra cardboard. To Jules, it looked like her fifth grader's diorama of a Japanese apartment.

"Add conference room rentals, special event hosting and special training seminars and we can easily grow to six figures in the first twenty-four months. I'm telling you Jules, this place has so much potential. I'm even looking into corporate sponsorships for our mentorship program."

He uses his pencil to point to each area of The Office.

"Just imagine, Jules. Here we have the Tennessee Titans West Wing, and over here, the Bell South Conference Room, and right here- the Nashville Symphony Fountain!"

Mitch was packing his notes into his brief case. "I have a meeting with Richard Sampson tomorrow."

"Richard who?"

Mitch had introduced Jules to so many colleagues over the years she couldn't keep them straight. And up until recently, she was usually distracted by one or two babies on her hip or at her heals that she'd forget their names almost immediately.

"Sampson, from the entrepreneurship group meetings I've been attending. I think I told you about him. He's an interesting guy. He owns several businesses in Nashville. He's a millionaire, but he started with nothing. He's going to let me pick his brain. I just know there's a way to do this, and I'm not giving up."

Richard Sampson was a smart man, 'brilliant at business', is how he described himself. His finest skill was recognizing the potential in an idea. He saw the potential in The Office immediately. He had heard about entrepreneurial centers, incubators, and other small business starters, but Nashville had not seen any of its kind.

Mitch had grasped on to a need in this city. A need for an affordable way to start a business, providing a space and support services, with limited overhead. It made perfect sense, and as Mitch poured over the details of his plan, Sampson realized the potential was far beyond even what Mitch could comprehend. Sampson's interest was peaked.

"I just don't know how to raise the capital, Dick. That's where my creativity ends. How does someone like me, in my situation, find the resources to start something like this?"

"Seems to me what you really need is the right partner, Mitch."

"Partner? I don't know, I've never really thought of that before. I'm not sure I'd really want to work with someone else. I mean, this is my project, my idea, my dream. I hate to sound like a spoiled child, but I don't think I'd like the idea of having to cooperate with someone else."

"Well that's what I mean by the *right* partner. Really, in my experience, the only good partner is a silent one. You need someone who can provide the financial resources in exchange for a cut in the profits. Someone who believes in what you are doing, sees the potential, and will let you run the business how you would run the business."

"A cut in the profits, eh? According to my calculations I could get this business off to a decent start in the first year, but if I had to share the profits it would be 3-4 years before we'd possibly take in enough revenue to support two owners!"

"Now see Mitch, this is why you came to me. You are far too near sighted. You don't look past the obvious when it comes to business. This will always keep you running at mediocre. What you need is a smart business partner who can think outside the box. You have a fantastic idea here. But there is so much more potential you haven't even recognized. The right partner is one who knows how to make money- and you need that more than anything else, my friend."

"You think The Office has more potential than everything I've laid out here tonight?" Mitch was starting to listen.

"Absolutely! I'll tell you what, give me a few days, I want to work with the ideas in my head, I may have just the right guy for you."

Within six months The Office was up and running. Eight young entrepreneurs sharing one large warehouse building, starting eight new businesses. Mitch was ecstatic. He was actually living out his dream of making a living helping others. He couldn't have done it without the help of his business partner, Richard Sampson.

Sampson was the silent partner. The one with the resources. With Mitch's vision and Sampson's money, The Office was a success even before it officially began. By the time The Office opened its doors on July 10, 2011, Mitch and Sampson had filled the offices to capacity and had a waiting list for six more clients. Mitch's vision was perfect except for one small detail, his partner. By September 10, 2011 Mitch and Sampson had split. It was a bitter, ugly separation, and a year later both parties were still in the middle of a nasty legal battle.

With the loss of his business, Mitch found himself out of work and looking for sales. This was unfamiliar territory. Mitch had never had to advertise, his business had been strictly word of mouth. Together, Mitch and Jules began brainstorming and eventually came up with a few strategies that were beginning to pay off, and the real estate market was picking up a little. While he hadn't built up enough business to move out of his mother's house, he was starting to see an increase in his client list. And his bank account had finally crept out of the red.

Four

WHEN SHE HADN'T returned home that afternoon, Stephanie's mother called the school. She was informed that Stephanie had not reported to homeroom that morning.

"But I sent her off to the bus this morning at 6:30. I watched her walk to the bus stop. Can you check the rolls again, she was assigned to Mrs. Walker's classroom." Her mother was sure the school had made a mistake.

"Mrs. Miller, I'm sorry but I've checked the rolls three times, Stephanie did not make it to homeroom today, nor did she report to any of her other classes. You should have received a phone call from our attendance office alerting you of her absence."

Susan Miller glanced down at the receiver of her cordless phone and saw the red light blinking, indicating voice mail messages.

"Ok, thank you." She hung up and immediately checked her voice mail. Surely there'd be a message from Stephanie that explained everything. There wasn't. She put the cordless phone back in the receiver, feeling a bit stunned. Where could Stephanie have gone? She left the house angry, was it possible she ran away?

Susan called Stephanie's cell phone and it went straight to voice mail. She called it again, and again. Susan knew a fourth time would produce the same results, but she called it again. Then she left her daughter a message, "Please call me, I love you."

Susan pulled out her own cell phone and began retrieving phone numbers from her contacts. She called each one of Stephanie's friends in Philadelphia. None had talked with Stephanie today, and none were aware of any plans she had to go back to Pennsylvania. Next she called the bus station, to see if a girl matching her daughter's description had purchased a ticket to Philly. She kept telling herself not to panic. Finally, she called her husband.

Jeff Miller arrived home to find his wife arguing with someone on the phone. Tears were streaming down her face.

"No, officer, I'm sure she did not run away. I've spoken with all of her friends. She has just vanished. I'm telling you, she was on her way to the bus stop and just disappeared. Something has happened to her. Are you going to help me or not?"

After a long pause Susan hung up the phone. The tears came faster now as she fell into her husband's arms.

"They won't do anything until she's been gone for 72 hours. They think she ran away. Oh my God, Jeff. She's only fourteen. Where do you think she could be?"

Jeff changed into a pair of jeans and a t-shirt and began canvassing the neighborhood. There were four teenage kids who lived on their block, three of whom went to West Franklin High. He only found one that was home and willing to talk, Donald Strickland.

"Yeah, I saw her. She left with the upperclassman." Donald's tone suggested he was perturbed. Stephanie had blown him off for older, popular boys.

"Upperclassman? What do you mean she left with them? Who are they? Did you know these guys?" Jeff was spewing out questions faster than Donald could comprehend.

Donald shrugged his shoulders. "I have no idea who they are. They looked like seniors. They came by in this fancy car, some kind of caddy, or something. It was a convertible. They offered her a ride to school and she got in with them."

Donald was a poor witness. He ID'd the car as a grey Cadillac convertible, old, he said, maybe a 1975, but he couldn't recall the plate numbers, or even if it was registered in Tennessee.

Jeff called the police as soon as he got home, but got the same runaround his wife received an hour earlier. His daughter was seen getting into the car of her own free will, there was no crime.

It was 8 pm by the time Jeff finished with the detective on the phone, and getting dark. Jeff went to the cupboard and found himself a bottle of scotch and poured himself a drink while Susan scoured Stephanie's room looking for a clue.

'What on Earth could she be thinking getting into that car? Who were those boys? I can't believe she would do something so stupid- I've told her a thousand times never to get in the car with strange boys.' Susan was punishing herself with answerless questions. She was filled with fear, confusion, and anger. Then she heard the front door open.

"Young lady, where the hell have you been?" Jeff's baritone voice echoed through the house. She smelled of cigarette smoke and alcohol, and her eyes looked dazed.

"Dad..." Stephanie slurred her words and looked at her father through half-closed eyes.

Susan took one look at her daughter and let out her famous "AAAAHHHHHHH! Oh my god have you been drinking? What on Earth have you been doing Stephanie? We were worried sick about you, and you're out partying? Who were those boys?"

Stephanie tried to talk again, but was unable to form an audible word.

"You know what, forget it Susan, it's not worth it, not tonight." Jeff was angry. He had tried to make this move easier on everyone, but he didn't have a choice, he needed this job. Stephanie had pissed and moaned every day for the past six months about the move. He was tired of it. Tired of her selfish attitude. He had worked his ass off for his family and was doing the best he could. And now, she repays him by the sneaking out, drinking and messing around with boys. He'd had enough.

"Stephanie, go to bed, we'll talk about this in the morning. But I'm telling you right now, you're grounded for the next month."

Stephanie looked at her mother with eyes that pleaded for help. A tear fell down her cheek. But her mother had had enough as well.

"You heard your dad. You've put us through enough misery for one day. Goodnight."

Stephanie began to sob as she shuffled down the hall. She had to keep a hand on the wall to steady herself. She turned into the bedroom and shut the door. Her body was tired, she hurt, and she was bleeding. She made her way to the bathroom and began to take off her clothes. She forced herself to look in the mirror. The bite marks on her breasts were turning purple, and the cigarette burns on her abdomen were starting to ooze. She climbed into the shower and watched the water turn red as it ran down her legs. Stephanie Miller hated the stuck-up suburbs.

Five

WHEN THEY arrived at 1023 Hilltop Road, Mitch pulled their Suburban into the long drive to the Perry's lakeside retreat, a 5,000 square foot log cabin nestled on three acres of waterfront property. The cabin was surrounded by an acre of open land that crept into a small forrest of trees. A wrap-around deck skirted the cabin, looking out onto the water. The back of the cabin opened up to a rock patio, outdoor kitchen, and fireplace. It was the ultimate party place.

A long pier led out to the boat dock, where all the real fun happened. Having grown up on the water, Jules missed spending her summers boating, skiing, and listening to the crash of the waves. Her lifelong dream had been to have her own waterfront property. For now, she has the luxury of using someone else's.

"Ok, rule number one- no cell phones!" Jules pulled the phone from Mitch's hand just as he was about to call the Johnstons.

"Jules, I really need to set up a meeting with Paul about the open house. How about a deal? I'll take care of this, and then agree to hang it up for the next twenty-four hours." Mitch Spalding was a consummate negotiator.

"Forty-eight"- Jules knew this game.

"Thirty-six" - Mitch was as stubborn as an ass.

"Ok, thirty-six. But if I catch you cheating on me, I'll throw it in the lake!"

Mitch gave her the thumbs up as he was already talking with Paul Johnston. He knew she was serious. Jules Spalding was ruthless when she wanted to be.

Jules finished unpacking the suitcases while Mitch finished his business. She put all of their clothes in the dresser, unpacked the toiletries in the bathroom, and pulled out a bottle of 1995 Navy Creek Merlot. This was the same year and vintage the two had shared on the night Mitch proposed. It took Jules several days and a good part of her meager savings to lay her hands on one.

There was a knock at the door just as Jules made her way into the kitchen. Odd, she thought, this was the off season and Monica told her that the neighbors would not be around.

"Monica and Douglas sent us a pizza!" Mitch came into the kitchen armed with the biggest and most amazing smelling Guido's pizza Jules had ever seen. She had given up pizza, among other things, in an attempt to keep up with the younger trainers at the gym. It had been six months. She wasn't sure whether to curse Monica, or give her a big fat hug!

"Well it will go great with this....." Jules handed Mitch a glass and held up the bottle of merlot.

"Navy Creek?" His eyes softened. Can you believe it's been fifteen years?" Mitch pulled Jules close, and suddenly she felt like she was twenty five again. The pizza would have to wait.

JULES WOKE at 2:00 am starving, stumbling and fumbling her way through the dark hall to the kitchen. She puled the pizza out of the fridge, took a slice and heated it in the oven. The first bite was like heaven. This was already a fantastic weekend.

She re-filled her wine glass, grabbed a blanket and headed out for the back patio. Douglas and Monica had thought of everything, even an outdoor wood burning fireplace with a gas starter. One push of a button and Jules was lounging beneath the stars next to a warm fire, drinking a fine glass of wine and dreaming of her future.

The quiet stillness of the night gave Jules perspective. It was tough living in her mother-in-laws' house. She felt the constant gnawing and yearning for her own home, and the discouragement in knowing that she would not have it for some time to come. With a foreclosure and a bankruptcy on her credit, it would be years before they would be able to qualify for a loan, and who knows when they would even be able to afford one.

She felt like a failure at forty years old, to be living in someone else's house- especially a parent's house. At this point in her life she should be enjoying a successful career, taking her children to karate, and vacationing in the Bahamas.

These thoughts seemed to crowd her days lately, and Mitch was beginning to worry she was depressed. It was beginning to affect her ability to work, and days would go by as she seemed lifeless, no passion, no purpose.

But out here in the middle of these woods in the cool night air she felt energized. She felt alive, and most of all she felt grateful. Suddenly she realized just how lucky she was to have a warm safe place to live, and a family that loved her. Few marriages could have survived what Jules and Mitch had been through in the last year, but today, they were stronger than ever. They were different people now. They both looked at the world differently, with more compassion, more love. She felt optimistic. Jules began to cry at the thought.

THE FIRST crack sounded like it was coming from somewhere out in left field. That is of course, if they were on a baseball field. The manicured lawn of the cabin would have ended just past the perimeter of the bases. At that point, the property was filled with tall grasses, brush and shrubs, and continued into a thick, wooded forrest. It sounded as if something was moving just past the point of visibility. Something large.

Dog ears, Mitch called them. Jules' sense of hearing was incredible. *All* of her senses were heightened, as a matter of fact. 'Hypersensitive' is what she had been called by her doctor. "Makes me sound like a petty school girl!" She told Mitch.

Jules' sense of smell was both a help and a hindrance. She always knew when her son was playing with matches, even from the other end of the house. But she also got headaches from her daughter's perfume and couldn't stand sleeping next to her husband after a night of cigars with the boys.

Tonight though, it was her ears that perked up. The sound came from about one hundred yards away. It was too big for a raccoon or coyote. It sounded like a person. Several footsteps at first, but when she sat up and took notice the footsteps stopped. Her heart pounded out of her chest and it felt as if she'd never gain control of her breath. Nothing.

She sat back in the recliner and took a deep breath. Something was out there, watching her. The moon was full tonight, she knew she was in plain sight. She closed her eyes, pretending to drift off, and waited. Nothing.

Then a stick breaking. Nothing. Seconds passed that felt like hours. Nothing. Still, her heart was racing but she took deep breaths. Slow, deep breaths. Nothing.

Jules opened her eyes and looked around. Getting out of her chair she went to the cabinets under the grill top, trying to appear casual. Inside she found the large black flashlight Douglas kept on the top shelf. As she walked out towards the woods her mind drifted back, she was in the sixth grade, cuddled up on the hideaway bed with Sharon and Erica watching the original Halloween.

"This one's the brave girl," Erica announced- referring to Jaime Lee Curtis' character. She had seen the movie before and felt the need to narrate. "There's always a brave girl in horror movies, they're the ones who go and investigate."

'I don't feel so brave now' Jules thought to herself. 'More like an idiot!'

As she walked toward the direction of the sound she suddenly heard a scuffle, and the sound of running through the dry leaves, sticks, and brush. She followed the direction of the sound but it was getting further and further away. He was faster than she was.

Several times she nearly lost her footing on vines and broken logs. This was unfamiliar terrane. The cracking and shuffling of leaves continued for another few minutes. She followed the sound like a trained hound dog following the scent of a fox. Scanning the flashlight she saw only woods. She kept running, following the sounds. Then the sounds stopped abruptly. She stopped and scanned. Nothing.

Six

"MORNING SUNSHINE!" Mitch exclaimed as he kissed Jules on the forehead and handed her a cup of coffee.

"Morning..." Jules replied, dazed and confused. It took her a minute or two to realize where she was. The sun was falling in through the sliding glass doors and through the glass she could see the water outside. It was absolutely beautiful. She glanced at the clock, it was 11:00 am.

Mitch left her with her coffee and her favorite magazine, opened the sliding glass door slightly to let in some fresh air, and went to the kitchen.

This was her favorite time of day. At home she would wake early, before everyone else, just to have some quiet time. A cup of coffee and her daily devotional- something she had been lax about lately. For the past six months or so she found herself sleeping as late as possible, and then moaning and groaning about having to get up. She missed the comfort of her own couch, her own living room.

This morning though, everything was perfect. The cool breeze, the sun, a good nights sleep. She felt completely refreshed. And then she remembered her visitor.

The thought of the early morning events sent chills up her spine. She closed her eyes and concentrated on her memories, trying to recall every detail. Was she dreaming? Was she drunk? Could it really have been a large squirrel, raccoon, a coyote even?

No, whatever she heard in those woods, whoever she heard in those woods was watching her. He, or she, or it, had run when she came to investigate. And then the sounds stopped as suddenly as they began. Who was out there and why? She was determined to find out.

"WHERE ARE YOU HEADED, ma'am?" She jumped as Mitch caught her heading outside, dressed in spandex and Nikes.

"I think I'll start with a run this morning. It's already 11:30, I need to get out of bed and move!"

"Give me a minute and I'll come with you." Mitch was already headed to the room to change.

"I think I need to take this one by myself- I won't be long." She kissed him and ran out the back door before he could object. She headed down the dirt driveway just far enough out of sight before heading into the woods. Mitch would never understand why she would be taking a run through the woods. She just wasn't ready to tell him about her early morning visitor. She had a feeling he wouldn't see things the same way.

She found her way to left field, her best guess of where the sounds originated. From there she had a clear view of the back patio, including the recliner in which she had sat much earlier that morning. The leaves had been falling for several weeks, and the woods were thin. Jules was sure whoever was out here could see her from this vantage point. He could also see clear into the cabin through the rear sliding glass doors. How long had he been watching?

She focused her eyes on the ground, and noticed broken twigs and disturbed brush. She felt like a TV CSI as she followed the newly broken trail through the woods. Around two hundred yards out, she came to a grassy clearing about a quarter of an acre square. Right in the center laid the remains of an old foundation. It must have been a tiny house, maybe a hunter's lodge, but it had obviously burned down many years ago. Evidence of decomposing charred wood lay around the broken cinderblock foundation. At the far right corner of the clearing Jules saw a large path. As she came closer she realized this was an old dirt and grass driveway. Fresh tire tracks lined the path.

Jules followed the driveway for approximately a quarter of a mile and found herself out on Hilltop Road, the main drag on this side of the lake. There was no mailbox for this property, no identifying markings of any kind. Just a small "No Trespassing" sign on the ground that looked as if it had been run over. Perhaps, by our early morning visitor. Jules took a left turn and proceeded to jog about a full mile before coming to the next driveway. This driveway was short, and she could see the small cabin from the road. An older man was outside, trimming the hedges.

"Excuse me. Hi, my name is Jules Spalding. I'm staying at the next cabin down the road." Jules pointed in the direction of Monica's place. "I heard some strange noises last night and I was wondering if you had heard or seen anything out of the ordinary?"

"I'm sorry Ma'am, I'm just the gardner. The Spencer's hire me to mind their property when they're gone. Is anything missing, or out of place?"

"Well no, and it was probably just an animal. We're not used to being out in middle of the woods like this." Jules said with a sheepish grin.

"In all of my sixty five years I ain't never had one report of a crime in these parts, ma'am. I'd say the critters are far more dangerous than the humans! You do want to keep your doors closed at night though. There've been a few cases where the 'coons have helped themselves to leftovers." As the gardener smiled, he revealed a wide gap in the front of his mouth where his two front teeth used to be. Jules had to stifle a giggle.

"Do you know anything about the next property over? It looks like there used to be a cabin there." She was not sure why she asked, but she wanted to know more about that place.

"That's the old Smithfield lodge. It burned down about twenty years ago. Old Doc Smithfield lived in Nashville and used to come down every weekend with his hunting buddies. Back then, half of these cabins weren't even built and those grounds were prime for hunting. The cabin burned down a few years before Doc died. His children own the land, but they live out of state. I wouldn't worry about those noises, probably just some critters."

"I'm sure that's just what it was. Thank you!" She excused herself and headed back on the road. She took note that the unmarked driveway was just a half mile from the driveway to Douglas and Monica's cabin.

"THIS IS gorgeous!" Being on the water always made Jules feel free. She loved the feel of the movement as the boat rocked gently along the wake of passing boats. She closed her eyes and bathed in the late fall sun. Growing up she loved spending time on her family's boat. On special weekends the Spencer family would pack it up and head out to sea.

In May they would travel up the Chesapeake Bay to Annapolis to watch the Blue Angels, the Navy's tactical fighter pilots, fly over the Naval Academy. On the Fourth of July, six families from her home town would caravan to Baltimore to see the fireworks. Jules loved watching fireworks from the water. When she watched the reflection on the water, she fantasized that there were hundreds of mermaids dancing an underwater ballet.

Once every summer, usually just before school started, these same six families would spend a weekend moored off of

Davenport Island, a small "double decker", uninhabited island about a mile off shore. The kids called it double decker because it had a small, narrow beach flanked by a cliff. Over the years people had carved out pathways up the cliffs. One side of the island looked like a giant rock wall. Only back then they didn't have rock walls, only double decker islands, and the very ambitious would climb their way to the top. On the other side of the island, a very narrow path was cut on the side of the cliff. The hundred yard ascent felt like miles as the kids sidestepped, their backs to the cliff, up to the grassy meadow above.

When Jules was young, going to Davenport Island felt like being in an episode of Gilligan's Island. The top of the island, while only about an acre in size, contained a large forrest (or jungle, in Jules' day), surrounded be a small meadow. Deep in the middle of the woods was a small pond. On most days the pond was dry, but after a few good rains, the pond became the "survivors" only water source.

As Jules grew older, the upper deck of the island took on a different role. This was the place where she first kissed Matt Jorgensen, her eighth grade sweetheart.

"You must really be enjoying yourself! " Mitch smirked.

"You just caught me daydreaming about you." Jules smiled at Mitch. Mitch actually reminded her of Matt. The blond hair and blue eyes, wavy hair and the big wide smile. That smile is what hooked Jules.

"Thank you for this. You really thought of everything! What a perfect way to spend the day." Jules leaned over and kissed Mitch on the forehead. He had planned the perfect surprise. When she had emerged from her post-run shower she found Mitch waiting with picnic basket, champagne, and a duffel full of supplies for a day on the lake.

They spent the afternoon exploring Old Hickory Lake, gawking at the massive lake-front mansions, dreaming about their own future lakeside retreat. Mitch took a turn at waterskiing, but Jules found the cold water much too uninhabitable this late in fall.

As evening began to settle in, Mitch docked the boat at the marina for dinner.

Harper's Walleye was named for the famed Mabry Harper, the Fresh Water Fishing Hall of Fame's World Record holder for catching the largest Walleye, right here on Old Hickory Lake in 1960. A controversial character, Mabry was stripped of his title in 1996 when a magazine reporter contested the reported size of Mabry's fish- a whopping twenty five pounds and forty one inches. The author contended that based on photographic analysis the fish could not have been that long. After the Tennessee Historical Society presented key evidence, pictures, and a signed affidavit from a Tennessee Game Warden verifying the size and weight, Harper was reinstated as the 'All Tackle World Record' holder. To this day, many fishermen throughout the country resent the reinstatement.

Proprietor Hollings Bentworth is not one of them. He knew Harper well. His father had been fishing buddies with Harper and frequently took Hollings along. Hollings was there that day "the fish" was caught, and was instantly smitten with the sport. "You learn to fish, and you'll never go hungry!" Harper told Bentworth, and he took those words to heart. He became a master fisherman by the time he was twenty one. Bentworth's other passion was cooking, and over the years he created a large repertoire of signature dishes. He opened Harper's Walleye at the age of 45, at the request of neighbors and friends who couldn't get enough.

Harper's Walleye was best known for its Stuffed Flounder and Parmesan Crusted Halibut, but the Deep Fried Walleye was 'to die for', according to the Hendersonville Gazette's food editor, and the Nashville Scene gave Harper's Walleye the "Best Of Seafood" award. Jules had just finished reading the story on the front page of the menu as Mitch cleared his throat.

"I talked with Sam today. We're not getting anywhere with the request for production. We're still waiting, and we can't prepare for the deposition without that information."

"How can he get away with ignoring the legal process?" Jules didn't really want to talk about this now, but once the topic was started she couldn't help herself. Mitch had made several requests for the production of documents, including the partnership agreements, several other legal papers, and all accounting records during the preparation for and operation of The Office. Sampson has ignored each request.

"We are going to have to petition the court to order the documents. That will compel Sampson to hand them over within thirty days of receipt. Sam will file that on Monday."

This is exactly what Jules had been dreading- progress. It's not that she didn't want to go through with the lawsuit. Sampson had lied, cheated, and tried to steal everything from Mitch, and he had used Jules to do it. Worse still, he had threatened them. He had threatened their family. Sampson was a bully and he needed to be stopped. Rumor had it this was not the first time he'd done this to a "business partner". She used the term lightly, as Richard Sampson seemed to have no respect for the word partner.

But moving forward with the lawsuit meant facing it. Until this point she could go on with her life, enjoy the progress she and Mitch were having, and live relatively stress free. Depositions, interrogatories, litigation- it dug up bad memories. It brought tension and stress back into their lives, their marriage. Just the mention of Sampson's name caused Mitch to tighten his jaw, furrow his brow. Jules didn't like what the thought of that man did to Mitch, or herself. The resentment, the anger and hatred toward another, these were feelings Jules was not used to, yet she wasn't ready to let them go. And that's what really disturbed her. She ordered another beer as they discussed their plans. It was going to be a long night.

Seven

STEPHANIE FELT like a total freak at school. Her eyes were bloodshot, and her head was pounding. Sitting was painful. And the memory of yesterday distracted her from Algebra and Biology. She begged her mother to let her stay home but her mother refused.

Her teachers had already labeled her a troublemaker, and the girls at school looked at her like she wore a large red A across her chest. Stephanie felt sure the other kids knew her secret, and were laughing.

At lunch Stephanie took a seat by herself, towards the back of the cafeteria. She didn't want to talk to anybody. She kept her head down and picked at her food. She didn't feel like eating. 'Sucky snotty suburbs', she thought. 'They probably all know and think its funny.' Stephanie looked up and saw two girls looking her way and whispering. She put her head back down into her beefaroni.

She didn't hear him coming, and jumped when he sat down across the table from her. It was him, the driver. She thought she had heard someone call him Tony, but she wasn't sure. He never gave her his name while he was raping her.

Tony placed an 8 X 10 envelope on the table and slid it over to her.

"What's this?" She asked, but she couldn't look him in the eye.

"Just a souvenir." Stephanie looked up at him curiously, and he winked at her. Then he stood and strolled away.

Stephanie looked all around to make sure no one was watching. When she was satisfied, she turned the envelope over and ripped open the seal. Stephanie peaked in the envelope and saw what looked like a color photograph. She slid the photograph out of the envelope just enough to reveal the grotesque image in front of her, a horrid reminder of the day before. She flipped the photo over quickly so no one else would see, and on the back of the picture were the words, "SHHHHH Steph. I won't tell if you won't."

Stephanie slid the photo back into the envelope and resealed the opening. She was stunned. She could not think. She did not want to remember those ten hours and God knows how many men. At least the drugs had helped her lose track of time.

THE DOG WAS barking hysterically as Mitch pulled into the driveway.

"What is wrong with her? I swear she's been so overly protective the past few months. The poor delivery man won't even come past the driveway anymore- he's afraid she'll eat him!" The Spalding's German shepherd, Sophie was an amazingly smart dog. Mitch had trained her well. She was also gentle, and would never hurt a fly- having been raised with four small, unruly children. She had endured make-overs by the oldest, Claire, taken Ian for elephant rides around the dining room table, and tucked Conner into bed every night. Most guests were greeted with wags and nudges- invitations for a back scratching. But lately, six year old Sophie treated everyone arriving to the Spalding house with the suspicious glare of the US Border Patrol.

"Welcome Home!" Carolyn Spalding whispered as she opened the door for Jules and Mitch. Mitch's mother was an amazing woman. She had raised eight children, buried two, and survived a nasty divorce. Now, she was hosting her middle-aged son and his family of six, and she welcomed them with open arms. No stranger to troubles, Carolyn understood the pain her son was going through, and took him in without judgement or conditions. Jules found this woman to be an inspirational role model.

"The kids are already in bed. I thought about keeping them up to see you, but they have had such a busy weekend with Monica and Douglas they needed their sleep. Plus I thought you could use one more quiet night."

"You are an angel, Carolyn, thank you so much!" Jules hugged her mother-in-law fiercely. As much as she hated having to live in someone else's home, Carolyn made her feel safe and secure, which is just what she needed right now.

MONDAY MORNING came much too early. It's amazing how much a weekend of relaxation can take out of you, Jules thought. This weekend, however, wasn't entirely relaxing. First 'the visitor', and then the two hour rehashing of the events of last year. She couldn't help thinking they were related. She would have to think about that later.

"Morning guys!" Jules called as she woke her children for school. How nice it was to see them lying in their beds. They were always angels when they were sleeping. Awake was another story.

"Ohhhhh, do we have to get up?" Six-year old Colin was the first to rouse. His hair was flying all over the place, and his eyes were all scrunched up like someone had shone a flashlight in his eyes. It was a terrific site.

"C'mon bud, didn't you miss me?" Jules smothered him with a giant bear hug and tickled him until he giggled.

"You, sleepyhead"- she threw a pillow at the oldest boy, Ian. "Wake up!"

Conner, the middle child, was already up and had his head buried in his mom's lap. Jules had to pull him off of her just to see his face.

"You didn't miss me one bit did you?" With a big smile Connor kissed his mom and went to the kitchen to make his breakfast.

Claire was snoring like a lion. She was such a sound sleeper.

"Good morning sweetheart." Jules cooed as she climbed into bed with her daughter. The thirteen year old seldom let Jules hug her, so she lavished all the time she could get to cuddle with her daughter before she woke up.

"Moooooommmmmmm!"

"Ok, its time to get up girl." Jules relinquished her position and left Claire her privacy. She needed coffee.

The buses finally came, picking up her four children to deliver them to their respective schools. Claire had one more year in middle school, which was hard to believe. How did thirteen years go by so quickly? Jules' reminiscing was interrupted by the phone.

"Hey Jules, Can we switch our therapy date to today? I just got a call from my agent, I've got an audition on Friday." Monica sounded out of breath.

"What are you doing, Mon, I can barely understand you."

"I'm on the treadmill, I have got to lose at least five pounds before Friday, you've got to help me, can you meet today instead of Wednesday, I need all the help I can get?" Monica, the drama queen, was back.

"Sure, after my 11:30 appointment."

"Great- see you then!" And Monica was gone.

Jules sighed. Back to life. She had five training appointments this morning at the gym. She loved being a personal trainer. There was just one small problem. Some days she didn't feel very motivated herself. Today was one of those days.

"You've got to fake it till you make it." her boss always said. "Trust me, it works. If you don't feel like being happy, if you don't feel energetic or optimistic, or even alive, you just have to fake it. Then, the strangest thing happens- you start feeling happy, energetic, optimistic and very much alive. The brain works in mysterious ways, Jules- mysterious ways. You really should try it!"

Tony Romano was a mysterious guy. She actually knew very little about him. He had an Italian name, but an Eastern European accent. He was olive skinned and dark headed. He loved boxing, and knew everything about every American boxer that ever lived. Tony had made references to his former business, without divulging the nature of the business. When she asked questions, he would give her vague answers and change the subject.

All Jules really knew about Tony was that he enjoyed his retirement by opening up his own gym. He seemed a genuinely happy man, but at times, Jules caught him looking pensive and a bit withdrawn. Tony had a secret, she just hadn't figured it out yet.

Today, Tony's advice was worth the price Jules paid for it. She conjured up some smiles, doped herself up on caffeine, and made the most of a busy morning. But by the time she left the gym, she still felt lousy. Her weekend at the lake left her feeling more stressed and uneasy than ever.

Jules headed straight for The Grind, without bothering to change out of her workout clothes. Today would be one of those days she chose to stay "comfortable."

"So, Monica, tell me about this audition. This is the first one in what, five years?"

In 1995 Monica Perry had her first role in a national TV commercial, which led to five more over then next year. From there her career blossomed and she landed the leading female role in a hit sitcom. The show ran for seven seasons. Like most good shows, the story lines and plots weakened with each season. ABC finally canned the show in 2003, in preparation for the hit Desperate Housewives. It was all in good time, as Monica's three year marriage to TV producer Douglas Perry had given her a son, Charlie. Monica was ready to settle down, and Douglas was ready to switch gears. They moved to Nashville, where Douglas began creating and producing independent films.

It didn't take long for Monica to get antsy. When Charlie turned two, Monica found a local agent, and started going on auditions. It had been ten years since she'd had to go through the grueling routine, and she was now in her thirties. "Too mature" was the politically correct phrase for too old. "A little too ..... average" was polite for overweight. She spent two years and gobs of money on gym memberships, specialty foods, and facials, but came home with the same disappointment every time. Eventually she gave up, and proclaimed that she was "retiring".

Despite her best efforts to convince everyone that she was ready to quit, Jules knew Monica would never be content without pursuing her passion. It was only a matter of time before she made another attempt.

"I know, right? I must be fooling myself, I'm too old, too fat, and way too out of practice for this! What am I thinking? But Jules I want this soooooo bad!"

"Well, tell me about it."

"Home Improvement Television has created a new show- its called "Make-Over *Your* Life". Each week, a team including a designer, a counselor, a life coach and a nutritionist and personal trainer work with a sad, sappy mom like me, and help her make-over her life. And they want me to be their host! They actually called my agent and requested me. According to Jen, the audition is just a formality. But I still have to knock their socks off- or they'll want to use me for their first subject, not the host. Oh, and I tried to get you in for the diet and exercise part- I really did, but they've already cast a woman named Tricia. Get this, they are calling her "Nutritia"!"

"Well, it sounds like we should be hitting the track, not the lattes. First, get rid of this!" Jules pulled the blueberry muffin from Monica's hand, just before it hit her lips. "No more sweets, no bread, no pasta or rice for you dear for the next five days!"

"Ughhhhh," Monica sighed, "this is the real reason I left TV."

Jules spent the next thirty minutes going over every aspect of Monica's emergency slim down plan, to which Monica grunted, snorted, or moaned at each suggestion.

"This is just for this week, Mon. Then we start a plan for life. I keep telling you that you can't go on eating junk every day. Now that you are going to have a camera in your face again, you'll appreciate the advice!"

"And speaking of diets, I can't believe you sent us that pizza! I think I completely blew twelve weeks of training in one weekend, I'm not sure if Mitch even got a whole slice for himself!"

"What are you talking about, Jules?" Monica was truly confused.

"The pizza you sent to the cabin Friday night- Guido's- my favorite! Don't pretend like you don't know what I'm talking about"

"Are you kidding? I don't! I know how hard you've worked. Do you really think I'd do that to you? Oh, I bet it was Mitch, you know he's been trying to fatten you up for years!"

"Yeah, I bet you're right. Sneaky little bastard!"

Eight

"FORGIVE ME, Señor, we must do this for security purposes."

The Chilean soldier held out a burlap sack. The American understood, and bent down slightly as the officer placed the sack over his head and led him into the vehicle. The drive took several hours. He was accompanied by two soldiers, one identified himself as Espiranza, the other Muniz. A few times Richard Sampson tried to make conversation, but received no response. After a few minutes he was instructed to drink through a straw. And then he dozed.

"Señor Sampson, Señor Sampson, we're here. You must get up Señor Sampson."

Richard felt a hand against his face. He opened his eyes but his vision was blurry. The soldiers flanked him on either side and hoisted him to his feet. As he swayed they held him up and began to drag his feet behind as they moved forward. Slowly, Richard roused and regained control of his body. He was on a farm. He saw fields and meadows and crops in the background. Ahead were buildings, small cottages with flower gardens. Chickens walked freely around his feet, and he could hear the sound of cows in the distance.

"Welcome to Colonia Dignidad, Señor Sampson, I am Alejandro Espiranza. The Colonel has told me much about you. We are looking forward to having you as part of our family."

"DICK?" A TALL, muscular, blond headed man was studying Richard Sampson intently. Sampson had been staring out the window at the field of yellow flowers. The flowers reminded him of the compound. It had been so peaceful during the daytime.

"Sarge, is there a problem?" Richard Sampson looked at his right hand man expectantly.

"I just heard from Alejandro. The next shipment won't be ready until next week."

"Fine," Sampson replied, returning his gaze to the field. "Alert the organizers and send out a memo to the clients that they will have to wait until the first for the next showing."

"Saddie is worried about the new inventory. She's afraid they won't stay fresh that long."

"Saddie will manage. I'm not worried. Just send out a memo outlining the new plan."

"Sure thing boss." The tall blond soldier left Richard Sampson, alone with his thoughts.

Nine

THE DRIVE TO Guatemala city went fast. At least it felt fast to Eliana. She had slept most of the way. There were others in the van with her. She doesn't remember talking to them. She doesn't remember much of the trip. She was sleepy and wanted to lie down. Mariana took her to a bed, where she woke several hours later.

The room was dark, hot, and smelled of must and body odor. Eliana heard voices all around her. There was laughter. But there was also screaming. In the distance she heard a girl yelling "No!" She heard a slap, a thud, and then the crying stopped. Eliana was afraid. She was in a "room" made of sheet curtains strewn across rope hung from the ceiling. It was just big enough for a cot and a little extra walking room. Light poured into the space through a small parting of the curtains. Eliana walked towards the light.

Outside her room Eliana found herself in a hallway. There were girls sitting against the walls. They didn't talk. They played with their hands, they would close their eyes and dream, and they stared at her. But they didn't talk. One of the girls pointed to her right.

Eliana walked in the direction shown to her by the girl in the hallway. She came to an open space, a kind of entrance way. There she found Mariana talking with a man. When Mariana saw Eliana she stopped talking and came to her.

"My child, what are you doing?" Mariana lovingly stroked Eliana's cheek.

"Where am I?" Eliana was confused.

"We are just staying her for the night. We have a long trip ahead. Stay here just a minute." Mariana left into a room off the entranceway and quickly returned with a soda.

"You must be thirsty. Here, have a drink of this and lie down. We will leave soon for America." Mariana lead Eliana back to her room, and eased her back onto the cot. Eliana had finished half of her soda and was tired again. She slept.

MITCH HAD SPENT all morning pouring over documents, contracts and financial reports. Everything he had left of The Office fit into one cardboard file box. All of his dreams, his effort, and all of his money, all in one cardboard box.

He found the pictures he had taken on that first day he toured the inside. It had all seemed absolutely perfect. He just knew it was a sign. This was the right place, and this was the right time- for the business, and for him. The fall in the real estate market, the recession, foreclosure and bankruptcy, it all seemed to have a purpose. Mitch had been stripped of everything. To the casual observer it may seem like a terrible defeat. But for Mitch, it gave him the freedom to pursue his dreams. "Jules, we literally have *nothing* to lose!" he had told her back then. He didn't realize how wrong he could be.

Mitch dreaded this work but knew he would have to go over every last detail to prepare for the deposition. If he did this job well enough, his case might not even go to trial. His case was solid- even Sam, his lawyer, felt so. Richard Sampson intentionally misled Mitch and Jules in an effort to unlawfully obtain full ownership of The Office. The facts were clear. Mitch just had to present the evidence.

That afternoon, Jules joined in the task. She brought in a new box full of financial papers to the table to review, and watched as a single piece of paper escaped the pile. The document was titled "The Office P&L".

'How did this get in here?', she thought to herself. She worked quietly while Mitch took a break.

Mitch and Sampson had an agreement that Jules would keep a copy of all financial documents. She wanted to have access to all financial information, online banking, and be included as a signer on all banking accounts. She had a knack for numbers and was detailed enough to keep the books for her husband's business and the family's finances. While she was happy Sampson was taking the responsibility for the bookkeeping and accounting for The Office, she insisted on full disclosure and accessibility. This was something Sampson initially agreed to without question. It wasn't until two months into the partnership that it became an issue.

The argument over the finances was actually the first sign of trouble between the co-owners of The Office. After Jules' repeated requests for copies of the financial documents were ignored, Mitch decided to step in.

"Dick, can you please send Jules the financial reports this week, she's really hounding me on this one."

"Mitch, you and Jules don't need to bother with the financials. That's why you have me. You just handle the PR side of things and let me worry about the busy work."

"Oh trust me, neither one of us want the responsibility of handling the books, Jules just wants copies for her records. "

"Why?" Sampson took on a suspicious tone.

"Well, because that was part of our original agreement. Total disclosure, remember? "

"It's not necessary, Mitch. I'm not asking you for an accounting of your duties. Tell Jules not to worry about it." Now Sampson was sounding irritated.

"I'm sorry, but that's not going to cut it with Jules. She's not going to let it go. And besides, we agreed to share all details with each other. What's the problem here?"

Sampson stood and approached Mitch, so close his hot breath brushed Mitch's cheek. "The problem is, I don't think you trust me and I don't like it one bit. I'm running the financial side of this business and you've received your checks on time and in full. If you've got a problem with trust, maybe we shouldn't be in business with each other!"

Mitch instinctively took a step back. "Whoa, what the hell, Dick? What's really going on here?"

Sampson retreated and paused for an exceptionally long time, rubbing his eyes. "Nothing. I'm sorry, I'm just under a lot of pressure with RSE. I'll get the reports to Jules. Just let her know I'll email them to her by the end of the week."

SHE HAD NEVER actually received all of the financial documents back then. She was overwhelmed with balancing her role as marketing manager in the business, the children's schedules, and her part time job. She didn't even realize she had never received them. She had forgotten about them. Looking back on this, Jules was ashamed of her lack of responsibility.

What Jules did remember is the feeling that the office seemed to be making more money than Mitch was receiving. She did the math in her head and she estimated that The Office made at least $9,050 that first month. Yet Mitch had only come home with just over two grand. It didn't make any sense.

Jules took a closer look. The items listed on the P&L statements did not make any sense either. There were income and expense categories that were not relevant to The Office. "Travel Expenses" paid out to a company called Transport Express, and income from "Retail Sales" were completely unexpected.

The numbers were outstanding. In July alone, Sampson's record showed The Office took in over fifteen thousand dollars, with the bulk of this coming from retail sales, support services and misc. income. When it came to the expenses, more money was spent on marketing and transportation than payroll.

'What the hell was going on in that place?' Jules was suddenly feeling sick, her previous suspicions heightened.

She had never actually considered the possibility that Sampson was cheating them financially. Now, she was beginning to wonder if he was honest about anything. She pondered over the document for another hour.

Jules was getting a headache and needed a break. She closed the files and left them on the dining room table. Mitch was already snoring when she climbed into bed. She would table her thoughts until another day. She didn't want to think about it any more tonight.

Ten

THE SUN WAS so strong as she headed east on HWY 100 towards the gym, she could barely see the road. She turned left onto Harpeth Hills Parkway a half mile from the gym. Thankfully, she was out of the sun and could see the cars in front or her. She took another sharp left into the parking lot at Ramano's.

It was an odd name for a gym. Jules thought it sounded more like an Italian restaurant, and always got a craving for pasta when she drove up and saw the neon sign announcing she had arrived at the "best little gym in Nashville".

It was a great gym, and Jules had seen plenty in her years. Ramano's Gym was run by Tony Ramano, boxer aficionado. Inside, the place looked like an old fashioned boxing gym. Right in the center Tony placed a two foot tall, twenty-four foot square mat surrounded by ropes. It was used for stretching and floor work, but looked just like a boxing ring.

Ramano was a stickler for cleanliness and his employees vacuumed, swept, and mopped daily. He made all the ladies happy by placing vanity mirrors in the women's locker room. The equipment was always new, replaced at the slightest sign of wear. And despite the old school feel and decor, Tony made sure his gym was always outfitted with the newest and coolest gadgets. One of his new favorites were the suspension bands that hung in the rear corner.

But the best thing about Ramano's wasn't the equipment or the amenities, it was Tony. Tony Ramano spent every day at that gym, he knew every member by name, and was known for surprising a member from time to time with a public posting of a birthday greeting or congratulation for a promotion or birth. He's even hosted charity events and has taken up collections for members in need.

The members at Ramano's stayed at Ramano's because it felt like a family. And that's why Jules stayed, even after several years of earning the same wage. She knew she could make more money at another gym, and even more if she trained from home. But her clients and her co-workers had become part of her extended family, and that was something better pay couldn't buy.

This morning she was about to meet a new member of the family, Tim Holloway. From his file she learned that Tim is thirty-six years old, a single dad, with high cholesterol and a family history of heart disease. Tim lived close by, and had listed 'self employed' as his employer. His occupation was listed as 'independent contractor'.

Jules began to wonder what type of work Tim Holloway did for a living. 'Independent contractor' sounded like code for drug dealer. Her mind began to wonder, and she envisioned herself entangled in a web of dark characters interrupting her training sessions to get what's owed to them from her new client.

"Jules?" The sound of Tony's voice made her jump. She had to laugh at herself for being so silly. "Tim is here."

"Tim- Hi I'm Jules Spalding, it's good to meet you."

"Well its good to meet you too, I hope you can do something with this old thing." Holloway pointed to his expanding gut, which was definitely in need of some work.

"Let's come in the office first and talk for a minute." Jules brought Tim Holloway into the training office and began reviewing his PAR-Q, the medical questionnaire and evaluation.

"Have you ever worked with a personal trainer before?"

"Nope, I've never worked out before. I'm not sure what to expect. I have to say I'm a little nervous."

Jules laughed. "There's no need for that. We'll take it easy on you, the first time at least."

Tim had an easy way that Jules enjoyed. She could tell she would like working with him. "You look really familiar. I feel like we've met before."

"I think I've seen you at my son's school- West Franklin Elementary?"

"That must be it- what grade?"

"I'm sorry?" Tim seemed legitimately confused.

"What grade is your son in?"

"Oh, he's in the third grade."

"Ah, he either has Ms. Whooten or Ms. Stone...."

"Stone"

"OOOH, so sorry for you!" Jules winced.

"Oh, well I really don't know much about that, I try to let Frankie's mother handle all the school stuff."

"Good move, you know how much Ms. Stone hates men. Is she fair to your son?"

"Uh, yeah, I guess, he doesn't ever complain."

"Lucky- I have several friends with boys who've had a terrible time with mistreatment. But enough of that, though, lets get started."

Their first session together was a good one, and Tim Holloway was much stronger than Jules expected. He said he had never worked out before, but he had strong shoulders and a well defined back. Despite the spare tire hanging around his middle, Tim Holloway looked like an old soldier who still did push-ups at home.

Jules decided he must do some sort of physical labor. She tried to get him to talk about himself during their session, but personal questions brought evasive answers. She didn't want to seem nosy or rude, so she let it go for now. She would just have to take her time getting to know him.

It was a short day at the gym, with just two appointments on the books, and as Jules was finishing with her last client she glanced outside to check the weather. The forecast had been for rain, but she was hoping it would wait till she got in an outdoor run. The temperature had been so warm for this time of year.

As she glanced out the front window she caught the tail end of a tan Mercedes SUV with tinted windows leaving the parking lot. Jules froze for several seconds and then stood up and ran to the front entrance. The car was on its way down Harpeth Hills Parkway before she was able to see the license plate.

"You OK Jules?" Her client, Suzie Reed, had a worried look on her face.

"Yeah, Suzie, I'm sorry, I just thought that I saw someone I knew."

"Are we done then?" Suzie loved to complain her way through the entire workout, and would skip out early every time if Jules would let her. Yet she continued to come back.

"Yes- you did awesome, sorry I cut it short. I'll give you an extra five next week!"

"HA! That's not necessary!"

ON THE WAY home from work, Jules stopped at the drugstore and bought a small memo book. She decided to start a journal. If these sightings were just a coincidence, than no harm done. But if this tan Mercedes really was following her, she needed to have proof. From memory Jules entered in the dates and times of the previous sighings.

October 20, 2012- 2 pm red minivan parked across the street from house- 2 hours- never saw driver- neighbors didn't know van

October 25, 2012- 12 pm- tan Mercedes SUV from church to neighborhood, drove past our house

October 29, 2012 - 9 am- tan Mercedes followed from neighborhood to The Grind, drove on past store

November 1, 2012-2:30 am someone was watching at the cabin, in the woods, ran when I came to find him / her???

November 5-, 2012- 10:30 am- tan Mercedes leaving Ramano's parking lot onto Harpeth Hills Parkway- headed north

Putting it on paper made it seem much more real to her. Six events! Was it possible? The first two could have been coincidences. The cars were not the same, and as Monica had pointed out, they could have just been at the same place at the same time as Jules. But the stalker at the cabin, and the tan Mercedes, now seen twice, definitely felt like something more. Monica teased her about faulty intuition but this time it felt very real.

Seeing the events on paper emboldened Jules. She had data, she had documentation. She needed more. She needed license plate numbers, faces, and she needed names. Suddenly Jules Spalding felt like Columbo. She tucked the memo book in her purse with a new mission. She was no longer creeped out, and even felt a little excited about another encounter with the tan Mercedes.

JULES DROVE slowly to the school, constantly checking her rearview mirror. Every tan car stood out to her, and she almost caused an accident straining to see what turned out to be a Navigator five cars behind. When she arrived at Franklin Middle

School, Jules fell in line with the rest of the cars waiting to pick up their adolescent children.

Claire Spalding looked a lot like her mother. She acted like her too. She was shy and introverted, and often mistaken for rude. But Jules understood. Jules remembered how uncomfortable she had felt when adults would talk to her. She didn't know how to relate. On the other hand, at school she was popular and outgoing. Among her peers, Jules Spalding was charismatic and flirty. She just didn't know how to act around adults.

And Claire was the same way. The more Jules tried to talk, the more Claire buttoned up. But Jules had her figured out. She found that if she wasn't the least bit interested in what Claire had to say, Claire would ramble on about anything and everything. The car was a great place for this, and today, Claire had a lot to say.

Her friend Brittney was breaking up with her boyfriend Jack, and that was a good thing because Brittney really liked Ben, but that was a bad thing because Ben really liked Jennifer. Ally was being a real pain - making up stories about her new stepfather, bragging about how rich they were now. And Clarissa had lied to the entire eighth grade class and told them she had cancer, just to get attention. When she was found out, she was bullied so badly her parents transferred her to another school. Jules thought she was very glad to be out of middle school.

The pickup line at the elementary school was much longer, and filled with mothers Jules was not interested in seeing. Going bankrupt, losing a business, and moving in with parents is just something that doesn't happen in the upper middle class neighborhoods of western Franklin. Jules' 12 year old suv, with peeling paint and duct-taped seat belts stood out like a sore thumb among the new Hummers and Escalades lining the parking lot at West Franklin Elementary School. She had some friends from school, but there were a lot of mothers who stopped calling when her fortune turned.

"Hey boys! Climb on in! We've got a surprise tonight. Dad closed on the Johnston house. We're meeting Dad at The Pizza Company to celebrate!"

The volume in the car escalated as the kids began to whoop and holler. The Spaldings didn't go out to eat, at least not in the last three years. The Pizza Company was practically the best pizza place in town, and even Jules was ready to break her pizza fast (again) to celebrate Mitch's success. This was the first big closing he had had in several years. It was a large commission that could support the family for several months on their current standard of living. Mitch and Jules had hoped that this was the first of many.

"I can see it from here with my new boculars, mom!" Colin was holding up a pair of black plastic binoculars.

"Bi-no-cu-lars." Jules had to stifle a laugh while she enunciated for Colin. "Where did you get those?"

"I filled up my good behavior chart and got to pick this out of the treasure chest!" Colin was extremely proud of himself. Jules wished adults got treats for being on their best behavior.

Eleven

AT EIGHTEEN, Tim Holloway was unsure of his future. His parents wanted him to go to college. His girlfriend wanted him to propose. His buddies wanted him to backpack across Europe. Tim didn't know what he wanted to do, so he joined the Army. For the first few years Ft. Campbell, Kentucky was his home. It was just an hour from his family in Nashville, but he found it was far enough away to gain some independence- and that was exhilarating.

His training as an infantryman was rigorous and often brutal. In just one year, a six foot tall, one hundred eighty-five pound boy was transformed into a two hundred thirty pound machine, trained in weaponry, hand to hand combat, explosives, and computers. When it was discovered he had a knack for languages, the US Army began grooming Tim Holloway for Special Forces. Within four years he became a Green Beret and began reconnaissance and counterintelligence training. He was heading up in the ranks quickly, and then he screwed it all up.

Tim Holloway was celebrating his twenty second birthday with some old high school buddies in Nashville. He was on leave, two days before a deployment to Kuwait- his first mission. As a part of Operation Desert Storm, the newly appointed Green Beret was commissioned to assist the American Army in intelligence gathering. His big sendoff ended abruptly however, when a barroom brawl ended in a visit to the ER and then the Nashville

City Penitentiary. After a quiet dishonorable discharge Holloway found himself an unemployed civilian.

The world was unkind to an over-qualified ex-soldier with a criminal record. Employers were not willing to take a chance on a man who looked like the incredible hulk, and had a rap sheet to match. He found himself working the bar at the same Nashville night spot in which his career had ended. The owner, Raul Torres had known Tim for several years and felt bad about his misfortune. He knew Tim had just been protecting his old girlfriend. The Son Of a Bitch who started the fight had been hitting on her all night, and had become increasingly aggressive, until Holloway intervened.

If Torres had had the opportunity to speak to the police on Holloway's behalf, he would have sworn Holloway deserved a medal. But there were too many witnesses that night who claimed it was Tim Holloway who started the fight responsible for splitting SOB's head open, leaving him with a concussion, a broken nose, and three cracked ribs. 'Holloway was a trained animal', thought Raul, 'our army needed more men like him'.

It was in Torres' bar that Holloway first met the soldier. Tim was serving drinks on a Saturday night when he came in and sat at the bar. The man's size got Tim's attention. At six foot four and two hundred sixty-five pounds, the soldier made Tim Holloway look like a little girl. The man was dressed simply, in dark blue jeans, a short sleeved ivory linen dress shirt and flip flops. His tan skin highlighted his muscular frame. But it was his tattoo that kept Tim's gaze.

As he extended his left arm to reach for his beer his shirt sleeve pulled back to expose a tattoo of two infantry rifles, crossed, with the insignia "De Oppresso Liber" written under the cross. "To Liberate the Oppressed". Tim knew the Latin words well. The phrase decorated his own arm. It was the motto of the Special Forces.

"Have you got something against soldiers son?" The soldier caught Tim by surprise. He didn't realize he had been staring.

"No, sir." Tim went on working as if he were not interested. He tried not to be interested, tried to forget the anger, frustration and disappointment he had felt when he had to leave the Army. For someone who started out so unsure of himself and his future, he found them both in the Army. In the army he found his true potential and discovered a world that not only recognized his talents, but needed his expertise. In one lousy instant, he destroyed the possibility for an experience he had never dreamed possible. And now, here, in the place it all happened, he was face to face with a man who had lived his dream.

He continued to serve drinks, take orders, clean the bar, and do the best he could to ignore the man at the corner with the army tattoo. But curiosity kept him stealing glances as often as possible. The man drank alone. He seemed completely content in his singleness, and occasionally glanced at the Tennessee Titans football game that had just started and was playing on the television above the bar. At times, he seemed far away, as if deep in thought, but came back to reality to give his neighbors a smile or nod after a good play.

As the bar filled for the game, Tim found himself so busy he soon forgot about the Special Forces soldier and was thankful for the arrival of Chuck Weeks. Chuck had only been at Raul's for a few weeks, but knew a bar like the back of his hand. Normally Chuck got on Tim's nerves. A small, wiry fellow, his personality fit his physical stature. He had a high voice for a man, and talked fast and incessantly. Typically he gossiped or talked about the patrons of the bar, mocking clothing choices, bad hair, and make-up don'ts. His incessant rambling drove Tim crazy. He never understood why people chose to feel better by berating others. To Tim, this was a sign of weakness. And weak people bothered Tim Holloway.

But tonight, Tim welcomed Weeks. Tim was in the weeds and he needed the help. He also needed someone else to serve the soldier. Every time Tim approached the man, he found himself tensing up and becoming distracted. He needed to get away from this man.

"Another Bud Light?" Weeks asked the large man as he held out an opened bottle.

"Sure, thanks." he reached out for the bottle with his left hand, exposing the tattoo.

"Hey, you're an Army man, eh?" Weeks had to open his mouth.

"That's right." The soldier stared at him, questionably.

"So is our Holloway, here. Green Beret, even. Ain't that right, Tim?"

Tim had no way out. Weeks had opened a door he hadn't wanted opened. Not that night. It had been exactly one year since his discharge.

Tim looked up to give the soldier a grin, but quickly averted his eyes and kept on working. He did his best to stay busy and out of the way the rest of the night, hoping to avoid any additional contact. Luckily, the soldier seemed uninterested. Occasionally Tim would steal a glance his way and find him watching the game, or lost in thought.

The Titans were losing miserably by the beginning of the fourth quarter, which meant the bar would be closing early as fans simply gave up and went home before the two minute warning. There would be no after-party tonight.

Tim didn't see the soldier as he took the trash out the back after closing, but he felt his presence. Despite the fact he had never actually practiced as a Special Forces agent, his training prepared him for moments just as this. He could hear his breathing, and smell his musk.

"So your an Army man too? Ft. Bragg?"

"Ft. Campbell" Tim replied as he continued to the dumpster without turning around to face the soldier.

"Why is a Green Beret, 5th Special Forces Group tending bar in Nashville TN? "

Tim paused for a long time, staring at the ground.

He looked the soldier square in the eye, "What's it any business of yours?", and walked back into the bar before the soldier could reply.

When Tim made it to his car at the end of his night, he found a business card under his windshield. The card included a list of ways to contact the soldier. Tim tossed the card on the ground, got into his car and drove home.

"YOU HAVE A VISITOR." The guard opened Tim's cell and led him down a long hallway. The Nashville City Penitentiary was cold; the walls were painted an awful institutional olive green, and the place smelled of urine. Along the walls he could see long continuous scratches, as if someone had drug their nails down the hallway as they were being hauled off to the death chair. They didn't actually have a death row at the Nashville Pen, the small prison was meant for less offensive crimes. But during his brief time inside those walls, Tim sometimes imagined what it may have been like to be a dead man walking.

They arrived at a large open area, filled with picnic tables. Other prisoners were sitting at the tables, across from their families. Some women were crying, others were arguing.

"Right over there", the guard pointed to a table in the far corner. Tim could see his parents sitting apprehensively on the other side.

"Hi Mom, Dad." Tim sat sheepishly across the table from his parents, who seemed to stare at him as if here were a stranger.

"Tim..." His dad started, "I don't even know what to say. What the hell were you thinking? Do you realize you've destroyed your entire career? I hope that piece of ass was worth it!"

"Dan!" Tim's mother pulled her hand from her husband's.

"Lois, its true. He's ruined everything- all for that girl. Honestly, Timothy. I thought maybe you had redeemed yourself when you became a Green Beret, but the fact is you've always been a screw up, and you still are. If you had just listened to me and gone to college, none of this would have happened. You could be working with me now and on your way to a fine life."

Dan Holloway paused and cleared his throat. "It was uncomfortable, but I've pulled some strings with the mayor's office, and we'll at least be able to get your sentence reduced. He thinks you'll get out of here with time served and probation, but you will always be a convicted felon. You are a seriously lucky young man. If it weren't for me and my connections, you'd be in this prison for the next five years."

"If it weren't for you, Dad, I never would have been here!" Tim Holloway stood up, called the guard and asked to be returned to his cell. His father watched him leave and was, for the first time in his life, speechless.

TWO MONTHS passed before Tim Holloway met up with the soldier again. It was Superbowl Sunday, and the bar was packed again. The Tennessee Titans were not in this game. The bar was divided in two colors. Sports announcers shouted in stereo from the ten television screens inside Raul's, and the crowd was drunk and excited.

The soldier found an empty seat at the bar at half-time. It wasn't until Tim was right in front of him that he recognized his next customer.

"Bud Light?"

"Yep." He smiled at Tim but let him do his job.

It was a close game, and the crowd cheered and booed with each touchdown and bad call. The last customers finally left at 2 am, singing and woohooing their way into a cab, called by Holloway. When he returned to the bar, he was sitting on a stool waiting for him.

"What do you want?" This time Tim looked him in the eyes.

"I came to offer you a job." The Soldier looked back.

"I've got a job."

"I'm here to offer you a real job, with decent hours and benefits."

"Well, I'm sorry you've gone to the trouble, cause I'm not fit for a job with decent hours and benefits." Tim started to walk away.

"That mark on your arm says otherwise."

Tim had removed his t-shirt after the last customer spilled his vodka all over him. He was dressed in a tank undershirt, and his tattoo was visible.

Tim turned back towards the Soldier. "I'm no soldier either. If you knew my story, you wouldn't be so interested."

"I do know your story. And I know Raul. He says your one real hero. The kind that sticks up for people who need help. You're strong, you're smart, and you are a trained Green Beret. You deserve the attention of someone who appreciates those skills. I do. And I need someone like you."

Tim turned towards the Soldier and listened. Outside the Army, no one had ever shared an interest in his potential. And the Army was unforgiving.

"What kind of work are we talking about?"

"Let's call you my assistant. A little bit of everything. It may not be glamorous. Some days I may need you to load boxes onto a truck. Other times I may need you to pick up my dry cleaning. But there will be days I need a security expert, a computer geek, or a skilled linguist. You will be my jack-of-all trades. If you are interested I assure you I will make it worth your while. I'm offering you a legitimate career."

"When do I start?" Tim finally smiled.

The soldier smiled back.

Twelve

The music startled her. She wasn't sure where it was coming from.

The words haunted her, the music disturbingly familiar. It was the song played over and over in Tony's car.

"........................Cause now I own you."

Her phone was in her bag at the end of the bed. The chorus played over and over as she rifled through make-up, pens, wallet, and hairbrush, and finally found the phone. She turned the phone face-side up to see his face looking back at her, singing "now I own you." Stephanie dropped the phone on the floor just as the song ended.

Her heart raced and a cold sweat broke out on her forehead. The objects in her bedroom faded into one grey mass that began to spin wildly. Stephanie closed her eyes and had to take a deep breath to keep from passing out. The text message alert roused her and returned her focus back to her IPhone. With shaky hands she reached down to the floor, picked up the phone, and unlocked the screen. When she opened her text he had written:

'bus stop at midnight'

Stephanie nearly passed out again. Her fear quickly turned to anger towards the boy on the other end. She would be defiant.

'cant im grounded'

'find a way' He wasn't going let her take control.

'no'

The next text Stephanie received from Tony was a multimedia message. She opened up a slideshow of images from the last night she'd spent with Tony. The caption read

'i own you'

HER RIDE was waiting for her when she arrived at 12:05. "You're late." Tony wasn't smiling this time.

"Get in." Tony's friend didn't open the door for her this time.

Stephanie helped herself into the back of the 1957 baby blue Chevy. This time she could only smell her own sweat and fear.

They drove about twenty five minutes north into Nashville. Stephanie had never seen this part of town. The houses were close together and small. There were sidewalks, but no gardens, no fountains, and no picket fences. Stephanie's mind wandered as she watched through the open roof of the convertible. She wondered why these people didn't cut their grass, why they kept old cars in the yard, and chained their dogs to posts so close to the street. She decided she liked the stuck-up suburbs much better than this place.

They pulled up to a pale blue cottage style home. Not the beautiful baby blue of the antique convertible, but a washed out silvery blue that looked as if one more rain might wash the house white. The house was completely dark, not a light visible from the inside, with the exception of a dim glow coming from the basement window well.

Tony and his friend led Stephanie by the arm into the house, which to Stephanie smelled of a combination of body odor and rotting vegetables. The house was dimly lit by the light of the streetlamp pouring in through curtain-less windows. There were no furnishings. The house was abandoned.

Tony walked behind Stephanie, keeping his hand on the small of her back, leading her through the main hallway into the kitchen at the back of the house. Here she heard voices, coming from behind a closed door. It was the door to the basement.

Tony's friend opened the basement door and immediately the smell of smoke and the sound of southern rock filled the air. Kid Rock was singing about his carefree teenage years.

Stephanie resisted Tony's gentle leading to the steps. He squeezed harder and pulled as he walked in front of her to the top step. Voices sang with the chorus.

"And we were trying different things, and we were smoking funny things, making love out by the lake to our favorite song"

Stephanie thought about kicking him down the stairs. She thought she would kick as hard as she could, shut the door and run like hell out of the house. Swiftly she yanked her arm away from him and raised her right foot. Then she felt a hand hard on her shoulder.

"What'r ya gonna do?" Tony's friend had a grip on her so strong she would later find finger shaped bruises on her left shoulder. He looked at her in anticipation of an answer. She had none.

This time Tony took her hand gently and led her down the stairs, and Stephanie did not resist.

Thirteen

WEDNESDAYS WERE early days for Jules, with her first personal training session starting at 5:00 am. She hated getting up this early, but by the time she finished with her last client, she was always in a better mood.

Waking was extra difficult this morning, after a night of celebration, so she packed a thermos full of coffee to go. She had a lot to talk about with Mitch, but he was still sleeping. She would have to wait until she was home from the gym.

Jules had just finished her training session with Tim Holloway when Monica entered the gym. She had just two days before her big audition.

"Is that the new guy?" Monica was staring at Tim as he sweated it out on the elliptical machine.

"Yeah, his name is Tim."

"He's hot!"

"I didn't think he'd be your type. I thought you only liked men who wore Italian suits and drove BMW's."

"Maybe this is just a mid-life crisis, but there is something about a man with big biceps and rough hands that I find really attractive!" Monica was still staring at Tim Holloway.

"This is why Doug built you that home-gym isn't it?"

"Ha, ha. The truth is ..... I don't get out much. I'm really looking forward to this job- God I hope I get it. I could really use some activity in my life!"

"Then lets get started sexy!"

Jules took Monica through a fat blasting, strength and circuit routine that must have burned a thousand calories. Monica was exhausted and wasn't sure she could even pick up her little boy as she drove to the school that afternoon. Despite Charlie's pleading, Monica insisted on holding his hand instead of the usual piggy back ride out of the school.

As the two walked towards the car in the parking lot, she found her eyes drawn to a man leaning against a light post in the next row. She felt she knew him, but just couldn't place the face at first. Then she realized it was the same man she had been fawning over that morning. Tim Holloway was in the parking lot of her child's school, looking in her direction.

Had he followed her? Maybe he noticed her looking at him and decided to check her out? Was he interested? Suddenly Tim smiled big and waved in her direction.

'Oh my God', she thought, 'maybe he got the wrong idea!"

Just as she was sure that he had followed her around all day and was waiting for her at the school, she saw him walk her way. He rushed passed her towards the school as she heard him exclaim "Susie! It's so good to see you!"

Monica was so embarrassed at the absurdity of her own thoughts she could't even turn around to check out Susie. She hurried towards her own car, helped Charlie buckle in, and pulled out of the school parking lot without glancing back. She prayed Tim hadn't noticed her.

Monica was so distracted by embarrassment she didn't notice the tan Mercedes SUV pull out behind her.

JULES RETURNED home to find Mitch surrounded by papers at the dining room table. He was organizing his files and gathering evidence against his former business partner Richard Sampson. She kissed him on the back of the head and sat down to join him.

"What are we into this morning?"

"Piles of shit. " He slammed a file folder on the table and ran his fingers through his hair, a classic sign that Mitch Spalding was stressed out. "All these documents, rental agreements, bank statements..., I'm getting a headache."

"Mitch, I think he is dealing drugs. I was up several hours the other night after you went to sleep. I've been over every possible scenario and I think he must be dealing."

Jules sat down at the table across from him, found the profit and loss statement in the pile, and handed it to Mitch.

"In July he ran $15,000 through The Office, and only about a third of that was legitimate. The detail section here has companies listed for each category. I think we need to check to see if they are real."

"Son of a bitch! Right under our noses."

Mitch stood up and went to the window, rubbed his hand through his hair again and sat his forehead against the glass. He had always loved the view from the top floor of his mother's house. But at this moment, his eyes stared off at nothing as his mind raced.

"Mitch, we need to talk with Shirley over at the bank and find out if he opened any other accounts." Shirley was the account manager at Tennessee Bank and Credit Union, where The Office's accounts were held. She and Jules had become friends during the early days of The Office.

"I'd also like to check out the companies listed and talk with the owners. Maybe they could shed some light on these other expenditures."

"No." For the first time since The Office partnership split, Mitch was beginning to feel as if he were in control. "Sampson thinks he's gotten away with all of this. If we start asking questions, it will get back to him and he'll know we're on to him. We need to stay quiet about this now and let it all come up in the deposition. I want to catch him off guard, and see him squirm when he realizes we know what he's been up to. We may even get the police involved, Jules. " Now Mitch was smiling.

Mitch took the P&L report and went to his make-shift office storage closet. It was a white melamine ready-to-assemble bookcase he had purchased at the Goodwill store, furnished with clear plastic shoeboxes as drawers, and clear plastic trays to hold paper. He pulled out a fax cover sheet and addressed it to his lawyer, Sam Hastings.

"Jules, can you fax this to Sam and then call him to set up an appointment ASAP? We need him to follow up on the judges orders for copies of all Sampson's financial records. We need to put more pressure on him to cooperate."

Mitch kissed Jules on the forehead and nearly skipped out of the room. He was on his way to the Lake. One of Douglas' weekend buddies was selling his lakeside property, and Douglass had hooked him up with Mitch. This was going to be a good commission. Things were really starting to look up.

Fourteen

FOR JORDAN JONES, it started with gaming. He got his first Nintendo-64 at age thirteen, and became a whiz at Super Mario Brothers. He discovered internet gaming during the summers when he would spend his days helping out at his father's trucking business.

JJ's father, Herman Jones created Transport Express, a local trucking and moving company, in 1978, five years before Jordan was born. His trucks were painted white, with a navy blue swoosh under the printed name "Transport Express". Herman had painted the first truck himself, and he would laugh recalling the time some teenagers criticized him for stealing the Nike logo. Herman Jones was not a wealthy man, he dressed his son in hand-me-downs and if they were lucky, clothes picked out of the Sears catalogue. He had never heard of Nike.

By the time Jordan was a teen, Herman had ten trucks, and twenty three employees. He had become a staple in Nashville, and in the '80's, if you needed a truck, Herman was your man. His clients were primarily moving companies, corporate relocation agencies, and realtors, but he also contracted with a few local florists and furniture retailers. Each of his trucks came with a team of two drivers / movers, and Herman rented them out daily.

Jordan loved working in his dad's office. His primary responsibilities included filing and cleaning. His dad had two rules- do the best job you can, and work comes before play.

Jordan learned efficiency was an asset. When he was finished with his jobs for the day, JJ loved to "play" on his dad's computer.

Herman kept an old Macintosh SE/30 computer just for JJ to play on after he had upgraded the rest of the office computers to the newer Power Mac 9500. When he tired of games, he began to play around with other programs. It was here that JJ learned about graphic design, Photoshop, video editing and web design. He had taught himself, using internet tutorials and experimentation. He had just begun working on the design of a new website for Transport Express when his father died suddenly, the week before his eighteenth birthday.

Herman's wife had died in childbirth, leaving Herman alone with their only child. While Herman Jones had been a huge success in life as an entrepreneur, he failed his son in death by leaving him without life insurance. JJ had a choice; he could continue running the family business to provide for himself, or he could liquidate the company assets and go to college.

JJ had already been accepted to Middle Tennessee State University, and had plans to study information technology. He had studied computers in high school, and already had enough college credits to count as a second semester freshman. In June of 2001, JJ sold all of Transport Express' assets, with the exception of one truck, and the warehouse property itself. He couldn't explain it, maybe it was the memory of his father receiving the deed to the property in the mail, his proud face and the tears in his eyes, but JJ couldn't part with it. He set up an account from which to pay the property taxes each year, put up some No Trespassing signs, and with his dad's Mac Powerbook G4 in hand, Jordan Jones headed to Murfreesboro, TN.

JJ used the remaining truck, and the name, Transport Express, to earn money on the weekends and over the summers hauling small loads. But that fall the World Trade Centers were attacked and the US declared war in Afghanistan. The recession that followed affected every aspect of the transportation industry.

Gas prices were steadily increasing, and consumers chose to do the work themselves. JJ found it difficult to find loads to haul.

He wasn't the only one, either. JJ noticed more and more bulletin boards around town and around campus filled with home-made flyers made by independents like him looking for someone to pay them to move a load. There were haulers of all kinds- flat bed trucks, large independent drivers with their own 18 wheeler, small trucks for local moves like JJ, and even college guys with pick-ups just looking for some extra cash. For JJ, an idea was born.

He started working on the website immediately. For a small monthly fee, independent truckers of all varieties could join his website and post their profile. A quick google search for mover, truck for hire, or large haul would direct a customer to the Transport Express bidding site, in which they could enter their needs on an electronic bulletin board. The customer would then choose among a group of interested bidders- truckers who post a profile and a bid for each particular job.

Upon completion of a satisfactory job, the customer pays Transport Express, and Transport Express pays the contractor / trucker. For a small commission for each transaction, and a monthly membership fee for the contractors, the Transport Express bidding site filled a need for struggling truckers, and for JJ. The business was extremely successful. So successful, JJ had to take a few years off of school just to handle the workload. By 2009, JJ had received a Bachelor of Science in computer science, and had taken his company to a national level. There was just one problem- he needed help.

JJ was completely overwhelmed with the success of Transport Express, which is why he joined the Nashville Entrepreneurs' Group. He had seen a poster for a guest speaker presentation titled "Managing the Growth of Your Business" in the local news section of the Starbucks' bulletin board. He was enamored with Richard Sampson the minute the man opened his mouth. 'This man can really help me!' JJ thought.

"It sounds like you're in way over your head, young man." Sampson had told him that evening after the talk. JJ was so enthusiastic about speaking with Richard Sampson he approached the business man almost before he had had a chance to leave the podium. The two discussed JJ's problems as they walked to the parking lot.

"Way over!" JJ replied. "I feel like I shouldn't be complaining, especially in this economy, but I need some serious help. I know I need to hire employees, but I don't know the first thing about hiring, about managing others, about payroll, you name it. I can run a complicated website in my sleep, but I have no idea how to run a business. The problem is, I don't even have the time to learn."

Sampson smiled. "I'd love to learn more about what you are doing, it sounds fascinating. Could I come by your office sometime and see the operation?"

"Sure, how about tomorrow?" JJ handed Sampson a card with his number and office address.

"Good- I look forward to it." Sampson shook JJ's hand and walked to his car.

JJ met Sampson the following day and showed him his entire operation. Sampson was immediately impressed with JJ's creation. Jordan Jones had successfully filled a niche that needed to be filled. He had found a way to serve both the consumer and the provider. He had created the perfect win-win. These were always profitable. Sampson wanted in, and JJ needed someone like Sampson.

Within a week, JJ and Sampson were filling out partnership agreements. JJ agreed to give Sampson twenty five percent of his company, in exchange for Sampson's expertise and experience, and a minimum of ten hours of work per week. JJ would have the option of buying Sampson out within the first five years.

Sampson's responsibilities would be to handle human resources, accounting and record-keeping, legal, and financial reporting. JJ would continue managing daily operations, web hosting, and work directly with the employees.

Transport Express hired five new employees; two IT guys, a receptionist, an office assistant, and a bookkeeper. JJ was finding time to breath. He found he had more time to spend improving the site, and increasing sales. In just six month's time, JJ's bottom line went from a comfortable $200,000 a year, to $500,000 a year. JJ purchased five more trucks, just like the original he inherited from his father, and began to revive the spirit of the original Transport Express.

While Richard Sampson maintained an office in the Transport Express warehouse, he was rarely found wondering the halls. Sampson made weekly appearances, spent a few hours at his desk or on the phone, but most of his time was spent managing his primary business-a healthcare company.

Occasionally Sampson would have meetings at his TE office with some of his health care colleagues. JJ didn't know a great deal about Richard Sampson's other business ventures, and he didn't care. Richard Sampson had been a tremendous asset to the growth and stability of TE, and that's all that mattered to JJ.

There was however, one incident that concerned JJ. It was late in October, and it was cold, so cold JJ could see his breath. It was their breath that caught his attention out in the parking lot. It was just after dusk, and in the dark, he could see the breath of three men by the loading dock. The street light shone onto Sampson's face, the other two men were hidden under the roof's awning. The only thing JJ could tell about the others is that they were very big. And Sampson looked scared.

That was something, because in the year and a half that JJ had known Richard Sampson he had never seen the man look even remotely intimidated. Richard Sampson was a rock- he was confident, bold, and intellectually arrogant. But fearful? Not Richard Sampson. This night, however, Sampson looked as if he were in real trouble.

JJ passed Sampson in the hallway fifteen minutes later, and Sampson was his old self. JJ looked at Sampson for a long time.

"What?" Sampson said, in his 'I don't have time for you' tone.

"Nothing, really. Everything ok?"

Sampson's mouth said, "It's fine." His eyes said 'Mind your fucking business.' JJ let it go.

IT WAS JUST AFTER the New Year when JJ found out. He had been out of the office for almost a week, and decided to come in the first Saturday he was back. He expected to find the place a wreck, but Staci, his assistant had kept everything just as he liked it.

His phone messages were stacked in a neat pile in the inbox marked "messages", and his mail in a separate box marked "mail". Everything was in order, the carpets were vacuumed and the shelves had been dusted. JJ's collection of vintage toy trucks was perfectly secure on the top shelf of his library.

"Ok- I guess they didn't need me after all." He said aloud to nobody. The warehouse was empty. JJ loved being at the warehouse alone. He would walk the halls and look at everything he had created and sometimes he would cry. He remembered that day he had auctioned off his father's trucks, and remembered the agony he felt when he watched the last truck drive off the lot. He had anger towards his father for not preparing for the worst, guilt for abandoning the business his father had built from the ground up, and freedom from the noose around his neck that was Herman's life. Despite the angst of leaving behind his father's legacy, JJ was determined to start his own life.

And indeed he had; only now he felt like he was truly honoring his fathers' memory. In the large hall that led to the corporate offices of Transport Express, Herman's picture was framed with the caption "Founder of Transport Express- Herman Jones, 1961-2001".

As JJ was admiring his father's picture, he noticed that Sampson's office door was slightly ajar. This was unusual, Sampson was a private man, and insisted on keeping his door locked at all times. JJ decided to take a peak. It was his company after all, and his building. Richard Sampson was only part owner, and his portion was small. JJ had already saved up the majority of the money he needed to buy Richard Sampson out of his share. Sampson had done his part, it was time for JJ to claim his company, the company of Herman Jones, back.

Sampson's office was large, with two hundred and fifty square feet to spread out in. He had it nicely decorated with a mahogany desk and chair, red patterned antique Persian rug, and a dark brown leather couch and matching chaise. The windows were dressed with silk drapery, which covered wood blinds. The office looked more like the office of a lawyer in a prestigious Second Ave building than an office in a warehouse on the south side of Nashville. Sampson had spent his first week at Transport Express with contractors and decorators. A little over the top, thought JJ, but it was on Sampson's dime, and if it made him feel good, than so be it.

JJ went around to the back side of Sampson's desk, and he noticed a pile of white dust on the floor by the back wall. As he examined the powder he realized it was drywall dust. He had seen plenty of this during the renovation of the warehouse. But that was over a year ago. He looked up at the wall in front of him and noticed a new painting that hung on the wall directly behind the desk. Nice he thought, but it was a little crooked. As he went to straighten the picture the whole thing fell into his hands.

That's when he noticed the real reason for the drywall dust. Behind the painting a large wall safe had been installed.

The label on the lower left corner of the safe read, 'New Sterling Safe Company, Ballistic Steel Armored'. This was not your typical house safe. Sampson was keeping something very important, and very private. JJ was intrigued, but not concerned. Sampson was a private man, but JJ had no reason not to trust him. He put the painting back on the hook, straight this time.

JJ sat down at Sampson's desk, and leaned back in the leather-backed office chair. He closed his eyes and imagined what it would be like to be a millionaire entrepreneur like Sampson. He ran his fingers over the rich dark wood of the desk. It looked as if it had just been polished. JJ's curiosity got the better of him and he pulled on the metal knob that opened the desk drawer. It was locked. JJ tried the other drawers, all locked. 'Paranoid!' JJ thought out loud.

"Who's paranoid?" JJ jumped at the sound of her voice. Penny, his girlfriend of two years was standing in the doorway.

"Jesus, Pen, you scared the crap out of me!"

"I caught you snooping?"

"Yeah, I guess so. Sampson never leaves his office unlocked and I just found the door open-so I just thought I'd have a look......"

"What do you think he'd say if he found you here?" Penny walked over to JJ and straddled him in the chair.

"I think he'd say I've been a very naughty boy!" He stroked her hair and kissed her on the mouth. Then he pulled away, curious.

"What are you doing here anyway?"

"I've been calling you for the last hour and I couldn't reach you. We are meeting the Kirby's out at P.F. Chang's tonight at 7- you have an hour to get ready!"

"Oh, shit, I forgot. My phone's been acting up- I'm missing about half my incoming calls!"

"Still? I thought you were going to get that fixed!"

"Tomorrow, I promise."

As Penny stood up she backed into Sampson's desk and knocked stack of mail onto the floor.

"I got it." JJ leaned over and picked up the envelopes. An open envelope spilled its contents. He picked the letter up and glanced at the heading.

The document was from the law offices of Henry Clay, Sampson's business attorney. Clay had drawn up the contracts joining the two in business.

"Dick," the letter started. "I'm enclosing copies of the legal documents you requested. According to Tennessee Code 34987, you are the primary owner of Transport Express, and you have fulfilled your obligations to the terms of your pre-arranged buyout. The company is yours as soon as you sign and return the required paperwork I've included. This can be wrapped up by the end of this month. Henry Clay, Atty"

JJ read the letter three times. He couldn't make heads or tales of it, as his college advisor used to say. It just didn't make any sense.

Sampson's lawyers had stated that Sampson was the primary owner of Transport Express? No! The partnership agreement was clear, Sampson only owned 25% of the company. JJ spent hours with his lawyer deciding on just the right percentage to give Sampson incentive to work for Transport Express, without jeopardizing JJ's ownership of the company.

"J - what is it?" Penny could see the strange expression on JJ's face and was worried.

"Hold on..........."

JJ dropped the letter and ran down the hall to his own office. He opened the bottom right drawer of his own utilitarian desk, and rifled through the files for the folder marked "legal".

JJ pulled the file folder out of the drawer and opened it on his desk. He was looking for his copy of the partnership agreement. It was gone. He thumbed through every paper in the file three times. It was simply gone. There was nothing his file that even remotely indicated he had a partnership agreement with Sampson. It had been his only copy.

"What the hell is this?" Penny had followed him into his office with the letter in her hands. "What is he doing? He can't possibly claim he owns the business?"

"It's gone, Penny- our partnership agreement. I kept it right here in this drawer, and it's gone."

"Maybe it just got misplaced." Penny came around to the back side of the desk and the two of them pulled out every file. They painstakingly went through every piece of paper in JJ's desk. The partnership agreement was gone.

JJ sank into his cheap office chair. "I think I need a lawyer."

Fifteen

THE LABORATORY stank of something Richard couldn't identify. It was a burning smell, but not the smell of wood or paper burning, it was chemical.   Richard chose to wear a respirator, although the others didn't. He was a novice. They teased him for being so cautious.

"It's ready, Señor." Richard's lab partner handed him a container of clear liquid and turned to their assistant. "I'll call the sprinter."

The lab partner picked up a telephone on the wall and in a matter of minutes a young blonde haired, blue eyed boy dressed in wool pants and suspenders arrived. Richard handed the boy the container with a list of detailed instructions. The boy nodded in agreement and turned and walked out the door.

It had taken months to develop the clear, odorless, and tasteless mixture. Richard wasn't quite sure what he was making but each time he provided the German with a product it was returned a day later with a rebuke.

The diarrhea started after the first week. It came on unexpected, and at times left Richard so weak he could barely stand. That's when he started wearing the respirator. The others seemed to be sick all the time, noses running, coughing, and often left at night with headaches so severe they couldn't think clearly.

Richard sent this mix off with a prayer that it would be the last. His days in the lab had been tedious, and he questioned his purpose in this strange place when he had the chance.

"Work is divine service, Richard." Replied the German. And he left it at that.

Divine service? Who was he serving? God? Man? Satan, perhaps? Thirty years later, Richard Sampson was sure it was the latter. He opened his office safe and pulled out another log book. After making ten entries, he returned the book to his safe and closed it up and left for the night.

SHE WASN'T SURE how long she had been on the bus. Hours? Days? It was hard to tell. It was hot, and it smelled of body odor. Eliana was tired, so tired she felt she couldn't hold up her head or open her eyes. But something was changing. The constant cadence of the bus changed. It slowed, and then stopped and started, and bumped, and stopped and started again. Occasionally there would be a sharp turn that carried Eliana's entire body to one side or the other, but she could not stop herself. She was resigned to dance to the rhythm of the road.

Then she was back home, with her father. It was planting season. Bromeliads were her favorite. "They look like fireworks." Papa was saying as he packed the displaced earth back around the root ball of the long stemmed perennial. The top of the stem was adorned with a spray of orange and yellow that mimicked a decorative explosion. Eliana reached out to hold his hand, but it slid through her grasp. Then he was gone.

Eliana fought to wake. She told her eyes to open and eventually they obeyed. The small slits revealed a dark bus, and a dark sky. There were few streetlights where they traveled. It was dark like her home, but she knew she was not home because the path was smooth under the bus's tires.

Eliana told her arm to move and eventually it obeyed, bringing relief to the itchy patch on her forehead. She was able to turn her head now and look around. She found herself sitting at the back of a small bus, with seven other girls. Most of them slept. Eliana caught the eyes of an older girl who sat two rows ahead. This girl had roused and was looking around as well. She was long and lean, and her shiny black hair was cut short. She was dressed in her best dress, and shoes that were only meant for church. This girl's eyes locked onto Eliana and lingered. Eliana thought she saw fear in those eyes. No, fear wasn't exactly the right word. Terror. Eliana had seen terror in the girl's eyes.

The bus turned one last time, and then stopped. Out the window Eliana saw a house. Eliana thought it was a mansion. She had never seen anything quite so big and sturdy. In her home, families lived in tiny shelters made from salvaged materials, and slept on dirt. This home was enormous, it had real windows and a roof made of shingles that seemed to touch the clouds. The perimeter of the property was marked by a large fence.

A tall thin woman came out from the house and walked towards the bus. She took a key from her apron pocket and used it to unlock the large gate that kept out the unwanted. Eliana thought she had arrived at the most amazing place. She promised herself that in return for the opportunity to live in such a place she would work as hard as she could every single day of her life. She owed it to Miss Mariana and Anna Sophia, her guardian angels.

The doors of the bus opened, and the tall, thin woman entered the bus. She spoke to the bus driver in English. Eliana didn't understand yet. The woman looked up and down the rows at the girls and smiled. Eliana thought she was proud of her new recruits. The woman spoke to the girls in English, but again, Eliana did not understand.

"I am Miss Sadie, welcome!" Eliana understood this.

As the girls filed out of the bus one by one, Miss Sadie hugged each one of them.

Eliana stepped out of the bus onto the concrete sidewalk, and looked around. The black iron fence towered above her. It too seemed to reach the heavens, with tips that sprayed the sky like a bromeliad. The house was lit with the help of two gas lamp sconces. It was an older, two story, clapboard home, with real working shutters and a large front porch.

Covering the front door and outside each of the windows were bars, iron bars. Eliana had seen barred windows before, in Guatemala City. Eliana thought the bars were strange. Why would someone want to live with their windows barred, like caged animals in the zoo? But it was just how they did it in the city. Anna Sophia had explained that the bars were for the protection of the precious children inside. She told Eliana that life in the city was different from life in her village. She would have to be more careful, and more protective.

The bars here though, were different. Intertwined through the bars were delicate flowers, orchids and lilies, forged out of black iron. It was as if the bars were flowering vines growing up the side of the house. Eliana thought it was beautiful, like an iron garden.

Sixteen

IT WAS EIGHT thirty before Jules had gotten all of the kids in bed, the dishes cleaned, and the clothes in the laundry. She was exhausted, but tense and edgy. Mitch was consumed with his newest contract, and barely glanced up as she kissed him and walked out the door.

She loved the gym this time of night. She had it all to herself. The after work crowd waned around 7:30, and the shift workers didn't make it in until midnight. Ramano's was open 24/7 to its members, which made it a real hit for the nurses, ER docs, and other medical staff that worked at one of the ten hospitals in the Nashville Metropolitan area. It wasn't uncommon to see men and women sweating it out on the treadmills in their scrubs.

Jules used her access card to open the front door and headed to the boss's office. She accessed Tony's computer and clicked on the radio tab. She turned on her favorite station, turned the volume up, and headed for the treadmill.

Tony was particular about the music, and had programmed the stations to change throughout the day. He had researched it extensively and experimented with it personally. Tony Romano discovered that if he played just the right music at just the right times, gym attendance improved.

The senior ladies' hour, for instance, was from 10:00 am to noon on weekdays. He found that if he played the oldies during these hours his sixty five and older membership increased. The seniors were a great demographic. They had lots of free time, incentive to stay fit, and they had lots of friends. Tony Ramano increased his senior membership by twenty five percent within 3 months of 'demographics targeted radio', as he called it.

Tonight, the only demographic was a forty year old stressed out woman, and she needed it loud and energetic. Her station included Pink, No Doubt, Pat Benetar, and a variety of other women who rock.

After three miles on the treadmill she hit the gym floor. Push-ups, pull-ups and squats. She focused on old school moves that represented strength. Working out for Jules reminded her she was alive, strong, and powerful. After an hour and a half, Jules Spalding felt like a new woman, and was ready to go home.

She unlocked Tony's office once more, changed Pandora back to 'today's hits' and lowered the volume. As she closed and locked the door behind her she had a strange feeling she was being watched. Out of the corner of her eye she saw a shadow run across the back wall. She walked in that direction.

"Hello? Is anyone else here?" She walked hesitantly around the ring and glanced all around. There was no one there. Then she heard a click behind her. When she turned she was faced with her own reflection in the mirrored wall. She was so startled she jumped about a foot in the air, but still there was no one there.

She walked the entire floor, checked to see that all of the office doors were locked, and even walked through the men's locker room before heading to the ladies' room. She wasn't quite satisfied it was all in her head. Jules gathered her things from the locker and headed out of the women's room so fast she ran right into him.

"Holy SHIT!" Jules screamed as her face flew into Tim Holloway's chest.

"Sorry, did I scare you?" Tim was laughing.

"Oh my god, when did you get here?" Jules heart rate was higher than it had ever been on any run or heavy workout.

"Just walked in the door, are you ok?"

"Yeah, fine. I thought I heard someone in here earlier, but no one was here, it just creeped me out a bit." Jules took a deep breath and gave Tim an embarrassed smile.

"Are you leaving? You look a little shaken up. Let me walk you to your car. "

"That would be great. I know I must sound crazy, it's just ...well, lets just say it's been a weird couple of weeks and I'm a little on edge."

"The world is filled with creepy people Jules, you should be careful. It's good to keep your guard up a little." Something in Tim's tone bothered Jules. It didn't sound like him, and it wasn't a concerned gesture. It almost sounded like a warning, or even a threat. Jules turned to look at Tim under the parking lot lights.

Tim smiled, and instantly he was back. "Hey, if you're interested, my buddy is playing at the Playground tomorrow night. I have two extra tickets. Why don't you come with your husband? I'll drop the tickets off here tomorrow morning."

"Maybe I will, thanks." Maybe she was going crazy.

FRIDAY MORNING came early. Monica Perry had one last chance to work out before her mid-day audition for 'Make-over *Your* Life'. She met Jules at the gym at 6:00 am.

"Are you ready?" Jules poked at Monica.

"As ready as I'll ever be. I can't remember the last time I was this nervous."

Jules and Monica spent forty five minutes on the treadmills together. Jules took Monica through thirty minutes of tough interval training, and then spent the remainder of the time walking and gossiping. Her job today was working out Monica's nerves, get her endorphins going, and maybe sweat out a few extra pounds of water weight.

When Jules felt she had properly prepared Monica for the day ahead, she sent her on her way. She spent the rest of the morning going through the motions with each client, counting reps and checking form. Her mind wasn't in the gym. She and Mitch had an appointment with their attorney, Sam Hastings, that afternoon.

Mitch met Jules at Sam's downtown Nashville office ten minutes early. Mitch was uptight and impatient. Hastings had left Mitch a voice mail stating that he had received some documentation from Sampson's lawyer. Sam hinted that Mitch might not like what he sees.

"Sampson's lawyer faxed these over to me this morning." Sam handed Mitch a stack of papers. "These are purchase orders and deposits you signed. They cover all of the expenses you flagged- landscaping, transportation, office furniture, and legal fees, as well as the accounts payable receipts. While there are no clear cut descriptions of each invoice, each one has been signed and authorized by you."

Mitch reviewed the purchase orders. The signatures were his. How? He had no idea what these purchase orders were for.

"I don't even understand why my signature is on these. Sampson is the one who usually signed for this kind of stuff. That was his business. In fact he insisted that all purchase orders go through him."

But then Mitch remembered. He was on the phone with a potential client when he noticed a commotion out his office window. He saw a very large, sturdy built blond man handling a dark headed, dark skinned young girl. She couldn't have been more than 14 years old. He had his big hand on her upper arm and Mitch could tell he was squeezing hard because the girl was squirming and pulling away. She looked scared.

It was the expression on her face that bothered Mitch the most. It was fear, but also contempt. This girl loathed and feared the man at the same time, and he was controlling her. Mitch excused himself from his conversation and headed down the hall towards the back door that led to the courtyard in which the man and girl were standing. He passed Sampson's office and saw Sampson looking at some papers on his desk.

"Hey- you should come see this." Mitch said without stopping.

Sampson followed Mitch down the hall to the rear entrance and saw the sight out the window. Mitch was on his way out the door when Sampson grabbed him by the arm and pulled him back in.

"Mitch," Sampson whispered. "Leave it, it's none of our business."

"None of our business? That girl is obviously afraid of that man- and it looks like he's abusive!"

"That girl has given her father a great deal of trouble, and last night he had to drive to the police station to pick her up after she was caught with drugs. Sarge is my best man at RSE, he's a good man and he's doing the best he can, but his daughter is out of control. He brought her with him today so he could keep an eye on her, but it looks like she's given him more trouble."

Mitch couldn't take his eyes off the scene outside. "This Sarge guy seems like a real thug if you ask me."

"Here, I'll go talk with him in a minute. If you could just sign these p.o.'s for me, I'll see if I can tame him down a bit."

Mitch's attention was divided between the man and his daughter and the papers Sampson was holding.

"Mitch, sign here." Sampson redirected his attention several times until Mitch looked at the documents.

"Wait, what are these?" Mitch finally focused on Sampson's priority.

"These are purchase orders and invoices for The Office, just basic accounts payables and expenses."

"Wait, I don't understand, why am I signing these?" Mitch held the documents and began to look a bit closer at them.

"Just to have you on record as a signer. It's good for the bank and the vendors to know both of us, that way they'll trust you when I'm not available. I'll keep copies of all of these in my desk." Sampson gathered the pages back from Mitch's hands, and turned and headed back to his office.

By the time Mitch looked back out the window, the blond man and his daughter were gone.

"SON OF A BITCH!" Mitch sank into the oversized leather chair in Hastings office and let his head fall into his hands. He realized he had been set up. Sampson had Mitch sign all of the accounts payable receipts and purchase orders so that he could't question them. If the authorities investigated the accounting records, Mitch could be implicated in illegal money laundering as well.

"Ok, what can we do about this? Clearly he tricked Mitch into this." Jules was trying to keep the focus positive.

"I'm afraid at this point there is not much we can do. We can argue this out in court, but this is really a he said-he said argument. Sampson will clearly argue that you agreed to these purchases. And we have little to dispute that. If your roles were clearly delineated in your partnership agreement than we could try to argue that Sampson was negligent in his duties in the business. It is a weak charge, but coupled with everything else, it could help your case.

Mitch and Jules walked to the parking lot in silence. Mitch was brewing something. He let it spill when they got to the car.

"I'm going to kill him, Jules. I'm serious. I have spent my whole life trying to do the right thing. I put values like honesty and integrity before personal gain. And look where it's gotten me? I am so tired of being the fool! He's played dirty this entire time. Maybe it's my turn."

"Mitch, we're going to fight this in court the right way. It's a no brainer, he's dirty. It will all come out, and you'll win The Office back. You just have to be patient."

Mitch looked Jules square in the eye, lowered his tone and slowed his words. "I'm done with being patient. I'm done being the bigger man. And I'm done playing it straight. I don't know how yet, but Richard Sampson is going down, soon."

Jules could see that Mitch was serious. And he was right, he had always done the right thing, always played it by the book, and made it a point to act fairly and legally in all of his transactions. Perhaps Sampson needed someone who could play on his own field. Perhaps he needed to be taught one of his own lessons.

Jules held Mitch by the shoulders and looked him in the eyes. She kissed him on the lips and held her forehead to his.

"You are a good man, and you deserve more. We're going to get him- I'm with you on that, I promise. Now what do you say you and me forget about all of this for one night and go out and have some fun. I've got tickets for the show at The Playground tonight."

Mitch sighed and stroked her hair. "I can't, remember? I have to go out to the lake this evening to go over the contracts with the Paulsons. They've invited me to stay in the house for the weekend, which might actually be a great idea. I can really get a good feel for the home. I've got two showings on Saturday and an Open House on Sunday."

"Right, I forgot."

"I have a surprise for you, though. Mom's taking the kids to see Dee Dee, Steve and the boys this weekend. You will have the house to yourself until Sunday afternoon!"

Dee Dee and Steve Spalding were Mitch's brother and sister-in-law, and they had three boys, aged seven to twelve. When all of the Spalding grandchildren got together, the neighbors would take cover. Dee Dee and Steve lived on a ten-acre estate, with horses, chickens and a few pigs. They had an Olympic sized swimming pool, a tennis court and an in-line skating platform. Jules' children loved to visit their cousins, and Jules' loved having a quiet break.

"Did I tell you you were a good man?" Jules hugged Mitch tight. "I only wish you were going to be here to enjoy it with me."

Seventeen

AT 1:15 pm JULES was getting into her car at the fourth street parking garage in Downtown Nashville when her cell phone rang. Monica Perry's face lit up her screen. Jules was surprised to hear from Monica. She was supposed to be at the audition for the Makeover *Your* Life TV show. Jules figured she needed a pep talk.

"It's over, Jules." Monica's tone was angry, bitter, and discouraged.

"The audition's over already? I thought it started at noon?"

"It did. There must have been over one hundred girls here, all waiting to audition. After forty five minutes, the casting director came out to the lobby and announced that the role had been cast. He thanked us for coming and told us we could go home."

"But your agent said you were hand-picked?"

"Apparently over one hundred women were 'hand-picked'." The sarcasm in her voice cut through the air and landed in Jules left ear.

"I'm sorry, Mon. That's just not right. You were meant for that part!"

"Apparently the twenty-something blond with the twenty inch waist was meant for the part. This over the hill fat-ass is meant to stay at home."

"Well, I have an idea. Why don't you come out with me tonight to the Playground? I have two tickets to the show tonight. Let's make it a girls' night."

"Only if you drive. I don't want to be responsible tonight."

"You've got it!"

ON THE DRIVE to Franklin, Jules passed a blue minivan on I-40 with a bumper sticker that read, "Life is Good". 'Shit!' She thought. 'Nothing good about this day'. First, the news from Mitch's lawyer, Sam Hastings, that Richard Sampson had implicated Mitch in his money laundering operation. Then Mitch's tantrum and threats to kill Sampson- which really worried her. And then her best friend Monica was rejected for her dream role in a new TV show. Her mind drifted over the past six years of her life, and all she could see was disappointment and pain. Jules tried to convince herself that life was good, but at the moment she had a hard time wrapping her heart around the thought.

When her children arrived home from school that afternoon, Carolyn Spalding had the car packed with blankets, pillows, the children's suitcases and enough snacks and treats for an entire month. The kids loved road trips with their granny. She had two built-in DVD players with individual headphones, and she let the kids eat candy and ice cream on the road. Jules watched her children's excitement and thought Carolyn was a very smart lady.

After the kids left, Jules and Mitch spent two hours in bed. It had been so long since they had complete privacy. Half of that time was spent in quiet, holding on tight. Neither one of them felt like talking. At six o'clock, Mitch pulled himself out of bed, got dressed, kissed his wife and left for the lake. Jules was alone.

She stayed in bed for another hour, not quite sure she still wanted to go out. But she knew from experience she was prone to isolation, and that withdrawing when she felt this way would only make things worse. She forced herself out of bed, made a pot of strong coffee, and took a shower. She put on skinny jeans, a sweater, and her favorite heels, and looked in the mirror- sexy without trying too hard- she liked it. The caffeine and the outfit were starting to kick in. She was ready to go.

THE PLAYGROUND was built in the 60's and was a Nashville classic. It was praised for its uniqueness at the time of its inception. It was a relatively small five thousand square feet, but the ambiance made it the perfect place for intimate gatherings and exclusive concerts. Tonight's entertainment included five songwriters. While the world might not recognize their names, their songs have been played billions of times in 65 different countries. This was the "Unsung Hero's Show".

"Ok, you didn't tell me HE was going to be here!" Monica caught sight of Tim Holloway as he waved Jules and Monica over to his table.

"That's because it's not about him, it's about you and me. He just gave me the tickets." Tim Holloway and another man were seated at a round table right in front.

"I think he has a thing for you, Jules." Monica nudged her in the side as they approached the table.

Jules shot her a censoring glance and then addressed Tim.

"Wow. This is a great spot, you must have gotten here early."

"No, we're just in with the band." Time winked at Jules, and Monica kicked at her heel. Jules felt like she was in high school. She wasn't sure this night was going to last very long. "Jules, Monica, this is Steve Nicholson, and old friend."

The four exchanged greetings and Monica and Jules made themselves comfortable. It was a sold out show and they had the best seats in the house. Monica ordered a pomegranate martini, which earned her a snicker and an eye roll from their server. By the time she ordered her second she didn't care. Jules stuck with her usual Sam Adams in a bottle.

As the show started the four adjusted their chairs to see the stage and Tim landed shoulder to shoulder with Jules. Throughout the show she noticed him getting closer and closer. First, he let his thigh lean against hers. Then, as he massaged his quadricep he let his fingers brush her thigh. Monica was getting drunk and singing loudly. The music was good, but Jules was so annoyed by the horny man on her left and the drunk drama queen on her right that the night was quickly losing it's charm.

After his third scotch Tim gathered enough courage to slide his entire hand onto her thigh. Monica had finished four martinis and was singing obnoxiously.

"I think I need to take her home," Jules said as she stood, and turned to Tim, "we've both had enough."

"Jules....hey I'm sorry. I didn't meant to......"

Jules put her hand up before he could finish. "It's been a long day, Tim. I just need to go home. Thank you for the tickets. Steve, it was very nice to meet you."

Monica protested as Jules helped her to her feet and walked her out the door to the parking lot. On the way to the car Jules had to stop and wait for Monica to throw up in the bushes.

"All right, come on now." Jules helped Monica in the car. Monica was babbling about how sorry she was for ruining the night. She was saying something about lost dreams and failures but Jules had tuned her out.

What a rotten night, she thought. The perfect way to end this completely rotten day. Jules was angry. For the first time, she was really angry. After the business split she had been discouraged, frustrated, and annoyed. She had cried so many tears. But today, she was angry. The kind of angry that stops a person from caring.

Jules started the car, made a visual check of her mirrors, put the car in reverse, and headed out of the parking space. She shifted into drive, and checked her mirrors one last time. She saw the tan Mercedes SUV parked five cars down the row. Now the back-up lights were on. 'Ok, I'm ready for you.' She thought.

Jules watched as the car followed her out of the parking lot. This time she wasn't scared. She welcomed a confrontation. The long stretch of two-lane highway between Green Hills and Franklin was dark, and Jules and her stalker were the only ones on the road.

She followed the speed limit and watched as the Mercedes stayed about five car lengths behind. He followed her through downtown Franklin, and then onto Carter's Creek Rd. Here the road narrowed and wound around horse farms and country estates. The tan Mercedes came in closer.

Jules instinctively sped up to create distance from the SUV. But the faster she drove, the closer the Mercedes came. The sound of the engine felt like hot breath on the back of her neck.

Jules was about five miles from the turn-off to Monica's home when she noticed the headlights in her rearview mirror seemed to grow bright and then shrink back in the distance. He was playing with her.

Monica had passed out several miles back, and was completely unaware of the situation. The impact woke her.

"Jules, what was that?"

"It's the tan Mercedes, Mon. He's following us."

"Did he just hit you?" Monica was starting to panic.

"Yeah." Jules sped up enough to see the lights in her mirror for a second, before the Mercedes was able to close the gap. He bumped her again. Monica was screaming now. Jules' 1999 Suburban was no match for the 2010 Mercedes G class SUV. The only thing Jules had on her side was an intimate knowledge of the roads ahead. She took a deep breath, coached herself to calm down, and began to think clearly.

"Monica, it's going to be ok, I promise, but if you keep screaming I'm going to crash and we're both going to die. Do you understand?"

"OK." Monica quieted herself, secured her seatbelt, and braced her hands and feet on the dash."

Jules kept her speed constant and held her ground as the driver of the tan Mercedes repeatedly slowed down, sped up, bumped her, then slowed down again. It was a game. The driver of the Mercedes wanted to scare Jules. She wasn't going to let him do it this time. Jules gradually accelerated as she headed south on Carters' Creek Road.

A mile ahead laid the exit ramp to the Rolling River Bypass, a new road still under construction that connected Franklin to Chattanooga. As she approached the exit to the Bypass, Jules hit the accelerator as hard as she could. The Suburban groaned as she coaxed it forward. Jules made the slight right at the last minute, crashed through the traffic cone barrier, then took her foot off the accelerator and let the truck decelerate down the exit ramp onto the newly paved highway.

About a tenth of a mile off the ramp was a gravel access road on the right. Jules eased onto the access road, traveled about 50 yards and made a sharp turn. She stopped the car behind a thicket of bushes and turned off her lights.

The driver of the tan Mercedes was caught off guard by the last minute detour. He traveled straight on Carters' Creek another five hundred yards before he was able to come to a complete stop. He put the car in reverse and traveled backwards to the Bypass exit.

"Monica, stay here and get down." Jules turned off her interior lights before she opened her door and got out of the Suburban. She followed the access road back towards the Bypass. Near the intersection of the two roads lay three traffic cones that had been scattered when Jules came through in the Suburban. She could see the headlights coming down the exit. Jules picked up two of the cones and placed them at the entrance of the access road and dove into the woods just as the headlights shone on the entrance.

The driver of the tan Mercedes slowed as he passed the access road. A flashlight shone down the gravel lined driveway and panned the edge of the woods. From behind a fallen tree Jules tried to catch a glimpse of the driver through the open passenger window, but the light was in her eyes. Her hot breath created a smoky cloud in the cold night air. Jules' heart nearly stopped at the sight, afraid it would give her away.

Before she could take another breath, the SUV moved on. The driver continued on the Bypass for another half of a mile, then turned the car around and followed the Bypass back up the exit to Carters' Creek Road. Jules watched him turn left onto Carters' Creek and head back towards Franklin. She stayed there for at least five minutes, sure he'd come back the minute she turned her back to the road. But he was gone.

When Jules returned to the Suburban she found Monica curled in a ball on the back floor of the truck, covered by one of the kids blankets.

"Mon, its ok. He's gone."

Monica stepped out of the truck and began vomiting in the woods. This time Jules joined her.

They traveled down the old gravel road that had been there long before the conception of the Bypass. The road belonged to Walter Dennis, the original Mr. Pepper.

Mr. Pepper was known for his Famous Fried Chicken to most Spring Hill natives. His grandson lived next door to Jules and Mitch in Franklin, and the two families had become friends.

Mr. Pepper was a true southern gentleman. He and his wife
Evelyn had entertained the Spalding family at their Spring Hill
farm on several occasions, and they had adopted the Spalding
children as their own grandchildren. Before the county started
construction on the Bypass, the access road was their driveway.

A year after construction on the Rolling River Bypass
commenced, Walter Dennis suffered a heart attack and died. Poor
Evelyn lasted another nine months before her own heart died of
loneliness. Their hundred acre estate now lays vacant while the
children try to decide whether to divide it up for themselves or sell
it to developers. The five siblings could not seem to agree on its
monetary or sentimental value. Tonight, Jules thought, the
property was priceless.

Jules stopped the truck as she approached the house to
gather herself. The tears that started a half mile back had turned
to sobbing, and had now settled into a deep shudder. She closed
her eyes and began to relax. After a few minutes Jules opened her
eyes. Monica was looking out the window.

Jules drove past the house and out the newly paved
driveway that led to the northern end of Carter's Creek Road. She
and Monica drove to Monica's house in silence. Jules watched
her rearview mirror the entire five mile route to the Perry's home.
No one was on the road. Jules dropped Monica off at 1:30 am and
headed back to her own home, despite Monica's insistence she
stay the night.

Jules needed to be in her own bed in her own home. Well,
at least her own borrowed bed in her own borrowed home. She
arrived at her mother-in-law's house at 1:55 am, double checked
the locks on all the doors, and climbed the stairs to her bedroom.
She took a moment to log the night's events into her memo book,
and fell into bed. She was asleep instantly.

Eighteen

SOME NIGHTS WERE better than others. But they were all hell nights. Stephanie would lay on the bed, unable to control her body. She would try to push them off, but her arms lacked the strength. It was if she were trying to lift them out of quick sand, but they only lay on the bed. She had control of her eyes at least. She could close her eyes, and avoid the looks of the men around her.

They laughed at her, called her a whore. They made fun of her small breasts, kicked and slapped her hard- just not on the face. Tony had given the men strict instructions to leave her face alone.

Ten to fifteen men a night, four nights a week, for the last three months. Stephanie tried to do the math in her head, but her head was fuzzy. She would lose concentration, and thankfully, time would pass rather quickly. During her lucid moments, she knew exactly what was going on, but lucidity came and went with each breath. During her lucid moments, she knew she would not remember much in the morning.

Tony had said he had given her the drugs to help her relax. That was a lie. She was not relaxed. Inside her heart was pounding, she could feel it. She could feel the panic at the site of knives, cigarettes, and fists. She just couldn't do anything about it.

When Stephanie's teachers complained to her mother that Stephanie was falling asleep in school her mother started asking questions. Stephanie told Tony she would not be able to work anymore without raising suspicions. She had hoped he would let her go. Instead, he found a new drug for her. This one gave her energy. And she was starting to like it. This drug made her feel invincible. Tonight, she felt she could take on anyone.

"Go ahead, slap me, cut me, I don't care. I can't feel a fucking thing!" She shouted at the red headed beast that was taking his turn with her.

He finished his business and scoffed off. "Crazy bitch!"

And then there he was. Mr. Sparks. He was next. He walked into the room with a greasy smile on his face.

"Hi Stephanie."

Stephanie's stomach turned. She knew there was something off about her freshman guidance counselor the moment she met him.

Mr. Sparks took out a long black knife. Stephanie had seen one like that before, at her Uncle's cabin at the lake. It was a filet knife- for skinning fish. Stephanie instinctively stood up, backed into the corner of the room and called out for Tony. Within seconds Mr. Sparks was upon her with his hand on her mouth and the knife at her neck, just behind her ear. He put his mouth to her ear and whispered to her.

"Now that's exactly what I *don't* want to happen." He pressed the blade hard into her skin and let the blood run through her blonde hair.

Tony stopped just outside the doorway. "You ok, Steph?"

"This is between you and me, understand?" Sparks whispered. He looked straight at her and his right eye twitched when he talked.

"I'm fine, Tony." Stephanie replied.

THE THERMOSTAT read one hundred and five degrees, but Tim Turner with Channel 2 news reported that the eighty percent humidity makes the "feels like" temperature one hundred and fifty degrees. September 10, 2011 would hit the record books as Nashville's hottest day in eighteen years. The air conditioner in Mitch's 1995 Jeep Cherokee had quit the week before, and he didn't have the seven hundred and fifty dollars it was going to take to fix it. He had spent the morning meeting with local businesses, promoting The Office meeting rooms and private party rentals, and had been in and out of the car for three hours. By the time he reached the air conditioning of his office, Mitch's navy blue, Men's Warehouse pin striped suit was soaked.

The heat put Mitch in a terrible mood. "You're a strong Pitta!" Jules had teased. She had been reading and studying the ancient science of Ayurveda, and had diagnosed her husband as a temperamental, fiery heat monster who required a cool environment, cold salads, and calming yoga to stay healthy and sane. This day was not for him. Even Sampson's deep belly laughs were pissing him off. He walked down the hall to investigate the inexcusable fun.

Mitch arrived in Sampson's office to find him deep in discussion with an old colleague, Dan Strauss. Dan was the commercial real estate broker that had helped Mitch when he first started in the business.

"Hey Dan, what brings you to this neck of the woods?"

"Mitch Spalding, so good to see you man!" Dan reached out for a hand shake.

"Dick was just showing me what you've done here, I'm really impressed. I think I have just the right spot for number two, and I have a few options for three and four, but they might not be ready for another six months." Dan pulled out a folder full of plats and arial photographs of buildings in Nashville.

"Two, three and four? These look great, but Dan, I'm sure Dick's told you we won't be ready for these for at least another six months, a year more likely."

Richard Sampson and Dan Strauss shared a look that made Mitch uneasy.

"Actually, Mitch, I've hired Dan to go ahead and secure number two. I'm working on the contract right now and plan to submit it by the end of the week."

Sampson's words took Mitch by surprise. "Dan, could you excuse us for a minute?"

"Sure, Mitch. Dick- I've got some calls to make. I'll be down at the coffee shop. Just send me a text when you're ready with the contract. Mitch, great to see you." Dan gave Mitch a wave as he hurried out of the office.

"What the hell is this, Dick? You set up this meeting without talking to me first? *You're* writing up a contract now? This is my business!"

"No," Sampson's tone was calm but condescending, as if he were speaking to one of his children. "this is *my* business, and it's time I stepped up before you run it into the ground. I'm making the decisions from now on, and you can either work with me, or move on."

Mitch laughed nervously. He was confused.

"What the hell are you talking about Dick? This is my company. I gave you thirty percent in exchange for your investment. All of which I intend to purchase back. That was our agreement. You are out of line!"

"No Mitch, you're out of line, and you are a fool." Richard Sampson opened a desk drawer and pulled out a folder, from which he handed Mitch a stapled document. "*This* is our agreement. I am controlling owner of The Office, and if you are unhappy with my decisions you are welcome to step out any time you'd like. That's what you agreed to- its right there."

Mitch held the document and followed the lines he had read so many times to the third paragraph titled "Management Duties and Restrictions". The agreement read, "The Office, LLC shall be owned and operated by the following parties. Richard Sampson shall own and operate seventy percent of The Office,

LLC, and have controlling interest. He shall have all authority to bind the Partnership in making contracts and incurring obligations in the name and on the credit of The Office, LLC. Mitch Spalding shall own and operate thirty percent interest in The Office, LLC. ....

"What is this? This isn't the partnership agreement I signed, you've made this up?"

"That's your signature, Mitch."

"No, I signed our original agreement, giving me 70% and you 30%. You've changed this."

"Mitch that is the original."

"I have the original in my desk." Mitch tore down the hallway to his office and opened his desk drawer. He pulled out the file folder marked "documents", opened it up and looked for the older marked "partnership agreement. It wasn't there. He searched his entire desk drawer. It was gone. Richard Sampson watched from the doorway.

"What are you up to Dick?" Mitch's anger was apparent. His blood pressure had spiked, his face was bright red and his hands were tied in fists.

"I don't know what you are talking about, and I don't like what you are implying. You need to calm down, and if you can't I will be forced to call the police. We don't need an incident, Mitch." Sampson was calm and peaceful, almost glib.

Mitch had nothing to say. Something had gone terribly wrong. Sampson had forged a partnership agreement claiming controlling ownership in The Office and stolen the original right out of Mitch's desk drawer. He looked Sampson in the eye and saw the amusement at his realization. He left without another word, locked his office door, and went out to his hot car.

116

"MITCH, I'M afraid this agreement supports Richard Sampson's claim that he is the legal owner of The Office. Unless you can prove it's a forgery, come up with your copy of the original, or somehow shed some doubt on its validity, this document has to be considered legal."

Mitch's lawyer, Sam Hastings was shaking his head apologetically.

"Sam, you know its a fake, you saw the original. I created The Office, it's my business, and those are my clients in there. He is literally stealing it out from under me and you're telling me there's nothing I can do?" Mitch was pulling on his hair.

"Nothing outside a civil ruling. You can sue him for ownership of the company. You will have to provide a compelling argument that The Office was your conception and that Sampson altered the partnership agreement. Without that agreement, this is a subjective argument Mitch, and the only way you are going to get back control is to convince the right people Sampson is a crook. You are going to have to go to court."

An hour later Mitch returned to The Office. He walked down the hall to Sampson's door. He paused to listen as he peered inside. Sampson was alone. Mitch stepped into the office, approached the large mahogany desk and reached his hand into his jacket. Without hesitation he pulled the Ruger 9 mm out of the interior pocket of his Mens Warehouse suit and aimed it at Sampson's head. Sampson opened his mouth to protest just in time to catch a bullet square in the forehead. He fell forward and hit the desk with a loud thud.

The thud jolted Mitch awake.

THE SOUND OF A door slamming woke Jules. In an instant she was out of bed and tiptoeing down the stairs. The only thing close to a weapon she could find on the way was Carolyn's crystal vase from the hallway. She held it above her head as she rounded the corner to the kitchen.

"I'm so sorry, I didn't mean to wake you." Monica was sitting at the bar watching the coffee brew. "I wanted to surprise you and I knocked over the book." The thousand page book she was referring to was Mitch's bound copy of volumes eight through twelve of the Tennessee Journal of Business Law.

"Jesus, Monica- I thought you were him. I was dreaming he was chasing me, and I was hiding and then I heard the bang. In my dream he had just broken down the door." Jules' hands were shaking. Monica handed her a cup of coffee with cream.

"Hey, its ok. We're ok." Ironically Monica was the calm one.

"Mon, this is out of hand. He was going to kill us!"

"No, Jules, he wasn't going to hurt anyone. He was just trying to scare you, trying to send you a message. If he really wanted to kill either one of us we wouldn't be sitting here right now."

Monica continued. "We should be asking ourselves, why? For the past month you've been sure Sampson has had someone follow you, but why? And are you sure it's him? Why would Sampson go to these lengths to scare you? What is it he wants to achieve?"

"Drugs."

"What?" Now Monica was confused.

"Mitch and I found a financial document that showed The Office took in over fifteen thousand dollars in one month, over three times the expected revenue at that stage in the business. I don't think he meant for us to have a copy of that document. Our requests for all of the financial documents have been ignored. Come to think of it, the stalking started after we pressed for him to produce the accounting records."

"What makes you think its drugs?" Monica was playing devil's advocate.

"What else could it be?" Jules had been so sure of herself up until now. What could Sampson be into that would bring in that kind of money that he would go to threats and intimidation to protect? His healthcare company was worth over a hundred million and he had a personal net worth of almost five million dollars. Fifteen thousand would have been pocket change for Richard Sampson. He didn't need to deal drugs for money.

Jules and Monica spent the next two hours discussing theories and ideas. Nothing really made sense, except that they now had an urgent desire to find out more. Before long, the two had concocted a plan.

THE NAVY BLUE Swoosh was almost as big as she was. Monica admired the Transport Express' logo on the side of a 24' truck as it was getting a wash in the back lot. She followed the arrows in the parking lot to the side entrance and walked to the front desk window. A young man named Jason asked if he could help her.

"Yeah, hi, my name is Susie Sparks." Monica smacked her gum and spoke with a thick Mississippi drawl. "I'm working with Chuck Swenson Productions. Chuck's going to be in town next month shooting a scene for his new movie, 'Call of the South'. We are looking to rent a few trucks for about a week, and I'd love to find out what you have available."

"Ok, sure, do you know what size you will need?"

"I really don't. I was hoping I could take a look at your stock and take some pictures to take back to Chuck."

"Uh, well I guess that would be ok. Hold on one second."

Jason went to the back room and retrieved a key. He led Monica through the back hall to the doors double doors that led to the large garage that held the Transport Express fleet.

"We have three sizes to choose from, the standard fourteen foot, which is what most do-it-yourselfers choose, a twenty four foot, and a twenty six footer. The twenty four and the twenty six footers have a fairly large mom's attic for extra storage. What will you be using them for?"

Monica was taking pictures of the trucks, and surveying the garage. The sight of the tan Mercedes G Class stopped her in her tracks. It was parked in the back, behind a fleet of 26' trucks.

"Ma'm?"

"Oh, I'm sorry, phew- it sure has been a crazy week. We will need a few trucks to haul equipment, props, you name it. But we also need a large truck, like that one over there, " Monica pointed to the twenty six foot truck parked next to the Mercedes, as a prop itself." Monica walked over to the twenty six footer. She positioned herself to take snapshots of the truck, but zoomed in to capture the Mercedes behind it.

The Mercedes was backed tightly into the garage, with the license plate facing the back wall. Monica walked to the truck and pulled the door handle.

"Do you have a key to this one? I'd love to get inside and take some shots of the interior."

"There's not much to see Ma'm. If you driven in a U-Haul its pretty much the same thing."

"Yea, but my boss is extremely picky, and I prefer to be thorough. Do you mind?"

"Sure, I'll have to get the key from the office. It will take just a minute."

Jason was getting a little impatient with Susie Sparks.

When he left the garage Monica started taking shots of the Mercedes. First the left side, then the right, and then the front. There were scratches along the front brush guard. The rear of the car was parked so close to the wall she could just barely make out the first and last digits of the license plate, Tennessee plates, Davidson County, number X....5.

The windows were tinted dark, but Monica could make out a coffee tumbler in the dashboard cup holder, a pack of Marlboro Reds in the console, and a red and grey workout bag in the back seat. On the drivers' side of the front window there was a small decal, a Metro Parking sticker. Monica took pictures of everything.

"Uh, Ma'm? The Mercedes is not for rent." Monica jumped at the sound of his voice.

"Oh, but it sure is pretty isn't it? Sorry, I got carried away in my own fantasy. I've always wanted one of these. Is it yours? You look like a man with good taste!" Monica could charm the stripes off a bumblebee.

"No, Ma'm, it belongs to one of my supervisors. Here's the key to the twenty six footer."

"Oh, right. I think I just need one more shot and I'll be done." Monica opened the drivers' side door, took a quick shot without taking the time to focus, and closed the door. She handed the key back to Jason.

"Did I see a bathroom down the hall?"

"Yes, its right down here on the way back to the office." Jason led Monica down the same hall to the first door on the right.

"I'll just be a minute, thank you."

"Uh, yes Ma'm, I'll be in the office."

Monica closed the door and waited a few minutes, flushed the toilet and ran the water. When she entered the hallway, Jason was gone. She walked slowly down the hall, peeking in the rooms she passed. The nameplate on the second office was "R. Sampson". The door was ajar. Monica pushed the door slightly and took a quick look, it was empty. She pulled out her digital camera and tried to get a good wide view. Just as she put the camera back in her bag she heard footsteps.

"Can I help you?" A tall, handsome man in his fifties came walking down the hall towards her.

Monica had studied improv at Berkley. She was a pro, and today was her best performance ever.

"Oh, I'm sorry, I was using your ladies room and I got caught up looking at the portraits. This one says JJ- founder- TE Online. Is he the owner?"

"JJ is Jordan Jones. His father created Transport Express, and JJ made it into what it is today. Unfortunately the pressure of running a business became too much for him. He went a little psycho, if you know what I mean. I'm Richard Sampson, the current CEO. You are?"

"Just a prospective customer. And I'm leaving. You have a great staff here, Jason has been a great help."

Monica turned and walked out of the building as fast as she could.

IT WAS 11:00 am BY the time Jules got to Tennessee Bank and Credit Union. It was Saturday, and the bank was open until 1:00 pm. Shirley was at her desk.

"Jules, how are you? I've missed you."

"Hey Shirley, me too. It's good to see you."

"You sound stressed, is everything alright?"

"Well, it's been tough since Mitch left The Office, but we're hanging in there."

"Between me and you, that Sampson guy's a creep. I hate what he did to you and Mitch, and I'm not sure the tenants are that happy either." Shirley was whispering.

"What makes you think that?"

"I don't know, just a feeling I get. Once in a while I pay them a visit on site. I've caught a few glances, a few grumbles. I don't think many of them like him."

"I'm not surprised. He's probably ripping them all off."

"Well if there's anything I can do to help you guys, please let me know. I'm cheering for you."

"Actually, that's why I'm here. Mitch and I have been going over the documents we have on file for the period of May through August of last year, and we're missing some of the statements. I was hoping you could get me copies."

"Sure, darlin'- what do you need?"

"I need copies of the business money market or savings accounts, and any other business accounts Sampson set up. I can't seem to find any of them."

Shirley turned to her desktop computer. "Richard didn't set up any savings accounts. I'm double checking, but I'm sure he didn't. I suggested it several times, and encouraged him to set aside money in a retained earnings account, but he basically told me to shut the hell up and mind my own business. Nope, see here, just one checking account for The Office, that's all. I guess that's why you couldn't find the statements." Shirley offered Jules a smile.

"I guess so. My head has not been completely screwed on these last few months. We are trying to get everything together, and my memory is a little fuzzy."

"Well, again, if there's anything I can do, legally, I mean...." Shirley winked at Jules "you just let me know. I'd love to see Mitch back in charge. He belongs there, Jules."

"Thank you Shirley. I really appreciate that, and I'll take you up on it for sure!" Jules hugged Shirley and then turned and headed for the car.

Nineteen

BY THE TIME MITCH returned home Sunday night the kids were tucked in bed and Jules was waiting with a cheap bottle of merlot.

It took just over thirty minutes for Jules to detail the events of the weekend. She shared with Mitch her journal that detailed each time she was followed. She had had the photos of the tan Mercedes SUV, the partial license plates, and the scratches on her Suburban printed at a one hour photo shop and passed them to Mitch.

"Do you still think I'm being paranoid?"

"No. I'm sorry I doubted you Jules." Mitch said the words, but his tone suggested he wasn't completely present. He was thinking.

Finally, he spoke directly to Jules.

"So Sampson's had you followed for the past month. And now, he's taken it to an entirely new level...." it was a statement and a question at the same time. Mitch was working it out in his head, out loud. And then he looked straight at Jules, excitedly.

"He's working really hard to intimidate you, to get me to back down, but it's not going to work. In fact, I think we can use this to stop him."

"What do you mean?"

"If Sampson wants to use fear and intimidation, let's give it right back to him. I have mp3 files of the threats he left on our voice mail the week he was served with the lawsuit. We also have your journal detailing the dates and times you were stalked by the tan Mercedes SUV. We have pictures connecting the SUV to Sampson's Transport Express garage. We have you and Monica to testify you were chased and almost killed by the same SUV, and the pictures of the scratches on both cars."

"So you think we should go to the police?"

"No. We go back to Sampson. It's time to end all of this right now. Sampson can settle this by handing over The Office to me free and clear, or we can go to the police and have him charged with harassment, stalking and attempted murder. It's time we put the pressure on him, and he's given us the leverage to do it."

The photos, the journal entries, and signed affidavits by Monica and Jules detailing the events of the car chase on Carter's Creek Road were sent to Sam Hastings, Mitch's attorney. Hasting's letter to Sampson's attorney, Henry Clay indicated that his client would be forced to make a formal police complaint if the two could not come to an amicable settlement agreement soon. He included a lengthy formal document detailing the transfer of ownership of The Office to Mitch Spalding, for Richard Sampson to sign.

RICHARD SAMPSON was born on April 28, 1955. His father, Malcolm Sampson, a heart surgeon from Toledo, Ohio, moved to Nashville, TN to work at Mid State Baptist Hospital in 1950, where he met a beautiful Chilean nurse named Francisca Diaz. Richard was the only child of the Sampson family, and was raised to respect his elders, work hard, and study even harder.

He was an excellent athlete. In spring he played baseball, but his real passion was wrestling. In his senior year of high school he scored the most wins by fall in his weight class and led his school to win the state tournament. He won a full scholarship to Virginia Tech, and was planning to attend in the fall of 1974 when life interrupted his plans.

Besides wrestling, Ricky Sampson's life was his girlfriend, Jenny Jones. She was an honor student, classically trained on the violin, a candy striper at Vanderbilt Medical Center, and pregnant at seventeen.

The debate over the pregnancy grew strong and heated as parents and grandparents fought over the fate of the child growing inside Jennifer Ashley Jones. Malcolm saw the pregnancy as a distraction, and pressed for an abortion. But Francisca was a devout catholic and refused to entertain the idea. On May 25, 1974- one week before graduation, Richard Sampson and Jenny Jones were wed during a private ceremony by Father Joseph Todd at the Vanderbilt University Chapel.

In August 1974, Richard Sampson reported to Fort Bragg, North Carolina for basic training. Richard Sampson flew through basic training. His athleticism proved he would make a strong infantryman. But his ties to South America, the Chilean army, and his proficiency in the vaseo Spanish dialect made him a perfect candidate for work in the US Special Forces operations in the Southern Cone- the south American countries of Chile, Argentina, Paraguay and Uruguay. With just the right strings pulled, Richard Sampson traveled to Chile in 1975 to be part of a top secret anti-communist operative. He stayed in Chile for four years.

When Richard Sampson returned, his baby girl was five years old. It was only out of favor to his grandfather that Richard Sampson had even seen or heard of Sophia Sampson. His mission in South America had been declared top secret, and correspondence with anyone outside the military was forbidden. He had received two letters from his wife in the four years he had been in Argentina. When he returned, he felt like a stranger.

Adjusting to this man in her life was hard for Jennifer. She had lived the majority of her adult life as a single mom. Ricky, the teenager she had known, had gone away and a strange man had taken his place. Sergeant Richard Sampson was quiet, cool, and aloof. He drank almost every night, and when his insomnia finally broke, Jennifer often found him crying in his sleep.

Richard Sampson fell instantly in love with Sophia. She had his mothers eyes, and her mothers beautiful strawberry blond hair. It was Sophia who had resurrected the spirit of the 18 year old boy he had been so long ago. By the mid 1980's, Richard, Jennifer, and Sophia Sampson had settled into a family life that looked and even sometimes felt normal.

Richard found a job working with a health insurance company. He was a fast learner and within a year he had recognized the shortfalls in the insurance industry. Richard Sampson realized that insurance companies were spending exorbitant amounts of money on services that were unnecessary. He also found that when he questioned the expenses, some doctors were willing to revise their course of treatment to make them more cost effective while maintaining quality of care. For Richard, an idea was born.

Pathways was Richard Sampson's first company, under the parent company Richard Sampson Enterprises, or RSE. Pathways was one of the first managed care organizations operating in the southeast, and serviced three major insurance companies. By the time Sophia was twelve years old, Richard Sampson was a millionaire.

The early days were a blur, working eighty hour weeks and living on caffeine, but they soon gave way to the happy, prosperous days. The days before The Ambassador re-entered his life. These were days of family vacations to Europe and fishing expeditions with his buddies.

He was longing for those days as he studied the photo on the wall. He and Henry had been in Sitka, Alaska fishing salmon. He caught his finest fish that trip, an eighty pound king salmon. And Richard's lawyer, Henry Clay had become his best friend. But the situation at hand called his attention back to present day.

"Henry, I can't afford to lose this one. I need you to do whatever it takes. Do you understand?" Sampson was pacing back and forth, and sweat was beading up on his forehead.

Henry Clay sat at his desk in his corner office of Clay and Associates. He was holding several photos of a tan Mercedes SUV.

"Dick, relax. This is nothing. These pictures mean nothing. There is no evidence of a crime here. We have two witnesses who will testify that Jules Spalding and Monica Perry were drunk on the night of the so called 'attempted murder'. I think I can have the photographs thrown out. If not, Spalding will have to prove the scratches on the Mercedes came from his wife's car. That will be expensive."

"Even if he can muster the resources for forensic testing, we can argue that one of your employees was involved in a traffic accident with Jules Spalding. We could even spin it as though she were at fault- a drunk driver backing into the SUV. I bet if the police searched the Suburban they'd find the owner of the SUV's insurance information scribbled on a napkin in her glove box. And the journal? By the time we are done with them, it will be one big joke. This all looks like the contrived scheme of a scorned business partner." Clay was smiling at Sampson.

Richard Sampson was beginning to feel a little bit better. He sat down in the leather arm chair in Clay's office and began to smile.

"So let me have it straight, Clay, what am I looking at? The big picture...."

"Dick, Spalding doesn't have a case. This is is a spat over ownership of a business. Mitch Spalding may present a heart felt plea loaded with sentimentality and filled with character witnesses, but he has no substance. If this were a he-said, she-said argument, he may be able to convince a jury to like him best. But you have documentation and evidence of ownership, and the resources to outlast him in court."

"Lets go for it then, Dick. How fast can we go to trial?"

"Whoa, slow down now, it still takes time to prepare for something like this. I'd like at least three to six months."

"I don't have six months, Clay. The Ambassador is breathing down my neck to stop this nonsense. The tenants are getting restless also. Some of them are suspicious. Have you seen the latest article in the City Journal?"

"You mean this one?" The headline read 'Rumors Abound about The Office CEO, Richard Sampson's Theft of the Business'.

"Spalding is hard at work to discredit you in the public arena, Dick. Maybe it's time you joined the game. I think I'll call the writer, Justin Toomey. Let's see if you can get your side of the story in."

"That's a good idea. Arrange that. But I also want this trial expedited. I need this over with ASAP. Can we schedule it for next month?"

Henry Clay took a deep breath and cocked a sideways smile at Sampson. "It will cost you extra."

"YOU WANTED TO SEE me sir?" Mr. Sparks popped his head into Principle Stallworth's office.

"Yes, please, Oliver, come in and sit down." Principle Stallworth pulled a file folder from his drawer and cleared his throat as the school guidance counselor took his seat.

"This is a bit uncomfortable, forgive me, but I have to address this with you." The principle handed the folder to his employee across his desk, and averted his eyes as Sparks opened the folder and reviewed its contents.

"I was afraid something like this would happen, Brent. This girl is seriously disturbed. I was really hoping I would be able to help her on my own, but now I'm not so sure." Sparks' voice communicated discouragement.

"Explain." Principle Stallworth was cautiously supportive.

"Well, she revealed to me her cutting habit at our first visit. She has struggled to deal with her anger towards her parents for moving her from Pennsylvania. So I suggested we meet weekly. I've had experience with teens who've cut before, and some good success with non-traditional therapies. But..." Mr. Sparks paused, "at our last meeting she was different. Instead of being withdrawn and angry, she became sexually aggressive and tried to seduce me. When I refused her advances she stormed out. I had hoped that she would have time to cool down before our next visit so that we could talk it out, but it seems she has trumped up these allegations in retaliation." Mr. Sparks sighed.

"These are serious claims she's making, Oliver. Why didn't you alert me of the situation when it happened?"

"I should have, I'm sorry. I really thought I had a handle on this. It's not unusual for a vulnerable girl to have sexual feelings for her counselor. This is usually a sign that she feels safe around him. I thought this was a good sign. I was mistaken."

"What do you suppose we do now? She has threatened to go to the police?"

"I believe we can handle this internally, Brent. I have extensive notes from our sessions detailing her behavior. I'll make copies for you today."

ELIANA TRIED her best to be brave. Miss Sadie told her to hold her head up high and look straight ahead. She told Eliana not to cry, and to do what the men told her to do. She told Eliana that if she didn't she would be beaten.

Eliana tried her best. But the man hurt her. He told her to do things she didn't want to do. She didn't know how. He had laughed at her.

"I'll show you how to be a woman." He said, and then he hurt her.

He hurt her in ways she could never have imagined. When she resisted, he hit her. She couldn't help but resist. It hurt so bad her body naturally resisted, and so he beat her more.

When he finished he left her on the dirty cot, in the cold room, bleeding, beaten, and alone.

Until the next one came. And then the next one. Over and over it happened. She begged them to stop, and sometimes she would faint from the pain. They didn't care that she was bleeding. They didn't care that she cried. They just kept coming.

Eliana cried out to God, wondering how it was that she had landed here, in this horrid place. Where was He and how could He leave her this way. Who were these men? These men that were not like her father. These men who were evil. They threaten and hurt her over and over. They laugh at her and leave her to die.

Eliana looked around at the other girls. Some had been in this place for years. They have no eyes, just empty spaces that occupy a face. Empty spaces that look out into nowhere, that say nothing, that no longer cry. Eliana wondered if someday her eyes will turn empty, and prayed to her Father she will never become one of these girls.

At twelve, she was the youngest girl at The House. That's what they called it, The House. It was not a mansion. Eliana knew that now. In the light of day it was an old, run down home with ten rooms. A kitchen, a bathroom, and eight 'bedrooms'. Each bedroom was a five foot by five foot curtained off area that contained nothing more than an old, dirty cot.

Eliana had been a virgin. She was considered special. And after she had been broken, Miss Sadie sewed her back up again, so she could stay special. Miss Sadie had done this before, had tied the girls down to the bed, stitching them up without an anesthetic. Miss Sadie had no feelings at all. She simply replied to protesting screams with "Special girl gets the special room!"

Her consolation was to put Eliana's cot next to a window, and she told her to be thankful for the accommodation. In the three weeks since Eliana arrived in Nashville, TN, she had spent 18 hours a day in her special room, "entertaining" up to 15 men a day.

Eliana would look towards the window, at her iron garden. She'd keep her eyes fixed on the vines and imagine them growing up and carrying her out of this place. She'd close her eyes and cling to the magic vines, letting her dreams take her far away from the horror of her reality.

Twenty

THE TRAFFIC on Second Avenue was heavy for ten am on a Thursday. Mitch watched the cars from the tenth story window. They just kept coming. When traffic stopped from one direction, it started from another. It all looked like a well choreographed dance from the sky's view. Even at one hundred and fifty feet up, the cars looked like toys. It was as if all of Colin's matchbox cars had come to life right before his eyes. Mitch preferred entertaining these thoughts to listening to the reality that was unfolding.

"Mitch, are you getting any of this?" Sam Hastings was looking at Mitch with concern.

"Yes Sam, unfortunately. You're telling me that Sampson is requesting an expedited trial by jury. The photos, the documentation, it meant nothing to him."

"His lawyer will first try to have the photos excluded as evidence- he is claiming that Monica used false pretenses to get into that garage, and therefore the photos are not admissible. Then he will discredit the testimony of Jules and Monica. He'll have witnesses testify they had been drinking the night of the chase. From what I hear, Monica made quite a spectacle of herself."

"And without the photos and reliable witnesses to the chase, Jules' journal is purely circumstantial. A good lawyer can spin this to look like you and Jules will go to any lengths to win the company from Sampson."

Mitch raised his eyebrows at Sam.

"It's what I would do, Mitch."

"What about the threats? I have them recorded. Sampson said, and I quote, 'if you 'try to take The Office away from me I will do whatever it takes to take you down', and then, ' if you don't drop this lawsuit I'll fucking make you wish you had!' What on earth do you call that?"

"Mitch, as part of a group of evidence of physical threats, stalking, and attempted murder those threats are compelling. But on their own, which they will be, a jury will see them as the rantings of an angry man."

"So that's it, then, it's over. Just like that he can create lies, fake documents, discredit the truth, and steal- all with the blessings of our wonderful judicial system and jury of my peers....." Mitch focused on the cars again. He wondered what the people in those cars were thinking.

Some of them have just received good news. One's having a baby, another just go a promotion. And another just won the lottery. None of them knew the agony he was going through at that moment. The anger, frustration and depression knowing he's been totally fucked and can't do a thing about it. The Ruger 9mm was starting to look a little better to him.

"No, Mitch, it's not over. What you do have is the truth. This won't be easy, but there is a chance. I have some ideas, but we are going to have to work around the clock on this if we want to pull it off in thirty days.

Mitch and Sam Hastings spent the next hour and a half working out Sam's plan. Mitch left the office with a lengthy to do list and a small degree of optimism.

HE STARTED WITH Jonathan Hess, a web designer from California. Jonathan was one of thousands of west coasters who flocked to Music City to enjoy the low cost of living and exceptional business environment. Hess was The Office's first client.

"Jonathan, its Mitch Spalding." It had been just over a year since he had spoken with Jonathan Hess. The last time they had seen each other was the day Mitch left Sampson in a fury. He hadn't seen the tenants watching. Mitch had made such a raucous each of them had come to their doorways to investigate. To an outside observer it must have looked like an unruly prisoner being carried down the hall to solitary, all the other inmates watching from the bars.

"Mitch, wow, its good to hear from you, how are you?"

"Good, Jon, I'm doing well. How about you? How's the business?"

"Its great, actually. I've been overworked, actually, and have had to subcontract out some of the menial stuff. Sarah and I just finished the addition on our home. I've built a huge office out the back with it's own entry. I love it!"

"That's great to hear, Jon. Look, I'm going to cut to the chase. I could really use your help. We are preparing for trial against Dick- I'm going to win The Office back. He's played some dirty tricks, and I've got a lot of work to do to prepare my case. I need to prove that The Office was my idea. I need you to testify that I approached you with this idea long before Sampson was involved. Do you think you could help me out?"

There was a long pause on the other line of the phone. Complete silence. For a moment Mitch thought they had been disconnected.

"Jon, are you there?"

"Yeah, Mitch. Listen, I would love to help you out. I'm real sorry you are facing this. The breakup was difficult for all of us, and it left a lot of scars. The rumors were fierce, and my business tanked for months from all of the bad publicity. I'm sorry Mitch, but I can't risk that again. We have a mortgage and a baby on the way. I know I must sound like a real prick, but I can't get involved, Mitch."

"Jon, you know he stole it from me. Sampson is a thief, and he's making a ton of money off of what I created. Jules and I are living with my mom! Please, I need your support."

"I can't, Mitch. I'm really sorry." Then the line went dead.

Mitch was dumbfounded. Jonathan Hess had been a good friend. Mitch was there when he cried over his first big client, and when he proposed to his girlfriend Sarah. How could he have turned his back on Mitch now?

He went to the next name on the list, Max Harrison. Max was a young real estate developer, and Mitch had a special liking for him. On several occasions, Mitch had stayed at The Office until the wee hours of the morning to help Max with a project.

"Hello, you've reached Harrison Development, please leave your name, number, and a brief message and I will get back with you within twenty four hours. Thank you and have a great day."

"Max- it's Mitch Spalding. When you have a moment, can you please give me a call back at this number? It's really important. Thanks!"

MITCH CONTINUED down the list of the remaining eight tenants of The Office. He had one more rejection, from Josh Hanover. It was similar to that of Hess. His business was thriving, and he couldn't stand the bad publicity of testifying or being involved in what he called a bitter 'custody battle'.

The rejections surprised Mitch. These men were not just clients of his. He had given them everything he had. He had put his heart into The Office and they knew it. In the short time he operated The Office, Mitch Spalding spent at least two hours every day directly with his clients, getting to know their business, and discovering how he could serve them better. He had entertained them at his home, and played with their children. Why would they turn their backs on him now?

Five days, and several more calls later and Mitch was still without a key witness to support his assertion that he created The Office. Each day that passed without a return call left Mitch more and more distressed.

While Mitch was impatiently waiting, Jules was putting together the documents on Mitch's list. She started with the timeline the two had created in preparation for the deposition.

"Mitch, what about depositions? With the trial less than a month away, shouldn't we have a date for the depositions scheduled by now?"

"We're not going to have a depo. Our plan is to surprise Sampson, catch him off guard. If he knows our strategy before we go to court, he'll have time to prepare. Sampson's a hothead. If we catch him in lies in court, he's likely to lose his temper. That will work in our favor."

"That sounds smart. Do you think it will work?"

"It could. If we ask the right questions."

"What are the right questions?"

"I don't know yet, Jules. That's where I'm really going to need help. Sampson has something to hide, I just don't know what. I'm not even sure where to begin, but we need to dig deep and find out as much as we can about him. There has to be something we can use against him. We'll win this case if we can convince the jury he is a con and a bully."

"But he's slick, he knows how to spin a wreck into a masterpiece."

"That's why we have to find his weakness."

As if on cue, the phone rang. It was Sam Hastings.

"Are you kidding me? Sam that's great. Yeah, we'll look into it, thank you." Mitch finished scribbling a name and number on a sticky note and handed it to Jules.

"What's this?"

"This is a start. Jordan Jones, the original owner of Transport Express. Sam just found out that Jones filed a civil suit against Sampson eighteen months ago in the Davidson County Circuit Court."

Mitch handed Jules the sticky note.

"According to Sam, Jordan Jones claims that Richard Sampson falsified documents, destroyed the originals, and stole ownership of Transport Express in July of 2009."

Jules was speechless.

"Where does this case stand now?"

"Chronic delays. Sampson is controlling this one. Word is that Jones has sold everything he has to support his case. He's not giving up."

Jules looked at the sticky note. "I'm on it!"

JULES SPOKE with Jordan Jones briefly before heading to the gym. At the mention of Richard Sampson, Jordan almost hung up on Jules. But she got his attention quickly at the mention of lawsuits, threats, and intimidation. Suddenly he didn't feel so alone. They agreed to meet the next day.

When she arrived at the gym she was feeling better, and intended on getting in a short workout herself before starting work. Then she stumbled into Tim Holloway.

"Jules, please, give me just a minute." Tim's humble pleading was effective.

"I know you put in a request to transfer me to another trainer, and I don't blame you. I was a complete jerk last weekend. I'm embarrassed, but mostly angry with myself for the relapse."

"Relapse?"

"Jules, I've been sober for 5 years. It has been my biggest accomplishment. Alcohol destroyed my marriage, my career, and almost took my life. I became a different person when I drank, as you saw that night at The Playground."

"Tim, I had no idea. Look, you don't have to tell me all of this."

"No, actually I do. I haven't shared my history with any of my friends. I've been too ashamed. That's why I agreed to drink with Steve that Friday night, I didn't want to admit my past. My sponsor told me that I need to have more accountability partners in my life. People like you, who are involved in my life in a healthy way that can help me stay on track."

Jules was taking all of this in. She found herself moving from anger to sympathy, and then she felt honored that he would consider her an important part of his recovery process.

"Please forgive my behavior last weekend. And if you're up for it, I would love if you would do me the honor of helping me keep my ass in line."

Jules was smiling now, like a parent proud of her a child who shows responsibility.

"How would you like me to do that?"

"Just knowing that you know I'm in recovery is a big help. But I'd love it if you would speak up if you see me headed in the wrong direction, give me a little reality check when I think I'm strong enough to handle just a little."

Tim looked at Jules expectantly, as if he was waiting for her to smack him across the face and walk off.

"Tim, thank you for sharing that with me. And I'd be happy to be your accountability partner." Jules laughed at the title.

"And I'll tell Tony to forget about the request for a new trainer."

"Good, 'cause I scheduled myself with you first thing in the morning."

Jules smiled and offered Tim a fist bump. Tim bumped back, picked up his gym bag, turned and walked out the door.

The gym bag. It was the same grey bag with a red stripe through the middle that Monica saw sitting in the back seat of the Tan Mercedes SUV. Jules knew that bag looked familiar. She froze as she watched Tim walk out to his car, a red minivan, and drive away.

"What's wrong dear?"

Tony Ramano's words startled Jules and she jumped. She turned to look him in the eye and forced a smile.

"Oh, no, you can't fake it with me. Come on inside and lets talk."

Tony walked Jules into his office and shut the door.

"Now what's been going on? You've been jumpy and edgy, and sometimes just plain dark."

Jules needed someone to talk to, and at this moment, Tony seemed like the perfect candidate. She sat in his chair and spilled her guts. She started at the beginning and detailed the stalking, the chase, and the discoveries at the Transport Express garage. She explained to him how she felt Tim Holloway may be connected to the whole ordeal, and apologized to him for getting the gym involved.

Tony smiled big, took Jules by the hand and reassured her.

"Jules, I've been waiting for something like this for a long time."

"What?......."

"In my country, we call men like this Sampson guy el bullo, a bully. And if there is one thing I really enjoy doing, it's putting a bully in its place. Do you know how to stop a bully?"

"How?"

"Bully him. Do you know how to stop a stalker?"

"Stalk him?"

"Now you're learning. How much information do you have on this car?"

"I know it is a tan Mercedes G Class SUV, and we have a partial license plate number. It is registered in Davidson County."

"That's a start. Can you get me that license plate number?"

"Yes, I have it written down at home, I can text it to you this afternoon. Why?"

"Because we are about to become the stalker."

TONY RAMANO opened his desk drawer and pulled out a photograph. They had been so young back then. Pete D'Amico had been his best friend, colleague and savior. The photo was a sober reminder of the fact that they were not as invincible as they once thought.

To the doctors, Tony Ramano was known as Rocco Lombardi, one of ten aliases. But to the nurses, Tony was simply known as "Amante" or lover. Even in a body cast, Tony Ramano had all of the young ladies in the Sicilian long term rehabilitation unit smitten.

The image of Tony and Pete surrounded by four beautiful nurses drinking champagne in the rehab lounge put a smile on Tony's face. He and Pete had only been in their 40's, but that last brush with death was enough to convince Tony he had enough of life as a special agent.

It took him five more years to persuade Pete to retire and move with him to the US, where he could walk freely without looking over his shoulder for Italian mobsters, opiate smugglers and guns for hire. At fifty, Tony Ramano, along with his wife and best friend, settled down in the comfort and anonymity of the small Tennessee town of Fairview, just a few miles West of Nashville.

Tony loved the quiet life, and he loved pursuing his other passion, fitness. His little gym became quite popular hangout for the West Nashville crowd. Tony loved people, and he loved the opportunity to serve them honestly, as himself.

He hadn't realized how much he missed the action and the adrenaline of his old life until today. Tony's instincts peaked when he saw the look on Jules' face. He recognized the forced smile and weary eyes. They inspired excitement in Tony, and he was eager to get involved.

Tony picked up his phone and dialed Pete's number.

"Eh, Tony, how are you?" Pete D'Amico was still in bed.

"Pete, I've got a job for you....."

Twenty One

THE MIDDLE SCHOOL called as Jules was leaving the gym, headed to meet Jordan Jones. Claire had been in the clinic all morning and needed to go home.

"Hey sweetie!" Jules arrived to find Clair resting on the nurse's couch.

"Mom........ my head hurts so bad!"

"Mrs. Spalding," The school nurse was an older woman in her sixties, with white hair tied in a bun, and white nurse's shoes. She made the perfect grandmother. "Claire has a fever of 101.1 degrees. She's been complaining of a headache and stomach ache all morning. It may be strep."

"Ok, let's get you home then."

Jules helped her daughter in the car and called the pediatrician on the way home. The Spalding children's pediatrician was a long-time family friend. Jules was able to describe the symptoms and give the school nurse's assessment and have the office call in a prescription before she arrived at the pharmacy.

Jules brought her daughter home, gave her some Tylenol and an antibiotic and kissed her forehead.

"Claire, I have to go. I have a meeting that I can't miss. I will be back as soon as I can, and Grandma is here if you need anything."

"Mom, please stay with me!"

It pulled at Jules' heart to leave her daughter. There were very few times Claire "needed" her mother, and Jules hated to let her down. But she couldn't miss her meeting with Jordan Jones.

"I promise, Claire, I would not be going if it wasn't absolutely necessary. When I get home you and I will spend the rest of the afternoon together. I promise!" Jules had to stifle a tear, which made Claire feel a little better.

Jules hugged her daughter, who struggled to hold on to her mother, and left. She called Jordan Jones to let him know she was finally on her way.

HIS APARTMENT was bare. He invited her in, and offered a plastic storage crate for a chair.

Jordan Jones was very handsome. But the stress of the past eighteen months had aged the twenty nine year old disproportionately. His dark brown hair was greying at the temples, and fine lines had formed at the corners of his deep green eyes, and around the corners of his mouth. His strong jawline showed signs of wear, as his jowls began to sag a bit.

"I'm sorry about the accommodations. I've sold everything, including the furniture."

There was a dark spot on the wall where a flat screen had hung, and voids in the dust on the shelves. A cheap lamp sat in the corner of the room next to a bean bag chair. Jordan picked up a stack of papers lying next to the bean bag and brought them over to Jules. He handed her stacks of papers one at a time. Jules did her best to focus.

"This is a copy of the lawsuit against Richard Sampson. This is my calendar, for the past eighteen months. Each date marked with a red pen is a deadline. Interrogatories, production requests, depos. All deadlines come and gone, all rescheduled, or often simply ignored. There seems to be no repercussions for rich men who chose to work on their own time schedule."

"Wow, you have a lot more experience with this man than we do. Where are you in the case?"

"We've spent the last six months trying to schedule a deposition. And with every phone call, every fax or email, my lawyer charges me another arm or leg. I don't have anything left to sell. So now, I'm at a standstill, and he's winning."

Jules leaned in towards JJ.

"Tell me about your company."

Jordan Jones spent the next thirty minutes explaining the vision of his father, the heartbreak of his father's death, the evolution of Transport Express, and how Richard Sampson stole it all away from him. And then he surprised her.

"I've been stalking him for six months now."

"What?"

JJ handed Jules a small notebook. Inside she found a list of dates with notations.

"He's into something really big, Jules. I just haven't figured it out yet."

"What is this, what is he into?"

"Look here," JJ pointed to Wednesday, June 15, 2011.

"Something big was happening at The Office. I drove by at 2 am and saw about fifty cars parked in the back lot. I stayed and watched for about thirty minutes. I could see shadows walking past the windows, but the blinds were drawn. I was about to get out of my car and walk closer to get a better look but two big thugs came out of the building and started to walk my way. I took off as fast as I could."

"Mitch and I think he's dealing drugs. Maybe this was one of his deals?"

"Doubtful, I've never seen or heard of a drug deal going down like this. About a week after I saw this I put a wireless security camera on a telephone pole across the street."

JJ turned the page on the notebook. He had still photographs taken from the video feed. The photos were dated June 29, 2011, a Wednesday.

"First, Sampson and his right hand man show up." The first dark, grainy photo showed Richard Sampson and a very large man following him into the rear entry of the building. The other man's face was obscured.

"Then the trucks start to show up." The next photo showed a Transport Express truck backed up to the loading dock.

"I have no idea what they unload off the trucks. I haven't been able to get close enough to put cameras on the loading dock. They keep the building pretty secure, and have their own sophisticated surveillance equipment. I'm working on hacking into their system to disable it so I can get in closer."

"Every second and fourth Wednesday is the same routine. Sampson and two of his employees show up around midnight, the trucks show up around 12:30 am, and then the cars start showing up at 1:00 am. By 2:30 am, the show is over and everyone leaves."

"I also have video cameras at the TE warehouse. Here's the really interesting part. Look at this."

JJ turned the page and showed Jules a black and white photo of Sampson, outside the TE garage, talking with two large, Latin American men. It is dark, but the three are directly under a street light.

"Every Thursday night, around midnight, these two thugs show up and meet Sampson for about thirty minutes. They go into the offices. I've spent several nights out there, and I can see the light in Sampson's office on. I've also watched them talk outside, under the street lamp. Sampson's afraid of these men. I can see it in his face."

"I'm working on securing more surveillance equipment. I have a buddy that transports for a security firm that imports its equipment from China. He pilfers a few things here and there, and writes the lost inventory off. He's getting me some button cams and a few other devices we can use. I should have everything by the beginning of next week. I have to get eyes and ears inside both buildings."

Jules watched JJ closely as he talked. Was he really an ally? While it seemed they were on the same side, Jordan Jones was obsessed. Jules feared he may be a little unbalanced.

"JJ, Do you think you are taking this too far? This seems a little dangerous. If you continue to press on this, you could risk losing a lot more than your company!"

"It's beyond that point already Jules."

JJ pulled out another folder from the stack. The first piece of paper he pulled out contained one word, each letter had been cut out of a newspaper, a black and white, all caps warning. STOP. JJ turned it over to reveal a date, written in pencil.

"This was the first one I received, just a week after I filed the lawsuit."

The next page was written in the same manner. Each letter cut out of a newspaper, or magazine. This time the letters were all different colors, and capitalization was optional. The warning read 'drop it now'.

There were twenty pages in all.

"I received one every week for the first two months, then they came less frequently, but more intense."

The messages became more threatening as time went along. Some were more like taunts, 'you'll never win'. Others were much more serious. 'Keep going and you'll regret it.'

"This came last week, after another attempt to schedule a deposition."

The most recent letter was the most ominous. In the center of the 8 1/2 X 11 inch piece of printer paper was a picture of a pretty woman, blond, in her mid twenties. He eyes were marked with red X's, and a red target was drawn over her chest. The text read, 'keep it up and she is history'.

"That's Penelope. She left me after I sold my grandmother's silver. I told her I had no use for silver. That wasn't really the point. She has been after me to drop the lawsuit and move on from day one. I was obsessed with this fight from the beginning, and she knew it was tearing me apart. She moved out three months ago. This picture was taken two weeks ago."

"Have you been to the police with this?"

"Three times. They tell me this is a civil matter. When it comes to 'going through the proper channels', as they say, this is a dead issue. Sampson has friends everywhere, even in the DA's office. I even tried to get a restraining order against him for Penny and me. I showed them this entire folder, and the bitch in the DA's office told me it wasn't enough to prove Sampson was a threat. They told me to take it to court."

"JJ, what do you plan to do once you know what's going on?"

JJ shrugged. "Honestly, I hadn't really thought that far. I guess it depends on what I find."

"Well, maybe we can help."

Jules and JJ spent the next two hours sharing ideas and talking strategy.

STEPHANIE WAS HOPEFUL for the first time in months. Principle Stallworth had found her note and had asked to speak with her. Perhaps now someone would listen. She had confided in that pig Sparks at their first meeting. He told her she had a vivid imagination for a fourteen year old. He had accused her of watching too much pornography. She called him an asshole and left. She had no idea how much of an asshole he was. Now she would get the opportunity to show the rest of them.

"Good morning, Stephanie!"

Stephanie could not believe her eyes. Mr. Asshole Sparks was sitting with Mr. Stallworth, smiling at himself like he was a prized pig.

Stephanie became lightheaded and lost her footing. She touched at the scab behind her ear. Mr. Stallworth stood and ran to her side. He extended his arm to her, but she brushed it aside and sat in the empty seat at his desk.

"Stephanie, Mr. Sparks and I have been discussing your current situation."

"My current situation?" Stephanie's venomous tone lingered in the air.

"Your past behaviors, your cutting issues, and your false allegations against Mr. Sparks?" Mr. Stallworth was becoming inpatient.

"Past behaviors? Cutting? What are you talking about? My allegations are the truth- this man is a perverted pig who likes to screw teenaged girls!" Stephanie was beginning to shout.

Mr. Stallworth stood and approached Stephanie. "Young lady, I will not tolerate that kind of disrespect in my office, and I expect you to lower your voice. Mr. Sparks is a respected counselor, and he has documented your self-destructive behavior and inappropriate conduct. It's time for you to sit and listen."

Stephanie sat down in her chair, not knowing what to say. They were winning once again.

Stallworth spoke again. "Now Mr. Sparks and I have spent a considerable amount of time discussing just how we should handle this situation. In my opinion, your parents should be called in at this point and we'd make a recommendation that you be committed to a psychiatric facility. But your counselor is a little more forgiving. He has proposed that we overlook your..."

Principle Stallworth paused to find the words, and opened the folder with Stephanie's note on his desk for her to see.

" ...antics, and opt for an in-house solution." He looked over to Sparks and nodded.

Mr. Sparks leaned forward as he addressed Stephanie. He leaned in so close she could feel his hot breath on her face, and smell the sour stench with each throaty word he uttered.

"Stephanie, I'm willing to give you a second chance. But, you have to be willing to commit to working with me. I'll give you a month to turn around. You will work with me one on one, once a week, in my office after school. I will explain to your parents that we will be working on dealing with your anger over the move. I'm sure they will be pleased with that." He sat back in his chair.

"If you cooperate, we'll forget this little incident." Oliver Sparks winked at Stephanie.

Twenty Two

VICTOR'S FATHER, Herman, worked in the mines. It was the profession of his father, his grandfather, and his great-grandfather. The saltpeter mines in the Atacama Desert were home to four generations of the Diaz family. Victor was expected to be the fifth.

It was a distressing thought for Victor. He had watched his father toil every day. Victor could feel the discouragement, the depression, and the dread in Herman as he would rise early each morning, and go to work.

Life in the mining towns was grueling and dangerous. The mining camps, known as officina's, were maintained by monopolizing organizations that exercised strict control over the lives of the miners. Miners and their families lived in small, army barrack-like "quarters" and were paid in tokens that were usable only in the confines of the officina. Miners worked eighteen hour days, often returning home injured, or suffering respiratory illnesses.

Herman Diaz considered himself a man trapped by the circumstances of his life. He was a victim of monopolies, corrupt men, and a government that failed to protect its citizens.

As his anger grew, Herman became active. He became a member of the Socialist Workers' Party in 1905, and witnessed the massacre of thousands of his fellow minors, striking and demonstrating for better wages in 1907.

Herman's first arrest was in 1910, and then again in 1912. He was proud of his involvement in what he considered a righteous movement, and began following the writings of communist activists like Luis Emilio Recabarren.

According to Herman, corruption and greed were natural instincts of man, and without governmental enforcement of 'fairness policies', societies would fall victim to the oppression of man.

Prior to the First World War, Germany was one of the leading importers of Chilean nitrates. But as the war progressed, Chilean nitrates were re-directed for use in explosives for the Allied war effort. This left Germany scrambling for supply. As a result, German scientists perfected their own substitute. In the process, Chile's share of the nitrate market began to fall, and eventually shrunk to nothing, leaving the Atacama Desert a ghost town.

Victor saw the German's move as the brilliance of innovation and a free market. He was inspired by the German scientists' adaptability, creativity, and ingenuity. And as he watched his parents sulk in self pity, Victor's disdain for socialism and communism grew.

In his teens, Victor moved with his family to the port city of Valparaiso where his father took a job working at the docks. It was there that Herman Diaz met and friended a young Salvador Allende, chairman of the Socialist Party of Chile. The Diaz home became an informal meeting house for members of the political left.

To Victor, the political climate in his own home was oppressive, and he longed to be free.

He found his opportunity in the army, where he studied economics, geopolitics, and intelligence, and met other like-minded men who shared his longing to create an abundant life.

Growing up a capitalist in a socialist home gave Victor a unique list of qualifications. As a teen and even as a young boy he found himself playing interference between his radical parents and a conservative authority. Twice he found himself appealing to the mine bosses for the continuation of his father's employment following his involvement in anti-establishment assemblies. Victor's keen sense of diplomacy and intimate knowledge, understanding and on occasion, empathy for the far left gained him the respect of his military superiors.

In his first year of service, Victor Diaz was sent to the United States to meet with a democratic Senator from Tennessee, Senator Wallace Benjamin. His objective was to establish a relationship with the Senator, who was openly anti-communist, and considering presidential candidacy.

Victor spent a month in Tennessee's capital, Nashville, and secured the relationship between the popular US senator and the Chilean army. He also succeeded in securing the relationship between himself and Frances Maria Conte, the eighteen year old daughter of the senator's housekeeper.

Victor and Frances were married the day before his return to his home country, and Frances gave birth to their daughter, Francisca Maria Diaz, nine months later.

Francisca was looked after by the Senator's family while Victor served his country thousands of miles away. Victor became known affectionately as the Senator's personal "Ambassador to Chile" and traveled to the United States four times a year for work and family. He established his service as a liaison between the Chilean and United States governments' anti-communist operations.

In 1959, Victor Diaz was stationed at General Headquarters of the 1st Army Division, based in Antofagasta, and served alongside Augusto Pinochet. The two were kindred spirits, and became instant friends. Victor's ties to the US were an asset to Pinochet, who needed US support to aid in his efforts. By the late 1960's, Colonel Victor Diaz had become one of General Pinochet's most trusted staff and advisors.

But Victor was tired, and ready to settle down. He was granted retirement from the Chilean army at the age of 60 and moved to the US to be with his family permanently, maintaining his relationship with General Pinochet and occasionally performing jobs for the leader as a consultant.

How wrong it had all turned out, he pondered, as he stood with his grandson now. Decades later Colonel Victor Diaz, The Ambassador, regretted the decisions he had made for his grandson that fall.

"THIS IS AN opportunity for you, Ricardo. This is possibly the most important movement in our history."

"In *your* history, Papa. I don't give a rat's ass about politics. My life is here, with Jenny."

"Ricardo, you are so young. You must understand, Chile is your history. And the politics of Chile are the politics of America. There is a tide coming, a strong tide that we must stop. These men are doing good work for us all. And they need you."

"But what about Jenny, the baby?"

"We will look after them here. They will be just fine until you return."

"But I can't see them?"

"We will work something out. It will only be for a time. You will come out of this experience a stronger man, Ricardo."

THE WORDS haunted the Ambassador. Had he known the full story he never would have sent young Richard Sampson to Chile.

Richard Sampson was just 19 years old when he landed in Santiago, Chile. He was greeted with warmth by The General himself. His fear rapidly turned to excitement, as he was treated with the respect of a prince. It seemed that being a descendent of the esteemed Colonel Diaz made for an enviable legacy.

"You are a special man, Ricardo." The General had said as he walked Richard down a long corridor towards a room at the end of the hall. "We have special plans for you."

The air was hot and humid. As the two approached the doorway Richard Sampson could smell sweat and tobacco, and hear the buzz of a fan. He entered a large office, dark, hot, and smoky. Light streamed in from louvered windows.

"Señor Sampson, it is a pleasure to meet you. I hope you have enjoyed your trip so far?"

The young Sampson was overwhelmed and unsure of himself. He knew very little about Chilean politics, only what his grandfather had told him.

Over the past eighteen months, the Chilean army, under the command of General Augusto Pinochet, had formed a junta and ousted the socialist Allende government. General Pinochet had been named the president of Chile. Richard Sampson was now standing in a small, filthy room with two of the most powerful men in South America, President Augusto Pinochet, and his friend and colleague, Colonel Manuel Contreras. It was Contreras who stood before him. He was a short, plump man. He spoke to Richard with warmth.

"You have entered our country at a most exciting time of reform. Unfortunately, we still have many citizens who do not understand, and we must continue to protect our interests. We are thankful for the Americans and their support of our efforts here in Chile, especially you. I am told you are a scientist?"

"Yes sir. Biology and chemistry were my best subjects in school. I had plans to study medicine, like my father."

"Ah, well.... you will do well here. You will be working with some of our brightest chemists in one of the finest labs in the country. I think you will find your work here very challenging."

Twenty Three

HIS PHONE RANG just as he was about to fall asleep. Mitch considered ignoring it until he looked at the caller ID.

"Max?" Mitch didn't have time for greetings.

"Mitch, hey, sorry it's so late. I just really needed to talk to you."

Max Harrison's voice was shaky and he was slurring his s's. There was a lot of noise in the background.

"Max, where are you, I can barely hear you."

"I'm out, Mitch. Can you meet me?"

"Now? Max it's after midnight."

"I know, but I think you'll want to hear what I have to say."

The Brewpub was crowded and loud, the perfect place to lose yourself. Max Harrison was sitting in a booth in the back of the bar, next to the arcade machines. He was drinking coffee.

"So Max, you ignore my phone calls for two weeks, and then you call me out here to talk about something so important it can't wait until the morning. What is going on?"

Max handed Mitch a large manilla envelope.

"What's this?" Mitch opened the envelope and found it full of 4X6 color photographs. The first two photographs were of a group of five girls, who looked around fifteen years old. The girls were dark skinned, they looked ethnic but Mitch could not place the nationality. They were all staring in one direction, and shared a strange expression on their faces. Mitch had seen that expression before, a combination of fear and contempt.

The next photograph was of Richard Sampson talking with a tall, thin, grey haired man. Mitch recognized him immediately as Mayor Tom Schoals. The two were smiling and Sampson was gesturing to their right. In the background Mitch saw more young girls standing with their arms crossed behind them.

The next photograph was a picture of two men. One of the men was a large, blond haired man that Mitch recognized from The Office. He was one of Sampson's men. He was the man Mitch had seen handling his daughter in the parking lot of The Office. The other man had his back to the camera, but Mitch could see that he was much shorter than Sarge, and was dark haired and dark skinned.

The rest of the photos were more of the same, girls, Sampson, and other men.

Mitch put the photographs down, and looked up at Max Harrison.

"Max, what are you showing me? What are these pictures?"

"These pictures belonged to Brian Fielding. I think these are what got him killed."

"Brian Fielding? The boy who worked the front desk? Killed? I'm lost. Brian Fielding left us in a lurch after just a few days. Jules had to step in to keep everything going. He's dead?"

"Mitch, Brian Fielding didn't quit like Sampson wanted us to believe. Sampson had him killed, because of these." Max held up the photographs.

"You are going to have to start at the beginning. What are these pictures of, and why do you think Brian Fielding was killed?"

Max whispered, "I'm not sure what's going on in these pictures. I found an SD card on the floor of my office the day after Fielding left. I wasn't sure where it came from so I just put it in my desk drawer and forgot about it. When I moved out of the office I found it again. At home I put the card into my digital camera and found the images. But that's not all."

Max handed Mitch a small Canon Power Shot and told him to press play.

Mitch saw Brian Fielding's face in the screen. " These pictures were taken by Brian Fielding at The Office, at 1121 Wilson Street, on Wednesday, July 30, 2011, 1:15 am. The individuals in the photos that I've been able to identify are Richard Sampson, "Sarge", and Alejandro Espiranza. I don't know what they are doing, but .."

At that point the video goes out.

Max leaned in close. "Brian Fielding never showed for work on July 31."

"I know that Sampson was worried about him, he called the police the day he didn't show up for work." Mitch was trying hard to remember.

"No, Sampson didn't call the police, Fielding's mother did. Sampson spun the situation and made it look like he was concerned. But I overhead him talking with the police in his office, and he lied to them. He told the police that Fielding made a big scene, complaining about his hourly rate, and that he told Sampson to F- off and left."

" I don't understand........"

"Mitch, Sampson is into something very dangerous, and he's willing to kill to keep it a secret. I believe Fielding wanted someone to find this because he knew he wouldn't be around to tell."

Mitch Spalding was beginning to see pieces of the puzzle. He just didn't know how they fit together. "This is what JJ was talking about."

Now Max was the one confused.

"What?"

"Jordan Jones, another former business partner of Sampson's. He has similar photos. But what is it? What is going on?"

"I'm not sure, but whatever it is, I don't want to get involved. That's why I didn't call you, Mitch. I'm sorry, I really am, but this is serious shit, and I'm not risking my life for it. I don't think you should either. That's why I decided to call you now. I wanted you to know what you are getting into."

"Do the other tenants know? Is that why nobody has called me back? And why Jon refused to talk to me?"

"Jon won't talk because he signed the same agreement I signed."

"What agreement?"

"After you left The Office, morale was pretty low. Several of us expressed frustration and Sampson offered to buy out our leases and let us go. He insisted we sign a non-disclosure agreement. He said it was in the best interest of The Office and the tenants who chose to stay, that we 'refrain from discussing The Office affairs'. We agreed not to talk with you, or anyone else about any and all experiences within The Office."

Mitch sat back in the booth and closed his eyes. The gravity of the situation was beginning to sink in, and it was shocking. What he thought was a simple dispute over a business was turning out to be a sordid tale involving illegal activity and murder. The business partner that he once trusted with his dream was more than just greedy and dishonest. He was devious and evil. Mitch excused himself, tucked the pictures into his jacket and headed out of the bar. Halfway to the car he stopped to vomit.

"THIS IS GETTING really out of hand." Jules looked at the first three photographs as she listened to Mitch retell the story he'd heard from Max, and dropped the rest on the bed as she faced Mitch.

"Do you want to stop now, Jules?"

"Hell, no."

WHEN HE WOKE it was 12:30 am. "Shit!" Brian
Fielding was messing up again.

At 18, Brian barely graduated from high school. He
wasn't college material, according to his guidance counselor, and
so he decided to venture out into the world of entrepreneurialism.
Brian's first venture was a multi-level marketing company. For
six months he walked door to door pawning cleaning supplies.
Who knew women rarely stayed home anymore, and those that
did didn't like to clean.

His second job involved selling memberships for a car
detailing service. He wasn't very good at that either.

His favorite job was in the magic shop. Unfortunately he
spent more time playing with the tricks than interacting with the
customers. It lasted two weeks.

After a year of frustration and a thousand dollars in debt,
Brian Fielding found himself desperate for work, any work.

The day he was fired from The Grind turned out to be one
of the best days of his life. Jules and Monica had been enjoying
one of their therapy sessions just as Brian was given the boot. He
wasn't very good at making lattes. He was, however, naturally
inclined to help people. When Jules left her wallet on the table,
Brian picked it up and followed her out the door.

"Ma'am, you left your wallet!"

"Oh, thank you! That was very sweet of you, not many
people would have been so honest." Jules was impressed.

"Just doing what I'd want someone else to do for me."

"I like that attitude, not many people have that anymore.
Do you work here? " Jules was looking at his uniform shirt. "I
don't think I've seen you before."

"I just started today- and ended today, too. I'm not very good at making coffee, I guess." Brian was embarrassed.

"Well what are you good at?" Jules was fishing.

"I'm not really sure yet. I like working with people, they make me happy. I know I want my own business someday, I'm just not sure what kind of business."

"Can you answer phones?" Jules had an idea.

"Sure!"

"Can you smile and be polite?"

"Absolutely!" Brian Smiled.

"How would you like to come work for me and my husband? It's not glamorous, we just need someone to answer phones and receive guests. But you will be surrounded by young entrepreneurs. You may get inspired."

Brian was ecstatic. Who would have thought getting fired from a coffee shop could end so perfectly?

Perfect until today, that was. Jules Spalding liked Brian Fielding. She liked his energy, and his demeanor. She liked how he treated visitors and was always courteous on the phone. But Richard Sampson disliked Brian from the beginning. He saw him as a snot-nosed kid with a history of screw-ups. Sampson wasn't one for second chances. And today, Sampson had caught Fielding coming in fifteen minutes late.

It didn't matter that his tire was flat when he came out to his car this morning, or that there was a wreck on I-65. It only mattered that this was his first week at work, and he was late.

Sampson didn't say a word, just looked at him with distaste and headed for his office. Later that evening he stopped at Brian's desk, five minutes before quitting time, and dropped a file about five inches thick on his desk.

"I need these copied and filed before tomorrow morning." Sampson didn't even look at Brian as he talked, then turned and walked out the door.

"He's giving me a second chance," Brian thought. "Maybe there's hope for me yet."

Brian didn't stop with the file on his desk. He continued to work through the night, organizing, filing, and finishing the large "to do" pile for The Office tenants. He was halfway through proofreading a large document for Max Henderson when he dozed at his desk.

"I need coffee." He said, to no one.

Brian Fielding left The Office and headed to the only late night coffee shop, several miles away. When he returned, there were several cars parked in the back lot. That was odd.

Brian parked across the street and took his camera out of the glove compartment. He placed the camera on auto mode and walked up to the building.

Brian entered through a side door. As he entered the building he heard many voices. He walked toward the voices, which were coming from the conference room at the end of the hall. When he got close enough, Brian ducked into an alcove and watched.

Brian took pictures of what he saw. There were so many girls. They all looked young, between fourteen and eighteen years old, maybe. Some spoke in Spanish. Then he saw Sampson. He was talking quietly with two other men. He didn't recognize the other men. He kept taking pictures. Then he saw the Mayor. 'What on earth?" he thought.

Brian changed the setting on his camera to video, and began his video documentation. The hand that grabbed the back of his neck felt like it was big enough to strangle a cow. The other hand, around his mouth almost covered his entire face. He was being dragged backwards, away from the party ahead.

"If you mumble a word, you're dead, understand?" The throaty voice whispered in his ear. Brian shook his head yes.

Once he was satisfied he had Brian under control, the large man turned Brian around and walked him towards the back entrance. As he passed the office of Max Henderson, Brian stumbled and fell. One quick move and he disengaged the SD card from the camera and slid it under Henderson's office door.

Brian's last thought was how much he'd learned in just two weeks at the magic shop.

Twenty Four

THE KNOCK at his door came at 2:00 am. The dog's barking woke Jenny.

"Richard, who is it?" Jenny called to her husband who was already at the front door.

Richard ran up the steps and whispered to his wife. "Go back to bed Jenny, its just Sarge. He's having a little relationship trouble. We'll go have a drink in my office."

Jenny went back to her room, and Richard Sampson went back down the stairs to face two men he'd hoped he'd never see again.

Richard Sampson opened the door to his office and let The Ambassador, and his two guests inside.

"Ricardo- it's good to see you again." Alejandro Espiranza had aged quite a bit in the last ten years. He kissed Richard Sampson on the cheek.

Frances Muniz took Richard's hand in his and offered an apology. "I'm sorry we are here so late, we have traveled a long distance. May we come in?"

Richard Sampson escorted the two Chilean soldiers to his office in the back of the house. He poured himself a scotch and offered some to his visitors.

"Thank you, Ricardo." Muniz spoke first, and took a drink. "We are here with a new assignment for you."

166

"Assignment?" Richard began to laugh. "I'm not in the Army anymore."

"Neither are we, Ricardo." Espiranzo spoke this time. "We are independent contractors now, and have decided to bring our enterprise to the United States. We are in the process of establishing contacts in various parts of your country."

"You're here with a business proposition for me?"

"That's correct, Señor. We want you to be our Southeast Distributor."

"Distributor of what?" Sampson was suspicious. He envisioned cheap plastic toys made by child laborers.

Espiranza handed Richard a folder. Richard opened the folder and began looking over several documents. There were financial reports, graphs, charts, and then several photographs. As he read through the pages his expression changed from confusion to disbelief. He turned to Espiranza.

"You've got to be kidding me!"

"As you can see, Ricardo, or business is quite lucrative. Those numbers reflect our business in the Southern Cone for the last year. We expect our American division will bring in at least twice that much. As our Southeastern distributor, we are willing to give you thirty percent of the deal."

"No. Sorry, I'm not interested. I finished with you the day I left Chile. Those days are long gone." Sampson was indignant.

Espiranza handed Richard another folder. " I think you may want to reconsider."

Richard Sampson opened up a file folder marked 'Sampson' and once again, thumbed through a stack of documents and photographs. He stared at the pages in disbelief, which quickly turned to fear, and then rage.

Richard sat down in his office chair, took a deep breath, and spoke in a quiet, but sharp tone. "You can't do this."

"Yes, Ricardo we can. You were very helpful to us in Chile. But we need your help again. If don't want to cooperate, we can send these files to the appropriate authorities."

Richard sat in silence for a minute, and then relaxed.

"Nice try." Richard dropped the file on his desk. "I'm protected. I have my own alliances boys. This will never go anywhere."

"Now that's not entirely correct, Ricardo." The Ambassador spoke this time, and handed Sampson another folder. This one contained more pictures. Pictures of Sophia. There was a picture of her with her grandfather, another of her leaving her dance class, one of her eating lunch on the patio of her school, and another of her at her bedroom window.

"Señor Sampson," Frances Muniz spoke, "your daughter is very beautiful. She would make a great asset to our company."

"You son of a bitch..." With one swift move Richard Sampson drew his weapon from his desk drawer, stood and approached Muniz but The Ambassador stepped in his way. With Sampson's Glock 17 aimed at his chest, Muniz looked at Richard Sampson calmly and showed a hint of a smile.

"Our colleagues back home have this information. This is just your copy to keep as an insurance policy. Your cooperation is not optional here. And if the two of us don't return with a satisfactory agreement, others will be sent to close this deal."

"HENRY, IT'S DICK. Did Spalding respond to our court date?" Richard Sampson sat at his desk with his lawyer on speaker phone.

"Uh, yeah. I have Hastings' reply right here. 'We have received your notice to appear in court on January 15, 2013. Thank you. We look forward to concluding this process in a timely manner. We will see you then, Sam Hastings.' Looks like we are a go!"

"Just like that? No discussion, no arguments? I didn't expect Spalding to be so cooperative."

"Dick, I think Mitch Spalding is as anxious to get this over with as you are. This is a good thing. A month from now, this will all be over."

"I wish I had your optimism Henry, but I don't trust the man. He hasn't approached any item on our agenda without opposition. He's up to something." The tension in Richard Sampson's neck was spreading down into his shoulders.

"Dick, you are reading too much into this. Spalding is a dunce. He has his head so far up his good-guy ass he is clueless. He believes he will win this on merit alone."

"Now you are being naive, Henry. Mitch Spalding is a smart man. If he is being quiet, he is up to something, and I'm not comfortable just leaving this one to chance."

"I can provide a distraction for you if you'd like." Henry Clay fingered a manilla envelope on his desk.

"Yes, I would like that, thank you Henry."

"Consider it my pleasure." Henry Clay smiled. He loved playing the bad guy.

Twenty Five

IT SEEMED unusually early for the school bus this afternoon. Jules had spent most of the day in bed, not really sleeping, but wishing she were. It had been a long night. The events of the previous day and last night brought a new meaning to the situation at hand. She and Mitch were no longer dealing with just an angered business partner. Sampson was truly evil.

She was still afraid, especially after learning of Brian Fielding's suspicious disappearance. But the possibility that Richard Sampson was using The Office as a means for something dark and evil fueled her desire to pursue their plan even further. Jules was more committed now than ever to find out just what Richard Sampson was doing, and stop him.

"Hey Mom, I got the mail." Claire came bouncing in the house in a great mood. She tossed a stack of mail on the kitchen table.

Jules gave her daughter a hug and then picked up the pile.

"Bills, junk, and more junk." She sighed. Then she came to a letter addressed to her. There was no postage and no return address. It had been hand delivered.

Jules opened the envelope and unfolded a piece of notebook paper. A photograph of Claire was pasted in the center. In cut-up magazine letters she read the words "STOP NOW". Her knees went weak instantly and she dropped the paper and sat in the chair.

"Mom? What is it?" Claire bent down to pick up the paper but Jules snatched it out of her hand.

"It's my friend Tanya, from high school. Her mom passed away last week." Jules couldn't look at her daughter, afraid her face would give away her fear. She put her face in her hands.

"Oh Mom, I'm sorry." Claire hugged her mother tightly. It was all too much for Jules. She began to cry, and Claire held on tighter. In this moment, Jules began to question her involvement with Richard Sampson. She thought she might be ready to let it all go. She discussed it with Mitch when he arrived home.

"We can't stop now, Jules. You said it yourself last night, we have to finish this. If we stop now he'll just find someone else to bully."

"So let him, Mitch. He's taken his threats to the next level. And if everything Max Harrison has told you is true, Richard Sampson is willing to kill to keep his secret in the dark. I'm not interested in putting my family at risk just to prove a point."

Mitch sat down across from Jules and took her hands in his. "Jules, this is serious, real serious. And you're right, he is a dangerous man. This is not just about proving a point. If I don't stand up to him now, I will always be watching my back, always waiting for him to resurface. We already know more than he wants us to know. If we don't put a stop to this now, he'll always be with us."

"I need some time to think. I'm going to the gym. Can you order a pizza for tonight?"

"Sure."

Jules kissed her husband on the forehead and walked out of the room. Her mind raced as she drove in the dark. Maybe if they just stopped everything right now, and let it all go, their lives would get back to normal. Maybe it was possible to forget about what they had seen and pretend it didn't exist. If they backed off the lawsuit, maybe Sampson would leave them alone. Jules told herself that she was wrong about people. Evil did exist, and it was everywhere. It would continue to exist regardless of what she did. Wasn't it more important for her to protect her family than try to get involved in something she had no control over in the first place?

When Jules pulled up to Ramano's Gym, Tim Holloway's red minivan was in the parking lot. It was a Friday evening, and the gym was full. Jules walked in the door and looked for Tim.

"Tim, how are you?" Jules had to force a smile. After her last encounter with Tim Holloway she pulled out the pictures from Transport Express. She committed the image of the black gym bag to memory. She was sure it belonged to Tim Holloway.

Tim was working with the squat rack. "Hey Jules, I'm great, how 'bout you?"

"I'm good- I'm sorry I missed our session the other day, my daughter was out for several days. I'm sure you know how that goes."

"Yeah, sick kids can really throw a kink into plans can't they? Hey, don't sweat it, I've had my share of last minute cancellations." Tim walked towards the ring for a post workout stretch.

Jules followed him. "Mind if I stretch with you? I could really use it. It's been a long week."

"Tough days at the office? " Tim managed a wink.

"No, at least not my office. My husband is having some trouble with his ex-business partner." Jules decided to fish.

"Oooh, business breakups are ugly, aren't they?"

"You know something about that?" Jules couldn't take her eyes off Tim. She was searching him.

"Not personally. I've never really been interested in being the boss, I don't mind working for someone else, it keeps things much simpler."

"What do you do, Tim?" Jules looked him square in the eye, and waited for his answer.

"I guess you could say I'm a jack of all trades. I work for a business man, and I do what he needs me to do."

"That sounds sinister..." Jules put on a playful, almost flirty tone. She was beginning to enjoy this.

"Ha! Hardly. Somedays I get to do some really cool things, like last week, I got to fly to South America. I had to escort some big whig my boss is trying to woo, to his office in Nashville. But yesterday, I was in charge of his dry cleaning and attending to his dogs. Its not always glamorous, but it definitely keeps me on my toes."

"South American big whigs, wow, what kind of business does your boss own?" Jules couldn't tell if he was telling the truth or just creating lies to distract her.

"He's into a lot of different things, including imports. Quite boring and uneventful, actually. With a son to support, it's perfect. I'm home at a decent hour every night, and I always know I'm safe." Tim stared straight into Jules' eyes. She felt he was sending her a warning.

She looked straight back at him and stood up. "Well, I've always found safe a little boring." Jules waved at Tim as she walked to the weight room floor. "I'll see you next week!"

JULES LEFT THE gym wanting to kick some ass. But the moment she stepped into the house and eyed the photographs of her children on the walls, she began to reconsider.

"Mitch, I'm just not sure I can do this. What are we getting into?"

"We're about to find out, Jules. I got a call from JJ when you were out. The surveillance equipment came in. He wants to meet tomorrow morning.

Hesitantly, Jules agreed. "I'll make him breakfast."

JULES MADE SURE Carolyn Spalding had left for her
Saturday morning tennis club before calling JJ to come over. She
did not want her mother-in-law involved in any of their plans.
The less Carolyn knew about what was going on the better.

Monica Perry arrived with Charlie just as Carolyn was
leaving.

"You're here early, Monica!" Mrs. Spalding was surprised
to see Monica out before 11 am.

"Oh, I know. Charlie couldn't wait to come play with Ian
and Conner. It was all I could do to get them to wait until after 9
o'clock!"

"Well it's good to see you. You girls have a good time!"
And Carolyn was gone.

JJ arrived shortly after and unpacked a large box of
equipment onto the floor of the Spalding's living room. It was a
tangled mess of buttons and wires that made absolutely no sense
to the others. He also unloaded several smoke detectors, two
digital desk clocks and three deluxe desk calculators.

"What is all this stuff, JJ?" Mitch was holding up a tiny
black button.

"These, my friends..." JJ proudly stated, "are our eyes and
ears inside Sampson's empire. We are hooked up with some of
the best technology and highest quality digital video and sound
out there. If we place them right, Sampson will never know we're
there."

"Ok, so just how do we place them?" Mitch was skeptical.

"I have a plan." JJ proceeded to share with the three his
plans for the following week. Jules, Mitch, and Monica listened
carefully, took notes, and asked questions. After three hours, each
one had a task, and was ready for action.

Twenty Six

JJ NEEDED CAFFEINE. As he sat at the window seat of the coffee shop, he thought about what he was about to do. The last two years of his life had been some of the most trying times he'd ever experienced. He wasn't sure he would be able to say the words he needed to say today. It was 9:00 am, time to go.

"Transport Express, can I help you?" Jason sounded unusually alert this morning.

"Jason, its Jordan Jones, how are you?"

"JJ? Dude! What's going on?" The twenty-one year old from Tallahassee, Florida was a career student. Going on his fifth year at Belmont University, he hadn't even completed enough credits to be considered a junior. But he was an asset to Transport Express, and had been ever since JJ met him. He was dedicated, and took an interested in the company. JJ always thought he'd make his way to manager one day.

"Jason, I need a favor. Is Sampson in?"

"Not yet, what's going on?" Jason sounded worried.

"I need to speak to him, do you know when he'll be in?"

"Said he'd be in around 11:00 this morning. He has a meeting at 1:00. You want me to call him in?"

"No, don't. I don't want him to know I'm coming. Can you just text me when he gets there? I will only take a few minutes."

"JJ, what are you up to? He's not worth it man."

"I just want to talk, I promise, I won't cause any problems, I just need five minutes, but I want to surprise him. Can you just let me know when he gets there?"

"Sure thing, bro. Hey, we miss you around here."

"Thanks, bud, me too."

JJ set his alarm for 10:45 and sent a text to Mitch.

MITCH SPALDING took one last look in the mirror before getting into the van. A week's worth of stubble, an old pair of bifocals, and a bottle of brown hair dye transformed him into someone he didn't recognize. The 'Metro Pest' decal he had created in Photoshop looked just like the real thing, and fit perfectly on the side of his rented painters' van. But Mitch was still nervous. It took him twenty-five minutes to get to Transport Express; it was 9:30 am.

He parked in the back lot, put his cell phone in his back pocket and went to the back of the van. Mitch loaded the backpack sprayer onto his back. He had filled it with water mixed with some yellow food coloring to give it a hint of color, and pasted a smaller version of the same 'Metro Pest' logo on the canister.

Mitch double checked that the cameras were in his shirt pocket, put on a pair of blue latex-free gloves, closed the van doors, and headed for the building.

He had seen exterminators spray his own home and The Office hundreds of times, and yet he was still nervous when he approached the structure. He aimed the sprayer at the base of the building and sprayed a long line of colored water along the ground as he walked the perimeter, just as practiced. As he approached the loading dock, Mitch drew his sprayer along the door frame.

He paused, looked intently at the corner of the frame, and turned and headed for his van.

Mitch retrieved a small ladder from the van and returned to the loading dock door. He opened the ladder and climbed up high enough to reach the top left corner of the garage door frame that opened to the loading dock. That's when he was interrupted.

"Excuse me, what are you doing?"

Mitch turned with a jump and saw Jason looking up at him. He closed his hand tight around the tiny camera.

"It looks like you've got evidence of a nest up here, I just needed to get a closer look." Mitch was starting to sweat.

"Nest? What are you talking about? Your guys were just here last week and we got a clean report. Dan, I think his name was, he told me that we were 'bug free.'" Jason made air quotes at the expression and imitated the exterminator who gave him the report.

"Yeah, I know. We gave a lot of clean reports recently, but we've had dozens of calls since, with complaints of Recluse infestations. They crop up quickly, and you can't be too careful with Recluses. A woman out in Springfield lost a huge chunk of her thigh just last month to a recluse bite, didn't you see that on the news? We've been sent out to all our businesses to re-spray and double inspect as a courtesy. You won't be charged for this."

"Well, ok dude. Do what you have to do."

"Will do. Oh, you should probably keep your employees away from the areas I'm spraying for at least a few hours until it dries. This stuff can be real toxic." Mitch surprised himself with his improv abilities.

"Gotcha." Jason trotted off.

It was 10:00 am. "Shit!" Mitch opened his fist and found the tiny button camera had been crushed. He only had five, and each had a specific placement. He would have to be more careful.

He pulled another camera from his pocket and inspected it. The tiny wireless camera was the size of a dime, but had a wide angle lens that could span the entire parking lot from this vantage point. It had night vision capabilities, and a smart motion sensor alert system. The camera could differentiate between the movements of small animals like squirrels and birds, and humans, and would sound an alert at the monitoring station when people entered the viewing area.

Mitch pulled a small box of wipes from his utility belt and pretended to wipe down the door frame as he fixed the camera to the top corner with putty, and then climbed down the ladder. From the ground, Mitch took a good look at the area and noted that the button cam blended in quite well with the surroundings.

For the next twenty minutes, Mitch patiently sprayed the remainder of the perimeter, and carefully inspected all window and door frames. Mitch had two cameras prepared for the front and rear entrances to the Transport Express warehouse. The rest of the cameras were needed at The Office. He had one damaged camera and would have to decide how to split the remaining cameras.

Mitch decided to save the remaining cameras for The Office, and forego placing a camera at the front entrance of Transport Express. JJ was insistent that all TE employees parked and entered through the back of the building, and JJ's previous surveillance had shown Sampson and his men using the rear entrance during their middle of the night encounters. Mitch felt confident he did not need a camera in front.

Mitch had made it full circle around the building and was headed back to the van when Sampson pulled into the parking lot. He was looking in Mitch's direction. Mitch could feel his pulse race and his body heat up, even on this crisp December morning. As he took the backpack sprayer from his back and placed it into the van Sampson was exiting his SUV and looking at Mitch with a puzzled expression. Despite the dark brown hair and beard, the hat and glasses, Mitch felt as if Sampson were looking directly into his eyes and recognized him. Mitch held up a hand in a Nashville wave and cocked his head to say hello. Sampson returned the head cock, turned, and walked to the rear entrance of the building. It was 10:45 am. Mitch headed for The Office.

JJ RECEIVED the text from Jason at 10:50. "Here now" is all it said.

He ran the wheels of the antique red metal model eighteen wheeler his father had given him over his hands one more time before leaving the window seat at the coffee shop.

"Son," Herman Jones had said, "this is what life is all about. Trucks- they make the world go 'round. Think about it. Where do you get your food, the grocery store? No, from California, and Florida, and East Tennessee farms. How about your clothes? The ones you're wearing now were likely made in Indonesia, and then flown in to California. We need trucks to bring us things, the things we need to live. And we need trucks to move our things, the things we want to take with us. This country can't survive without trucks- and we're here to provide this country with what she needs!" Herman Jones had given his son the old toy when he was ten years old. It wasn't worth much to the world, but it was worth the world to JJ.

JJ walked into the front door of Transport Express and exchanged glances with Jason.

"He's in his office." Jason was eyeing the truck and JJ with a suspicious glance.

"Alone?" JJ whispered.

Jason nodded, and winked at JJ for good luck.

"What the hell?.............." Richard Sampson stood up and started to come around from behind his desk when JJ held up his hand.

"I've come in peace, Richard. Please, sit down and hear me out."

Sampson didn't trust JJ. But he backed up and sat down in his chair, his eyes focused on the red shiny object in JJ's hand.

JJ stood across the desk from Sampson.

"I've come to let you know it's yours. I'm done fighting. I realize that continuing this fight with you is not honoring my father's memory. He was a peaceful man, and would rather hand the business over to someone who could run it well than possibly ruin the whole thing over bad publicity and a public trial." JJ had never worked so hard to control his emotions, he felt as if he were going to vomit.

Sampson stared at JJ, not sure what to believe.

"Here, I brought you this a peace offering." JJ leaned over the desk and held the truck in his open palm for Sampson to take. As he handed the truck to Sampson with his left hand, he used his right hand to place the tiny button sized wireless camera. The self adhesive backing was undetectable, and the round black camera looked like one of several buttons and knobs along the black desk speaker tethered to Sampson's desktop computer.

The camera, with its 180 degree wide angle lens would capture everything that went on behind Sampson's desk. The second camera JJ placed on the back side of the desk looked like a decorative piece of hardware. It worked perfectly with Sampson's mahogany masterpiece.

Sampson was still speechless, staring at JJ quizatively.

"I have a meeting with my lawyer next week, and we'll draw up the papers. I plan on dropping the lawsuit and moving on. I just thought I'd tell you in person."

Finally Sampson smiled. "You're doing the right thing, JJ." Sampson stood and offered his hand to JJ.

"I know I am." JJ ignored the hand and walked out.

Twenty Seven

MONICA PERRY loved flowers. She could have picked
one of the arrangements in the cooler, but instead insisted on
picking out each individual flower herself to create a sophisticated
display of three dozen perfect white roses. She picked out a sleek,
contemporary white vase, and tied a black satin ribbon into a bow
around the neck.

"Would you like a card from our selection to place in a
cardholder?" The clerk at the florist was holding a long plastic
cardholder and pointing to a rack of cheesy pre-made thank you's,
get well soon, and happy birthday greetings.

"I've got my own card, but I'll take this, thank you."
Monica took the cardholder, paid for the flowers and was out the
door.

Douglas' Cube provided the perfect transportation for
"Belle Meade Flower Company". Monica had the magnet made
by her friend Noel at the prop shop. It fit perfectly on the drivers'
side door of the Cube. Monica put on her apron, with the Flower
Company logo ironed on the front, and drove to The Office.

"I have a delivery for Richard Sampson." Monica held out
the beautiful floral display for the receptionist, Celia to see.

"Those are beautiful. You can put them right here and I'll
make sure he gets them."

"No, I have very specific orders from our client to place
these in his office personally." Monica looked around, hunched

over towards Celia and whispered "Jenny can be pretty persistent you know."

Celia was familiar with Mrs. Sampson's insistence for having things done her way, and had experienced her displeasure and rebuke for ignoring direction on more than one occasion.

"I understand. I'll have to let you in his office, let me get my the key."

Celia turned to the wall behind her to a small reproduction of Monet's Waterlilies. She pulled on the right side of the painting and the whole thing opened up to reveal a key rack, with several keys labeled. Celia took a key off the hook labeled 'Sampson' and closed the panel.

"It's right down here." Celia led Monica down the hall to Sampson's office, and opened the door.

Monica turned to Celia. "Thank you. I'll just be a minute."

Celia lingered and watched Monica. She wasn't getting the hint.

Monica put the flowers on Sampson's large desk, took a step back and shook her head in exaggerated exasperation. "No, that won't work." She turned to look at Celia.

"I can lock the door when I'm finished, if you'd like. It may take me a little while to find just the right placement. Jenny asked me to make sure I gave it my decorator's touch."

Celia didn't like the idea. Richard Sampson didn't like anyone in his office when he wasn't around. Butt then the door chimed, indicating a visitor had arrived at the front desk.

"Well, ok. But check in with me when you're finished." Celia hurried back to the reception.

Monica took a good look around, and placed the flowers at eye level on a shelf on the back wall across from the doorway. She fixed the black button cam on the center of the bow on the vase. The 180 degree lens should catch all angles of the room, including Sampson's desk. Before she left she picked up his office phone and installed a bugging device, just as JJ had showed her. It took 3 seconds.

Monica left Sampson's office, locked and shut the door, and returned to the reception, where she found Celia in a conversation with a stinky man in work clothes. He carried a long ladder in one arm and a tool box in the other.

"I'm telling you, we got a call from the fire marshall stating that your smoke detectors are not up to codes. They were placed here and inspected by our department ten months ago, but since then Metro has upgraded their standards. We have to replace the existing units in the next two weeks."

"Well then you are going to have to come back, sir, until I can clear this with the owner. He's not in yet today. I will have to call him and get his approval first before anybody does any work in this building." Celia was picking up her phone and beginning to dial.

The man took the phone out of Celia's hands and placed it back on the receiver.

"Ma'am, I'm under orders from the Metro Davidson County Fire Marshall." The man pulled a log book out from under his left arm and opened the pages for Celia. "I have an extensive list of work orders that have to be completed in the next ten days. If you hold me up I will have to work overtime, and cost you and your tax-paying boss twice as much in unnecessary expenses. Do you think your boss would approve of that?"

Celia knew he would not. Sampson grumbled incessantly about wasted government spending.

"Well, ok. But only in the common areas."

"I have orders to replace all existing devices in this hallway, and in the conference room, can you show me that area?"

"Sure, it's at the end of this hallway, that door on the left." Celia was pointing to an open door at the other end of the building.

"Thank you, Ma'am." The stinky man got to work, and switched out five smoke detectors.

The large hallway in The Office was a common area approximately thirty feet wide, and three hundred yards long. It was the hallway from which each office is accessed. It served as a community space, with waiting areas for each individual office. One weekend a month, tables and chairs were brought in for seminars and hands-on learning sessions. It had even been the venue of one tenant's wedding, with the reception held in the conference room.

The man switched out a smoke detector in three of the four corners of the long hallway, and one on the long wall mid-way down the center. He installed the fifth smoke detector at the narrow end of the conference room. As he finished, the stinky man placed the smoke detectors he had removed into his backpack, thanked Celia for her cooperation, and left the building with his ladder, backpack and tool box. Celia opened the door for him. He almost tripped over the exterminator's pack as he left the front patio.

"Asshole!" He sneered at Mitch as he headed to his pickup.

Mitch raised his eyebrows at Celia and the two of them laughed.

"He sure is having a bad day isn't he?" Mitch joked with Celia as he handed her the inspection notice.

"No kidding, poor guy though. Wouldn't want his job. Is it time for our inspection already? "

"Yep- you passed, no problems today." Mitch's confidence was growing. He had successfully placed the remaining three motion sensor surveillance cameras around the exterior of The Office without generating suspicion.

"Phew. I saw you really inspecting the doorways, thanks. The spiders really creep me out." Celia exaggerated a shudder and smiled at Mitch as he waved good-by and left The Office.

METH WAS a funny thing. It kept you up. And it kept you thin. Stephanie was learning to like it. There was just one problem. It was expensive, and Stephanie had racked up a debt to Tony so high, she would be working for him for the next ten years just to pay it off.

Most days, this didn't bother her. Most days, Stephanie didn't care anymore. Nothing mattered but the score, and she'd do anything for the next one.

But today was her birthday.

"Good morning Steph!" Susan Miller entered her daughter's room carrying a large tray. She sat the tray on Stephanie's bedside table and sat at the edge of the bed.

Susan forced a smile as she brushed the hair out of Stephanie's face. She stroked her head and winced as strands of her daughter's hair fell out in her hand. Stephanie had lost at least fifteen pounds in the last five months, and her teeth had yellowed. Susan Miller knew her daughter was in trouble. But she was tired of fighting.

She began questioning when Stephanie's clothes started to fall off her shrinking frame. Susan thought her daughter had been dieting, or worse, purging, as a form of rebellion. Stephanie's anger seemed to grow daily, and her moods vacillated between solemn and rage depending on the hour.

Susan tried to take her daughter to a doctor, and a psychologist, but Stephanie refused to go and threatened she'd run away if her mom tried to force her. Susan attempted to ground Stephanie indefinitely if she didn't change her attitude, but Stephanie said she didn't care, she had nowhere to go anyways.

Oddly enough Stephanie's grades were good, and her guidance counselor reported that she was making progress in their after school sessions. Susan Miller was sure her daughter was taking her anger out on her parents with rebellion. She had read about teens starving themselves, purging, and even cutting their own skin as a form of dealing with emotional pain. And Susan

Miller was convinced she had caused her daughter anger and pain by dragging her away from everything she knew and loved in Pennsylvania.

Now her destructive behavior had affected her health. Susan was desperate to help her daughter, but didn't know how.

"Try loving her." Susan's pastor told her one Sunday after church.

"I do love her!" Susan was offended.

"Of course you love her. But what I mean is, stop trying to fight her behavior, and just take the time to show her love. Stop using punishment as a deterrent, and start showing her love, no matter how she treats you. I promise, you will see a remarkable turnaround, in a short period of time."

So Susan Miller began loving her daughter, no matter what. It felt so strange to touch and feel the skin of a teen that felt like that of an 80 year old. It made Susan's heart sink, and she cried at the thought of her daughter suffering so terribly that she would do such things to her body.

"Mom, go away!" Stephanie rolled over and pulled the covers over her head. She could not face her mother this morning.

"Ok, sweetie. You can sleep as long as you want today. And if you feel like it later, I'll take you to the mall and you can pick out your present. Love you!" Susan kissed Stephanie's head through the comforter and left the room.

When the door closed Stephanie sat up. She looked at the tray on her bedside table. Chocolate chip waffles, her favorite. Without touching the waffles she reached for her laptop from her desk, powered it up, opened up her internet browser and began her search- 'how to commit suicide'.

Twenty Eight

MITCH LEFT The Office parking lot and headed towards the riverfront. He crossed the Shelby Street Bridge, turned right onto First Street, and pulled into the old Goodwill parking lot. Mitch pulled off his work shirt and cargo pants to reveal a thermal dry-fit top and black running tights. He placed the work shirt and pants into a black construction trash bag. He got out of the van, took off the fake decal and placed it in the trash bag. Then he opened the back doors and took out the backpack sprayer and utility belt and placed them in the trash bag with the rest, and brought them to the dumpster.

The dumpster at the Goodwill parking lot was emptied on Tuesday afternoons. Mitch and Jules learned this while shopping there for The Office. Every second Tuesday at the Goodwill was Super Tuesday, and business owners received fifty percent off of every sale. Mitch and Jules were broke, and fifty percent off Goodwill clothing fit right into their budget.

He returned the rental van, got into his Cherokee and headed to the meet-up.

JJ, Monica, and Jules were already at JJ's apartment when Mitch arrived. JJ had three large monitors on a card table, and was manipulating the windows on one of them.

"How are they working?" Mitch rushed to the table to see the results of his handiwork.

"Awesome, Mitch. You did great. I brought in three monitors so that we can view all of the video feeds at once. They are all connected to my laptop. The exterior cams are on this monitor, and I can toggle between them using this menu, or I can split the screen to show all windows at once." JJ showed Mitch how to navigate between the different camera views.

"View one is at the rear of Transport Express, view three is the loading dock of The Office, view four is of the side entrance of The Office, and view five is of the front entrance of The Office."

The group watched view 1 as an employee stepped out of his car and walked up to the rear entrance of Transport Express. As he approached the door, his face was clearly visible and identifiable.

"But I'm not getting a signal from camera two, from the front entrance of Transport Express?" JJ was looking at Mitch.

"Oh yeah, sorry. I had some technical difficulties" Mitch pulled the crushed camera out of the pocket of his running tights and handed it to JJ.

JJ laughed. "No worries, Mitch. I think we've got enough. Check this out."

JJ pointed to the second monitor, which was capturing activity in Sampson's office at Transport Express.

"This monitor gives us the feed for the two button cams I put in Sampson's office at Transport Express. Right here we have a full view of the safe."

The view from the button cam placed on Sampson's computer was perfect. The wide angle lens caught Sampson's desk, and the entire back wall of his office, including the safe.

"And here..." JJ clicked on the second camera icon and another view popped into the screen, "we have the back side of the office."

The camera JJ placed on the back of Sampson's desk caught the rest of his office, including the entrance to the hall.

"Whatever happens in this office on Thursday nights will be caught by these two cameras."

"On monitor three, we've got the feeds from The Office. Cameras one through four are from the smoke detector cams my buddy Lawrence placed, and camera five is the button cam inside Sampson's office- perfect job, by the way, Mon." JJ gave Monica a high five.

"All the cameras send a live feed to a secure server that will record and store the footage, so that it can be accessed from my laptop and phone at any time."

JJ opened his laptop, accessed the secure site and logged on. He showed Mitch, Jules, and Monica how to log onto the server, and how to navigate between the different video feeds.

"There will be a time and date stamp on every feed, as well as the camera number. I've created this cheat sheet for you to have with you. It has the site address, the login information, and the location of each camera."

JJ handed them each an index card with the information needed to access the video.

"And now?" Jules was looking at JJ.

"Now, we just wait. The action starts around midnight tomorrow night. I suggest we act as normal as possible in the meantime and stick with the usual routine."

SHE WAS AWOKEN by a tickle on her chin. When she opened her eyes, the sun shone in through the window beautifully. Eliana could hear the birds singing in the trees. And then the tickle again. As she sat up the vine beckoned. Her iron garden. It's outstretched hands motioned 'come here child'. Eliana pushed her sheet aside and stood at the window.

Before her eyes the flowering vines enveloped her and carried her up as the window opened and exposed Eliana to the warmth of the early winter sun. She held onto the vine that was no longer iron, but something organic, strong, yet gentle. It carried her up into the sky, through the clouds, and into a brilliant white light.

As the clouds separated, Eliana found herself in a lush, flowering, green meadow, full of her favorite reds, pinks, and yellows. There were other children playing games, and old men and women holding hands. And on the far end, she saw someone she knew.

"Papa!" Eliana ran to her father and he scooped her up in his arms. She felt the warmth of his hands around her shoulder, and his soft cheek next to hers.

Suddenly Eliana was filled with shame. She could not look her father in the eyes after what she had done. She wriggled out of his arms and ran behind a tree.

"Eliana..." her father called to her sweetly. When she opened her eyes he was crouched down in front of her. He took her face in his hands and gently brought it up to meet him.

"Papa, I am so ashamed!" Tears fell down the child's face.

"Eliana, precious daughter. You are a child of God. You are perfect. And you are going to be ok. I promise." Eliana's father smiled at Eliana, and instantly she knew he was right.

The Iron Garden became Eliana's refuge. She visited often. In the garden, Eliana would walk with her father, plant, water, weed, and feel at peace. She looked forward to these times, and oddly began to appreciate Miss Sadie for giving her that gift.

Twenty Nine

AT 2:00 PM ON WEDNESDAY, JJ's cell phone alerted him. Sampson had just walked into his office at Transport Express. JJ watched as he sat his case on the desk, and then turned his back to the camera. Sampson removed the painting from the wall behind his desk and began opening his safe.

"Bingo!" JJ screamed aloud. He had placed his button cam in just the right location to catch Richard Sampson opening his safe. From the vantage point of Sampson's desk speaker, every turn of the safe combination lock was visible. He would have to enhance the picture some, and slow the speed to get an accurate combination, but JJ was confident he had just gained access into Richard Sampson's safe.

From the safe, Richard Sampson removed a large file folder and placed it on his desk. With an unobscured view of the safe opening, JJ could see that it was relatively large, approximately two feet wide, two feet tall, and maybe eighteen inches deep.

Inside JJ could make out a long row of books, each one the size of a one and a half inch wide three ring binder. He also saw stacks of papers, folders, and a large box.

Richard Sampson sat at his desk and opened the folder in front of him. He pulled a piece of paper from the folder and held it in front of his face. JJ could only see the back of the paper. The words 'Baker Brothers, Aug. '12 were written diagonally across the back. The button cam was placed just a few inches above the top of Sampson's desk. From this perspective, JJ could tell that the paper Sampson was holding was a photograph, but JJ could not decipher the picture. He had a perfect shot of Sampson's face, now looking down at the next photograph on the desk. JJ was startled by what he saw. It looked like sadness.

Richard Sampson's face had never communicated any emotion to JJ other than pride, arrogance, anger, and contempt. Perhaps in the beginning Sampson had appeared genial, but JJ suspected it was all a front. Once Sampson began working with JJ at Transport Express, his true colors appeared. What JJ witnessed now was completely foreign to him.

He watched without blinking, the man on his monitor, as he picked up photograph after photograph, each one bearing a name and date on the back. Richard Sampson's expression was undoubtedly sadness. Several times he paused to close his eyes. He appeared to shudder his breath on occasion. By the time Richard Sampson was halfway through the pile of photographs, there were tears in his eyes.

Abruptly Sampson closed the folder and picked up his desk phone and began to dial. JJ switched on monitor two and clicked on the audio menu.

"Hello?" It was a woman's voice.

"Darling it's me." Darling? JJ was floored.

"Richard, what time will you be home? Sophia and Daniel are coming over at 8:00 pm." It was his wife.

"Jenny, it's Wednesday." Sampson was rubbing his forehead, and a tear fell down his cheek.

"Oh dear, honey, I'm sorry. I always forget. I'll cancel and we'll do it next week, ok?"

"Sure. I just called to tell you I love you. I'll miss you tonight. Give Sophia my love, please?"

JJ could not even begin to comprehend what he was hearing. The hard nosed intimidator was acting in a completely unfamiliar manner. Who was this man? And even more curious, what were in those photographs that made that nasty son of a bitch cry? JJ could not wait to find out.

AFTER DINNER, Mitch put on a pot of coffee.

"You're not supposed to drink coffee after three o'clock, Daddy!" Colin was pulling on Mitch's shirt to get his attention.

"You're right, buddy, but your mom and I have a lot of work to do tonight, so we're planning on staying up late, and we're going to need the extra caffeine."

"Can I stay up with you?" Colin asked his mom.

"Nice try young man, but no. Now go brush your teeth, I'll be in to tuck you in in a few minutes." Jules gave her son a hug and sent him to up to the bathroom.

Once all of the kids were in bed, Jules and Mitch set up Mitch's laptop on their bed and logged on to the secure server JJ had set up.

Both had struggled all day to resist the temptation to tune in and watch what was happening in The Office. Jules had had a busy morning at the gym, but since 1:00 pm that afternoon she had fiddled around the house, checking in every five minutes to see if anything new had happened.

There seemed to be a lot of activity at The Office. She saw many faces she didn't recognize. All but one of the original tenants had vacated their offices, and new ones filled their spaces. Men and women stopped to greet each other in the halls. They sat on benches, ate their lunches in the community areas, and shook hands when they said good-by. It was all rather boring and uneventful. Jules was disappointed.

It wasn't that she expected to see anything exciting or revealing going on at this hour of the day. She was disappointed that the sights she saw were uninspiring. While the professionals milling around the common areas of The Office seemed pleasant and content, there was something missing. Something lacking. She just couldn't place what it was.

At 10:00 pm, The Office was quiet. The hallway was dim, lit only from the security lights. There was no movement. Mitch switched over to the feed from the button cam in Sampson's office at Transport Express. JJ had sent him a text to go back and watch the video from 2:02 pm through 2:12 pm. Jules and Mitch sat and watched an unfamiliar Richard Sampson cry. The two sat in silence for several minutes, then looked at each other, not knowing what to say.

They went through several scenarios, trying to guess just what Richard Sampson saw in the photos. Mitch played back the video several times, trying to get a better glimpse of the photographs, but it was futile.

It was disconcerting to see this side of Richard Sampson. For the past fourteen months, Jules had hated this man. He had deceived her and Mitch, had stolen Mitch's business and his dream. He was greedy, arrogant, dishonest, and criminal. And most important, he had threatened her and her family. But here, she saw a side of him that appeared to be human. She did not like seeing Sampson as a man capable of love. She needed anger and hate to fuel her courage for the task at hand.

They threw ideas back and forth, but nothing seemed plausible. They would have to wait to get into the safe to know the truth.

"MON, ARE YOU coming to bed?" Douglas was in the doorway, waiting for Monica to get off her computer and join him.

I'm kind of into this right now, honey, I think I'll be up late. I'm sorry. I'll make it up to you later, I promise." Monica winked at him, and nudged him to go to bed. She could not tear herself away from her monitor. It was 11:45 pm.

Monica had not told Douglas what was going on. She never planned to keep anything from him, she just knew he would worry. So when she and Jules were chased down Carter's Creek, she told herself it was an isolated incident. And when she learned of JJ's surveillance videos, she thought she would stay out of it. And now that she had become part of a plan to take down a dangerous killer, well, she figured it was too late to try to explain everything.

"So, what exactly is this you're watching? Paranormal Office Activity?"

Douglas' voice made Monica jump. She hadn't heard him return to the living room.

"Mon, what's really going on? You've been sneaking around with Jules for the past two weeks. What are you two into?"

Monica took a deep breath and finally told Douglas everything.

"So what can I do?" Douglas was on board.

"IT'S YOUR TURN, Baby." Miss Sadie called Eliana.

Eliana looked up at Miss Sadie with confusion.

"C'mon special girl, you got lucky! Now let me help you fix yourself up."

Miss Sadie took Eliana into the bathroom and put her into the shower, the third shower she had had since arriving at The House. Eliana sat under the hot water and let it pour down her face. It felt like heaven. Tears fell down her face as she thanked God for small blessings.

"That's enough now, you've got to get!" Miss Sadie pulled Eliana out of the shower and handed her a towel, then a clean dress.

"Put this on and comb your hair. Hurry now."

When Eliana had finished getting dressed Miss Sadie took her to the front door and walked her out to the driveway where a tall dark headed man waited for her.

"Come with me." The tall man reached out and took Eliana by the hand to the car.

Eliana stepped up into the large SUV and the man shut the door.

"If you smile real pretty, you just might get lucky!" Said the man.

Eliana felt a pang as she watched her iron garden disappear in the darkness as the car pulled away. She wondered if her father was watching.

THE ALERT went off at 12:02 am. Sampson was two minutes late. He arrived at The Office alone tonight, through the loading dock entrance, and went directly into his office. JJ created a split screen on his monitor so that he could view each camera feed simultaneously. Sampson sat in his desk and closed his eyes. He sat there like that for eight minutes, until something stirred him.

He opened his eyes, stood up and walked out into the hallway to greet two large men, two of his employees JJ recognized from Transport Express. One of the men shook Sampson's hand. He was extremely muscular. His large hands look like giant claws as he grasped Sampson by the shoulders.

The smoke detector cam caught Sampson's flinch at the man's touch.

At 12:24 am, a Transport Express truck backed up to the loading dock. The button cam on the loading dock garage door entrance captured the truck reverse up to the building. After five minutes, the smoke detector cam inside the hallway activated.

The girls were young, possibly as young as twelve or thirteen years old, none over seventeen. They were dark skinned, like the girls in the photographs JJ had shown Mitch and Jules. They filed into the common hallway, one in front of the other, and were lead into the conference room by one of Sampson's men.

In the conference room, the smoke detector cam caught the girls as they lined up along the back wall in groups of ten. They were scared. They kept their eyes towards the ground. Some were crying. The second man, the muscular one, walked down the line and carefully inspected each girl. He pushed their shoulders back and forced them to stand up straight. He pulled their faces to meet his, and gestured for them to look him in the eye. He offered tissues to those that were crying.

One of the girls would not stop crying. The muscular one placed his claw under her chin and raised her head to meet him. She was petite, and looked like a mouse in front of the huge man. She was afraid. He spoke to her. There was no sound, but her reaction communicated she did not like what she heard. She shook her head no. The claw released her jaw and relaxed at his side. When the girl began to sob, the muscular one slapped her and she fell to the ground. He kneeled down and put his head close to hers and spoke again. Within thirty seconds the girl stood, faced forward, and stopped crying.

Cars began pulling into the parking lot between 12:50 am and 1:00 am, but the men stayed in their cars until precisely 1:00 am. At that time they entered the building through the loading dock entrance, and turned right into the conference room.

There were tables and chairs set up in the conference room. The girls remained lined up along the back wall.

Sampson's man inspected each one once again, and whispered in their ears. Some began to smile.

There were over thirty men in all, each having arrived by 1:05 am, and at 1:08 am, Richard Sampson entered the conference room and spoke to his guests. The men were standing, and sitting facing the girls. Richard was smiling now. He gestured towards the girls, and nodded to the men.

One by one, the men got up and walked towards the girls. One man took the petite girl by the hand. She looked as if she was twelve years old. He led her to a table and they sat down. He was talking to her, watching her and smiling. She forced herself to look at him, but could not smile. She did not talk back to him.

After three minutes, he stood, took her by the hand and led her to Sampson. The man pulled a manilla envelope from his jacket pocket. He handed the envelope to Sampson, who opened the envelope, inspected its contents, and made a mark in a book the size of a one and a half inch three ring binder. The man lead the girl out of the conference room, out the loading dock door, to his car, and off the premises.

JJ, Jules, Mitch, Monica and Douglas all watched in horror as more men chose a girl, payed Sampson and left with their purchase. Several men left with three or four girls. It was a scene reminiscent of a silent auction, only the items for sale were humans. Child humans. As the girls came in closer view from the smoke detector cams, some appeared to have bruises on their arms. Two of them had black eyes. One left with a large bandage on her neck.

By 2:00 am, all fifty of the girls, and all thirty of the guests had left. Sampson's men helped him put all of the envelopes containing cash, along with the log book, into a large duffel bag. They turned off the lights in the conference room. Sampson turned the lights off in his office and locked the door. The three men left the building together through the loading dock door.

The exterior cam caught Sampson talking with the two men briefly outside, and then the three parted. Sampson walked alone to his car, while the other two traveled together in a black H2 Hummer.

By 2:15 am, The Office was deserted.

At 2:30 am, Richard Sampson entered his office at Transport Express, placed the contents of his duffel in the safe, and left.

Thirty

HE TOLD HER to stop crying but she couldn't. She tried but she couldn't. The tears would not stop, and she felt as if she would smother in her fear. The blow knocked her down, knocked the wind out of her.

"If you don't get up and stop crying now, I will kill you right here and send you back to your mother in pieces." He spoke to her in Spanish. His breath was hot and rotten.

Eliana stood and stopped crying. She stared off in the distance made herself blank. She had to do that a lot lately, make herself blank, it was the only way she was able to not feel anything. She wasn't supposed to be here. She was supposed to be cleaning toilets, serving eggs and bacon to rich hotel patrons, and sending well-earned money to her mother in Guatemala. She shouldn't know the things she has learned over the past month. Not at twelve years old.

The man who picked her was old. He had white hair. She didn't understand his English. He smiled at her, like the others had. They all smiled when they wanted something. It wasn't the smile of her best friend Alicia, which told her she could be trusted. It wasn't the smile of her teacher, which said 'I'm proud of you'. It wasn't the smile of her mother, who loved her. It was the smile of a hunter, whose skilled hands hold a long bow trained on its prey, anticipating the feast that would follow.

JJ'S ALERT woke him at 11:45 pm Thursday night.

"Damnit!" He had fallen asleep in his chair. It was the first sleep he'd had in almost 48 hours.

He woke his monitor and clicked on the view for Sampson's office at TE. Sampson had arrived at 11:45 pm and sat down at his desk.

Two Latinos walked in and greeted Sampson. They sat across from him at his desk. Sampson handed the taller one a page containing words the camera could not make out. The two men looked over the page carefully before returning it to Sampson. Sampson opened his safe and retrieved the duffel full of cash, opened it and placed it on the desk. The two Latinos took the money out and counted out the stacks. When they were satisfied, the taller one handed a few stacks back to Sampson, and placed the rest back into the duffel.

And then the men got up, exchanged good-bys with Sampson, and left with the duffel. Richard Sampson stayed in his office for five more minutes, straightened his desk, put his cash back into the safe before closing and locking the door, powered down his computer, turned off the lights and was out the door at 12:03 am.

NO ONE SLEPT. Not Wednesday night, or Thursday night. They could not keep their eyes off the monitors. And when nothing was happening, they would replay the scene of the auction, over and over. When they stopped watching, they lay awake, thinking but not wanting to think, about the atrocities that were happening in their own city, in their own businesses.

Jules finally dozed around 5:30 am Friday morning, but was awakened sharply by Claire's alarm at 6:00am. She felt dizzy and nauseated. She fell back in and out of sleep but was awoken again for good by her mobile alarm at 8:30 am. Sampson had entered his office at Transport Express. He closed the door, walked to his desk and turned to face the wall. He took the painting off the wall and opened the safe.

Richard Sampson removed the cash and placed it into a briefcase on his desk. He closed the case and placed it on the ground before closing and locking the safe, and replacing the painting on the wall. He left his office at 8:40 am with briefcase in hand.

Jules picked up her cell phone and texted JJ.

"u getting this"

"yep"

"hes leaving with the money"

"i know. im on it."

"what. where are you"

"im outside te. slept here last night. following now. talk later."

JJ followed Sampson's car from a distance, out of the parking lot of Transport Express, towards downtown Nashville. He turned onto Broadway and headed away from the river. A right turn onto Second Avenue led Sampson to Tennessee Bank and Credit Union. Sampson found a parking space on the street in front of the bank and parked.

JJ turned down an alley and parked illegally in a fire zone. He hopped out of his blue Ford Taurus and ran back to Second Ave. JJ pulled his hood low on his head and headed into the bank. A quick scan revealed Sampson was not in the lobby. JJ looked towards the special services offices in the back. There he was, talking with a blond woman in the corner office, his back to JJ, separated from the lobby by a large plate glass wall.

JJ walked towards the office and sat down on a couch in the waiting area just outside. JJ was wearing a black hooded sweatshirt and blue jeans. He had spent the night in his car, and had coffee and food spills on the legs of his pants. He smelled. He realized he looked incredibly suspicious but didn't care. He craned his neck to hear, while pretending to be engrossed in a game of solitaire on his Iphone.

"Shirley, I expect you'll have this cleared by noon?" Sampson had resumed his usual dictator tone, communicating his authority over the world.

"Sure thing, Dick. You know we appreciate your business!" She sounded as if she were flirting.

"Good, I'll see you in a few weeks, then." Sampson slid something under her desk blotter, and winked at Shirley as he stood to leave her office.

JJ heard Sampson push his chair back and stand to walk out. He put his head down focused on his game as Sampson walked past him.

"Can I help you, sugar?" Shirley's voice was sweet as syrup.

When JJ was sure Sampson was out of the bank he turned to Shirley and smiled.

"I'm sorry, I think I forgot to bring my documents. I'll have to come back another day." JJ turned and headed for the door. He slowed his pace to make sure Sampson had pulled out of the parking space and was headed down Second Avenue before he exited the bank.

Shirley watched him in confusion. 'Maybe he's on drugs' she told herself, shrugged, and walked back to her desk.

JJ SPENT the afternoon at his computer. He had spent the last five hours hacking into the Tennessee Bank and Credit Union computer system. It wasn't difficult to locate the accounts of Richard Sampson. They were set up under the umbrella RSE, or Richard Sampson Enterprises. He had basic checking accounts for both The Office and Transport Express. He also had a basic business account and money market account set up under the name "Pathways". There were no other accounts associated with RSE, or Richard Sampson.

JJ pulled Sampson's social security number from his business accounts and searched for any accounts associated with that number and came up empty. He looked for any accounts associated with Sampson's address, his phone numbers, and then his birthday. A quick internet search led him to Sampson's wife's personal information, so JJ searched the bank's database for any accounts associated with Jennifer Sampson. Still nothing.

JJ pushed himself away from his card table desk and paced the floor to think. He returned to his laptop and conducted a search for all transactions at the Second Avenue branch between 8:30 am and 9:30 am this morning. There were hundreds. As he scrolled through he looked for anything that might stand out.

And there it was. At 9:15 am, "Trans-American Imports" made a deposit of $10,000 cash. JJ opened up the TAI account and reviewed the transactions. For the past year, TAI made deposits every two weeks, in amounts ranging from $10,000 to $20,000. The most recent deposit occurred today, and had already cleared. That was unusual, especially for an amount that large.

"She's working with him. I can't believe it, even Shirley is in on it." Mitch had arrived and was looking over the account information with JJ.

"Look at this."

JJ diverted Mitch's attention back to the computer screen.

"The deposit made at 9:20 am this morning was for $10,000. Then, at noon central time, a transfer was made from TN Bank and Credit Union to this account, here. This is an offshore account, the Caymans, judging by the numbers."

"How do you know so much about off-shore bank accounts?" Mitch was looking at JJ with surprise.

"That's just what happens when computer geeks get bored." JJ continued to scroll through the screens.

"So Sampson's making almost half a million dollars a year trafficking young girls into America." Mitch was trying to put the pieces together.

"These records go back 5 years. In the earlier years the deposits are less, some as little as $5,000." JJ pulled out his cell phone and clicked on the calculator function. After a few minutes he leaned back in his chair.

"With interest he could have three of four million stashed away in that account."

WHEN MITCH returned home that night Monica and Jules were drinking whiskey by the fireplace while the kids watched movies in the playroom.

Mitch filled Jules and Monica in on what he and JJ had uncovered. He shared with him how JJ had followed Sampson into the credit union and how Shirley helped him launder the money he had received from the johns two nights earlier.

Jules and Monica filled Mitch in on what they had learned that day. Jules pulled out her laptop and logged onto the internet. She opened a website for the agency End Slavery Tennessee (ESTN), a non-profit organization that fights against human trafficking, and provides aids to survivors. The website was filled with information on human trafficking.

According to the United Nations' office on Drugs and Crime, sexual exploitation of women and girls is the most common form of human trafficking. Around the world, twenty-seven million people are trapped in slavery today. Approximately eighty percent of these victims are female, and at least fifty percent of these victims are children.

One hundred sixty one countries around the world are affected by human trafficking, which is a thirty two billion dollar a year industry. Almost half of all trafficking occurs in industrialized countries. The average age of females forced into prostitution is twelve to fourteen years old.

The information was overwhelming. Jules now had a name, definition, and sickening statistics for what she had witnessed on the video monitors. The things she learned about human trafficking would be difficult for her to believe if she hadn't seen the girls being sold for herself. It was almost more than she could take. The only thing keeping Jules from completely falling apart was the glass of whiskey in her hands, and a determination to make sure she did everything in her power to stand up to this horror. Her children would never be safe in a world where this was allowed to go on. Her decision had been made.

"We need to go to the police, Mitch."

"Yes, we do, but not yet, Jules. It's pretty clear that Sampson's just the middle man. He's not the one in control here. If we take him out, his bosses will just find someone else. Right now, we need more information."

Thirty One

SHE FONDLED the blade, allowed it to pierce the tip of her pointer and watched as a tiny drop of blood formed a bead that ran down her finger. She imagined the blood trails flowing down her forearm into the bathwater, and visualized the entire tub turning pink, then bright red as she sinks below the surface. Wouldn't her mother be surprised?

Stephanie reveled in the thought. Then her mother would really be sorry. A sorry ass mother! Susan Miller didn't deserve the title 'Mother'. Every day was the same story.

"Mrs. Schultz called today; she said you fell asleep again in Algebra. What is going on with you, Stephanie? Do you have any idea how embarrassing it is to have your teacher call me repeatedly? And look at you! You look like a street person. I don't even want to be seen with you out in public. Honestly Steph you need to get it together."

And with that, Susan Miller walked off in a huff. There was a time when her mother used to care; she used to at least try to help. But now? She never asks if Stephanie is ok anymore. She has just given up. Susan Miller quit her daughter.

Yes, Stephanie Miller enjoyed the thought of shocking her mother. She especially enjoyed the image of her mother trying to explain her daughter's suicide to her stuck-up suburban friends. Stephanie smiled for the first time in months.

JUSTIN TOOMEY was just six months into his first journalistic position since graduating from MTSU. A bi-weekly publication, the Nashville City Journal highlights local businesses and keeps business owners abreast of changes in local and national business law. It was Mitch Spalding who introduced Toomey to Howard Lieberman, Editor in Chief of the Journal. Toomey liked Mitch, and his gratitude towards him made the task at hand all the more difficult.

"Toomey, you're a journalist, you have to resist the lean towards bias. You have to be able to adequately present all sides of an issue, otherwise you're no better than those TV knuckleheads who spend more time fighting to prove they're right, than actually getting to the real truth. You have to stick with journalistic ethics here. Print it."

Lieberman was referring to a letter Toomey had received from Richard Sampson. It was a glowing review of The Office, complete with complements from Mayor Schoals, the Nashville Chamber of Commerce, and the Better Business Bureau.

"The Office is a sort of incubator for small businesses, providing the resources every small business owner needs to grow and thrive. We are so thankful for the introduction of this concept into our city." - Mayor Tom Schoals.

"We have found a way to foster the development of new ideas and bring a rich new culture of opportunities to Nashville. As an entrepreneur, there really is nothing better than that." - Richard Sampson

Toomey sat at his desk for hours, looking at his computer screen, trying to conjure up the words to adequately serve both his boss, and his conscience, until he found a way to satisfy them both.

"Change is inevitable. We grow, we fall, we learn and evolve, and grow some more. We see this in our children, in our gardens, and even in our businesses. Some will tell you change is good, and

some will complain about the loss of consistency, but all will agree, it happens nonetheless.

Richard Sampson knows something about change. He has witnessed the constant flux of his business, The Office, over the past year as individuals, businesses and opportunities have walked in and out of its doors. Just two months after opening, The Office experienced its first major change, the disintegration of the partnership between its creator, Mitch Spalding, and current owner, Richard Sampson. According to Sampson,

"There have been some growing pains, but The Office remains a strong, grounded essential in the growth of small business today. I'm proud to offer a service that nurtures the development of new commerce through innovation, cooperation, and determination. Growth of new businesses is not just good for the business itself, its good for our local economy. Small businesses are a key driving force in fueling economic growth."

Sampson also states that he expects there will continue to be more changes at The Office, and he welcomes them.

Richard Sampson is the founder and CEO of Pathways, a managed care company, and current owner of Transport Express, a trucking company. He opened The Office, in July 2011, along with The Office creator, Real Estate Entrepreneur Mitch Spalding.

Currently the ownership of The Office is under legal dispute. According to court documents, Mitch Spalding has filed suit against Richard Sampson for intentional fraud and misrepresentation. In his lawsuit, Spalding asserts that Richard Sampson falsified legal documents and destroyed original agreements in an effort to fraudulently gain control of The Office.

In an official comment, Mitch Spalding states, "I believe that the truth will be heard by this court, and a just resolution will be achieved within the next six months." He continued to state that he wishes the resolution to be amicable. The City Journal will continue to follow this story, and update you on any new information we receive.

THEY HAD a little less than two weeks to prepare for what would happen next. To Jules it felt like preparing for a final exam that would determine the rest of her life. The next twelve days would seem like an eternity. She would have to go to work, mother the kids, and maintain business as usual to the outside world. But in private, she was plotting to take down a criminal. The gravity of the task at hand kept her up at night.

They were dealing with people who routinely tortured and murdered other people for money. Jules had to keep herself distracted from this thought in order to continue. Mitch was right. At this point, if they chose to give up, they would always be looking in their rear view mirror for the tan Mercedes SUV. They would not be able to rest until Sampson and his entire operation were dealt with by the proper authorities.

Jules started her preparation by finding alternative homes for her kids for a few days while she and Mitch took care of business. Winter break would start that week, so she called a friend.

"Stella, hey it's Jules. I was wondering if you could do me a favor, and I promise to do the same for you. Can the boys stay with your boys a few days next week? Mitch and I have made special plans for a getaway."

"Sure Jules. Tim and Craig would love to have the Spalding boys over. They've been asking for a sleepover for the past few weeks. We'd love it."

'That was easy' Thought Jules. Now for Claire. Claire had become very close with Chloe Wilson, who lived three doors down. Jules liked Chloe, but she didn't know her mother well. She called their home and left a voice mail for Chloe's mother.

On her way from work that afternoon, Jules stopped by the drugstore and paid cash for a pre-paid cellular phone.

Jules spent the rest of the afternoon on the internet. She searched the ESTN website for more information. She created a new file, and included names, phone numbers and addresses of local contacts. From her new phone, Jules dialed the reporting hotline.

"Hello, I was calling to find out who I need to talk with to make a report. I think I may know someone involved in human trafficking."

MONICA PERRY loved to travel. On Monday she powered up her laptop, opened up the web browser, and logged on to her favorite travel site. The Caymans seemed like the perfect destination to celebrate her tenth wedding anniversary.

JJ REPLAYED the video over and over until he was sure of the numbers. 33 right, 28 left, 16 right, 10 right. He made Mitch review the video separately and the two compared notes-

they both came up with the same combination. It had to be right.
They only had one chance, and JJ was not a safe cracker.

MONICA WAS enjoying herself. It took an hour to
transform Douglas into Devin Trousdale. Devin Trousdale was a
balding red head with freckles, and spectacles that looked like
he'd purchased in 1985. Devin had his picture made for a new ID,
which indicated he was born on July 18, 1970, was five feet, ten
inches tall and weighed one hundred and seventy eight pounds.

The real Devin Trousdale had died in an automobile
accident in 2008. Douglas would only need his social security
number for a short period of time.

RICHARD SAMPSON was a little more difficult to
imitate. Douglas was slightly smaller than the veteran soldier. A
padded body suit and lifts borrowed from Douglas' production
crew, along with temporary hair plugs and colored contacts helped
him pass a physical description. In Photoshop, JJ was able to
merge photos of the real Richard Sampson from DMV records
with the image of Douglas posing as Richard Sampson. The result
was a photo that held a strong enough resemblance to both the real
Sampson, and the Douglas Sampson, that one could rationalize the
differences due to age.

JJ SENT the email and crossed his fingers. Three hours later his inbox alerted him with a ding.

From: Richard Sampson
Date: December 12, 2012
To: Jordan Jones
Subject: could not open

JJ, I have been unable to open the document link you sent. Just have the originals sent via currier. Richard.

It worked. Now JJ just had to see if he could figure out how to use it.

For five hundred dollars, anyone can obtain a pirated copy of Zeus, a Trojan horse malware program used to gain access to another's computer. Jordan Jones didn't have five hundred dollars, but he did have what Scooter Dickens wanted- a view inside the Tennessee Titans Cheerleaders locker room. It was a fair trade, according to Dickens- who's infatuation with the cheerleaders had grown into an obsession over the past year. JJ convinced himself it was for a good cause, and planned to scramble the video feed as soon as his job was done.

Scooter's instructions were perfect, and within minutes JJ had access to Sampson's login credentials for his local online banking, and to his offshore account.

JJ stored this information in a locked file on his hard drive and continued to browse the contents of Sampson's computer. If Sampson surfed the internet, he didn't use his office computer. With the exception of banking transfers, Sampson's internet history was limited to travel sites, Map quest, and the Weather Channel website.

Richard Sampson was old school. He preferred written letters, memos, and facsimiles over emails. His email folder was full of spam, with the occasional invitation to link in with other business owners and individuals interested in becoming part of Richard Sampson's circle. There were no personal messages, and the rare professional emails were responded to with a "call me" reply.

Sampson's hard drive looked as if he'd never taken the computer out of the box. The applications folder contained the computer's default applications, Mozilla Firefox, Adobe Acrobat, Flash, Windows Live, Microsoft Office, etc.

JJ opened the documents folder and finally found what he was looking for. There were only two sub-folders in the documents folder, one for Transport Express, the other for The Office. JJ opened each sub-folder and viewed the contents. Both were relatively similar- accounting reports created from Quickbooks, bank statements downloaded from the credit union, various blank business forms, and finally, the partnership agreements. JJ saved copies of each of these to his desktop. He would review them with Mitch later.

When the time was right, JJ would be able to control all of Richard Sampson's bank accounts, including his private offshore savings. He would also be able to regain control of his business, and begin to put his life back together.

It was difficult to wait. JJ thought of a hundred ways to screw Sampson tonight. But they had a plan. A plan that would accomplish this and more, and the time wasn't right. He had to be patient. It was still a week away.

THE GRANDFATHER CLOCK ticked the seconds away as snow began to fall outside. Richard couldn't remember the last time he'd seen snow in December. The flakes fell in large clumps, and glistened as they caught the light from the porch lamp. It was surreal, and fitting this evening.

"I think it's time." The Ambassador was pacing.

"No, I'm not ready." Richard Sampson sat down at his desk resolutely. He sat in the same chair in his home office that he had sat in so many years ago when he was first visited by the Chileans.

"They will find out and they will burry you."

"I have this under control, you don't have to worry."

"You do not have this under control, Ricardo. Stop stalling!"

"I'm not stalling. I sent the word this week to go forward within the month. This should satisfy them for the time being, and give me some more time to prepare."

"Ricardo, you fool. They are not stupid. They will see through your schemes in short time. You must not act as if time is on your side."

"Papa, don't lecture me."

Richard could not stand the way his grandfather spoke to him, as if he were a child. He had managed to survive as long as he had on his own accord, not because of, but rather in spite of his grandfather's interference.

"I will lecture a fool. You, Ricardo, are a fool to let this go on one minute longer. Think of Jenny, think of Sophia!"

"Who did *you* think of, Papa? Who do *you* think of?"

The Ambassador was silent.

Thirty Two

JULES WAS DISTRACTED. She went through the motions, but her mind was somewhere else. As she was finishing up with her last client, Tony Ramano caught her attention. He motioned for her to join him in his office when she finished.

"Hey boss." Jules poked her head into Tony's office door.

"Come on in, shut the door." Tony pulled a file from his drawer and opened it up on his desk.

"You were right to be concerned. The Mercedes is registered to Tim Holloway. So is the red minivan he drives here every day. The address he gave us is phony. He is single, never been married, and has no children."

The realization that she had been deceived so easily was difficult for Jules to accept. She sat in silence, not sure how to respond.

"Jules, I'm not sure if he's dangerous, but you definitely cannot trust him."

Tony passed Jules the open folder. It was full of photos. An apartment complex. The Mercedes SUV. Tim at Transport Express. Tim leaving a club at night.

"What is this?" Jules looked at Tony, confused.

"Normal activity, really. He goes to work, comes home around 6:00 pm, goes out to the bar. He seems to live the typical life of a bachelor."

"You're following him?"

"Not me personally. I have an old friend helping me out. So far he seems squeaky clean, but based on what you've told me, it's a matter of time before we catch him up to something. For now, you can feel secure knowing we've got eyes on him. If I think you're in any kind of danger you will be the first to know. Just keep working with him. It will be our little secret." Tony winked at Jules his famous Ramano wink. He was telling her the conversation was over.

"Thanks, Tony." Jules left the office, left the gym and headed for home. It was Friday, just five days before Wednesday.

AT 9:00 AM ON Monday morning, Devin Trousdale walked into the Tennessee Bank and Credit Union on Second Avenue and walked to the back. He sat down on one of the chairs in the special services lounge and picked up a brochure informing customers of their banking options.

"Can I help you, sir?" The thin blond dressed in a navy blue pencil skirt and white cashmere sweater greeted Devin in a syrupy sweet southern draw that indicated she may have come from Mississippi.

"Yes, please. I'd like to open an account."

"Well come on in, I can help you with that." Shirley Upkins led Devin Trousdale into her office and offered him a chair.

MITCH LOOKED at the document for the third time. He could not believe how easy it had been. Sampson had taken the original partnership agreement and simply switched the names. Where the original document listed Mitch Spalding as owning seventy percent of the business, and Richard Sampson owning thirty percent, the fraudulent document switched the numbers, indicating that Sampson maintained controlling interest.

"I can't believe it. I just can't believe it." Mitch repeated him several times before JJ interrupted.

"Believe what, Mitch?"

"It's so simple. So incredibly simple. How is it that one person can take down another with a plan so simple my fifth grader could have created it?"

"It's one of the first laws of innovation. KISS."

"What?"

"Keep it simple, stupid. All good plans are simple. Complexity brings with it problems that trip us up and keep us from forging ahead. Simple- like this."

JJ pointed to his computer screen. He had simply switched the names on the partnership agreement back to the original form. He did the same with his own partnership agreement, and then, with a few clicks, replaced the documents on Sampson's hard drive with the new originals. JJ printed two copies of each agreement, placed them in a folder marked "documents", and put the file on his card table.

"We're almost there, Mitch. We could stop here. We could present the court with these documents, close our cases and stop right here."

"No, I'm not ready to quit. Not after everything I've seen."

"Good. I'm with you. Now, I estimate it will take five minutes to get in and out. While you access the safe, I'll retrieve the surveillance cameras. We'll have just five hours to sort through what we find and put together all the evidence. I've been working on the video files. By Thursday morning I'll have them burned onto discs and ready to send to TBI."

"And the accounts?"

"Doug's ready. We've gone over his part several times. He knows what to do."

"So we're ready?" Mitch looked JJ in the eye, looking for some form of reservation, but instead he saw only commitment.

"Ready."

WEDNESDAY MORNING came sooner than she expected. The alarm surprised her. Surprised that she had actually slept the night before. Jules had three clients that morning, including Tim Holloway.

"Good morning. How are you today?" Jules was surprisingly at ease. The days leading up to this were torture. But today, Jules had the calm reserve of a woman who was in charge.

"'Morning Jules. Are you ready to kick my ass?"

'Damn straight!' Jules thought. But she maintained her composure and professionalism and proceeded to train Tim Holloway the way she would have any other day. She kept him occupied and working hard, and avoided small talk. When they were finished she said,

"Great Job, I'll see you Friday!" At this, Jules winked. She had never felt so confident, so prepared to take on a task as she did today.

TIM WAS SUSPICIOUS. He had never seen Jules this way. She wasn't just confident, she was a bit arrogant, and something else he couldn't quite define. She had a Mona Lisa smile, the kind that makes you nervous. Like she knows something she's not supposed to know, but won't share it with you.

He thought about calling his boss. Sampson had been on edge for the past few weeks, and overly concerned about the operation. He was worried Mitch and Jules were getting too close. Tim felt he should share his feelings with Sampson. There might be something to it.

In the rear of the gym a back hall led to an emergency exit. It also led to a storage closet and laundry facility. Tim walked down the hall and into the laundry room for privacy and pulled his phone out of his pocket. Before he could dial Sampson's number, he heard voices coming his way.

"Yes, we're still tailing him, but so far, we haven't seen anything out of the ordinary. Why?" It was Tony Ramano's voice.

"Tonight's the night." It was Jules.

Tim ducked behind the open door and hid between the door and the wall as the two talked in the back hall. He held his breath and listened.

"What are your plans, Jules?"

"We're meeting up at Transport Express, around 3:00 am, after everyone's gone. It will just take a few minutes, but we have to get into Sampson's safe and get out."

"And what will you do with what you find?"

"We'll go to TBI. At 4:00 pm tomorrow, a package will be delivered to Agent Robert Aguirre. We'll provide them with a detailed list of everyone involved, including video and still images of the trafficking operation. They will intercept Sampson and his contacts at the Transport Express office at midnight tomorrow."

"And what about Holloway, will you be safe after tonight?" Tony talked with Jules like a father. This angered Tim.

"We have enough evidence to put them all away. We just have to pull this off without a hitch. If you can keep an eye on Tim for the next twenty four hours we should be fine."

"That's no problem, Jules- I've got your back."

"Thank you Tony."

Tim could hear the sounds of a hug, a hand brushing a back. Tim became even more resentful as he imagined a relationship he had always longed for. He deserved a father. He deserved someone telling him they had his back. Instead he lived with a constant gnawing and unmet desire. His own father considered Tim a failure, and his boss thought him nothing more than a hired hand.

For over ten years Holloway had been been Sampson's lap dog, waiting on him hand and foot. It was always, 'Sarge, I need this done now! I need you here. Go pick up the merchandise. Go clean up that mess.' Whatever shitty job Richard Sampson needed done, Sarge did it. He had been loyal to his boss like a dog to his master. For what? A five figure salary and a nice car?

Richard Sampson thought of Tim Holloway as a moron, a brut, good for nothing but menial or violent tasks. But he was wrong. Tim had watched every move Sampson made. He knew everything about Sampson, and Sampson's business. Holloway knew about Sampson's money, knew where he kept it, and he knew the combination to Sampson's safe. He also knew how afraid Sampson was of the Chileans.

No, Tim Holloway thought. He would not tell his boss about what he knew this time. This time it was his turn to be in control, his turn to take matters into his own hands and come out the winner. Hell, maybe he could even take over the entire operation. He knew the in's and out' better than Sampson himself, and had a better working relationship with Espiranza and Muniz. He should be the one making all the money.

Yes, Tim Holloway decided, tonight was the night he was going to get his due.

Thirty Three

CLAIRE WAS PACKING her bag when her cell phone vibrated. It was a text from Chloe.

"shawn j will b there!!!!!"

Shawn Jamison. He was so hot. Claire had had a crush on him since the third grade. Now he was fifteen, and had started to bulk up. He played football and swam, had broad shoulders and a wide smile, like her father's. He was the most popular boy in school and everyone liked him. Claire hadn't told Chloe she liked him. She hadn't told anyone she liked him. She couldn't dare, she was too shy. But maybe tonight she could find the courage to talk to him.

"wat r u wearing?" Claire texted back.

"pink swtr sknys and boots"

Claire scanned her closet and tried on almost everything she owned. It was pointless, she thought. Nothing was right. All of her clothes were three years old, and a little too small. The few things she had purchased recently were second hand, and at least two seasons old. She snuck into her mother's room while Jules was downstairs on the phone. Her mom had one pair of good jeans and they fit Claire just right. She found the jeans, and one of her mom's tops and ran back into her room to pack them away.

"What time are you going to Chloe's?" The sound of her mom's voice made her jump. Had she seen Claire sneak the clothes?

"When she gets home from dance, around four." Claire played nonchalant.

"Ok, well I'm going to take the boys over to Stella's. I'll be back by 3:00 pm so I'll see you before you go." Jules came into the room and hugged her daughter.

"Ok." Claire pulled away from a hug that felt uncomfortably long.

TONY RAMANO'S cell phone rang at 1:30 pm. It was Pete.

"Tony, hey it's Pete. Can I take a rain check for dinner tonight? My mother's ill and I really need to go see her."

Pete was talking in code. In reality, Pete had a date that evening and wanted some time off of Holloway detail. Even after 20 years, Pete still talked like an agent.

"Sure, Pete, I'll cover you." Tony was online watching the gps monitor track Holloway's minivan. He had followed Holloway virtually, from the gym, to his home, switch into the SUV, and now he was traveling east on Interstate 40, towards downtown Nashville.

Tony packed up his desk, turned off the light in his office and locked the door.

"Josh, I'm taking off early today." Tony said to the front desk manager.

"Ok, sure boss! Have a good evening." Josh was stunned. In the five years he had worked for Tony Ramano, Josh had never seen him leave before 7:00 pm.

Tony made his way to the interstate, and eventually caught up with Holloway. He was parked outside the Transport Express office. At 4:00 pm, Holloway left the office and travelled the interstate, headed west. Tony followed Holloway off I-40 and onto I-440, then onto I-65 south. They traveled ten miles before exiting onto Old Hickory Blvd west. From here, Holloway made several turns, followed back roads and traveled up and down hills. On Franklin Road in Brentwood, Tim Holloway made a stop at a small gas station convenience store. Tony Ramano parked around the left side of the building, far back near a dumpster to avoid being noticed.

HOLLOWAY SAW HIM about five cars behind. He had noticed the car parked across the street from Transport Express. He had never seen that car before, and Transport Express didn't usually draw in the general public. As he exited I-65 Tim altered his speed, made last minute turns on unexpected roads, and tried to outrun him on the hilly turns of the Forrest Hills back roads. But this guy was good, and Tim just couldn't lose him. As a last resort he pulled into a gas station.

Tim pulled into a parking spot right in front of the building. He paused and fished out a small black case from his glove compartment, then waited until his tail pulled in and parked around the corner. Perfect, Tim thought.

Tim Holloway walked into the convenience store and went up to the counter.

"Hey Mark! How's it going?" The proprietor, Mark Collins, was an old friend of Tim's, and ran a Friday night poker club in his basement.

"Holloway- good to see you man! What's been going on? I haven't seen you in what, six months?"

"I know, dude, I'm sorry, I've just been busy. But let the guys know I'll be back next month. I think you still owe me a few hundred!"

"More like fifty! But who's counting right?" Mark replied while ringing up cigarettes for a kid who looked about twelve.

When the boy left with his smokes, Tim approached Mark and spoke quietly to him.

"Tell you what, Mark. I'll call it even if you let me walk out your back door."

"What?" Mark was confused.

"No biggie, I just want to prank a friend who followed me here. Can I sneak out the back?"

"Sure thing man, and we're even?"

"Even!" Tim walked down the back hall of the store and exited quietly out the back door.

TONY WAITED patiently outside the convenience store. He had forgotten how much he hated stakeouts. He positioned himself so that he lay across the front bench seat of his 1988 El Camino. He had purchased the car the year he moved to America. It was perfect for lounging, and today he opened his window and rested his head on the sill, and stretched out so that his feet hung out the passenger window. If anyone were to see him they would think he was a day laborer taking a siesta.

But Tony Ramano's eyes remained open and fixed on the tail end of the tan Mercedes SUV, just visible past the front left corner of the building. As soon as Holloway was on the move, Tony Ramano would follow.

Tony's cell phone vibrated. He pulled it from his pocket and saw a text from Jules.

"everything ok?"

"fine, im on it. let you know if there's a problem"

"thnx"

Tony replaced the phone in his pocket and resumed his position.

At first he wasn't sure what bit him, but the sting on his neck felt like a wasp. He jumped and slapped at his neck, then felt the tiny sharp object. He pulled the dart out of his neck and looked at it up close. His vision blurred quickly, but he knew what it was. Before he could reach for his phone, Tony fell unconscious.

"STUPID WOP!" Uttered Tim. He placed his hat over Tony's face, and walked casually to his SUV. The tranquilizer should last several hours, he would have plenty of time to get on with it without interruption. Tim walked to the passenger side of the Mercedes and reached under the wheel well to retrieve the gps monitor. It had been fixed to the steel frame of the car with a powerful magnet. He pretended to be inspecting his tire. A quick look around assured him no one was looking.

When he stood up he scanned the parking lot. At the other end of the building he spotted a light colored Cadillac Escalade parked near the air machine. 'Perfect' he said to himself. He walked past the car and pretended to inspect the air machine.

"A buck-fifty, can you believe it? The one down the road is free!" Tim shook his head and complained to a passerby who had been watching him.

As he approached the Escalade he dropped his keys on the ground. Picking up the keys with his left hand, Tim used his right hand to place the magnet inside the wheel well. 'That will keep him busy.' Tim Holloway smiled at his cleverness, climbed back into his Mercedes, and went on his way.

"YOU KNOW how much I love you?" Jules had made her way home and was sitting on Claire's bed while Claire put on her makeup.

"Moooommm!" Claire rolled her eyes at her mother. She was being exceptionally sentimental and clingy today.

"More than thiiiiiiiiiiis much!!!" Jules held both arms out wide and exaggerated a measure of her love for her daughter. It was a tradition she had held with her daughter since she was a baby, and it used to make Claire smile.

Claire put her makeup in her bag, stood, and turned to her mother.

"I'm going now, ok?"

"Want me to drive you?"

"Mom, its three houses down."

"Ok, want me to walk you?"

"Mom!"

"Ok, ok, just be careful! I love you!"

Jules refrained from grabbing her daughter and holding on for dear life. She wasn't sure if it was the stories of the traffickers or the fear of her own fate that evening, but she felt an ominous wave come over her. She was afraid for her daughter.

'Probably just paranoid' she told herself. After this week, they would all be safe. And tonight, her children were under the careful watch of trusted friends. Everything would be fine.

WHEN TONY WOKE, it was 10:15 pm. It took him several minutes to fully rouse. He had been made. It wasn't the first time, but he felt foolish. He unlocked his phone and opened his gps app. Holloway was located in Nashville, near the Greyhound bus station on 8th Avenue South.

Tony sent a text to Jules.

"all ok?"

"yep on sched. still with th?"

"watching him now- keep you posted"

Tony sighed and took his first real breath since waking. Holloway had gotten away, but only temporarily. He would have to be more careful from now on. He got out of the car, went into the store and poured himself the last of the thick sludge that had once been coffee. He needed to shake off this hangover.

When Tony returned to his car, his gps app alerted movement. Holloway was traveling north on 8th Avenue. Tony started the car and headed in that direction.

Thirty Four

AT 11:00 PM, Jules and Mitch arrived at JJ's apartment. Monica and Douglas were already there. They had brought with them two air mattresses, blankets, a variety of folding lawn chairs, and a pound of gourmet coffee. It was going to be a long night.

"Coffee?" Monica handed Jules a cup and poured another for Mitch. The five of them sat down on the lawn chairs and drank their coffee in silence.

Finally JJ spoke. "Ok, Douglas and Monica, are you two good with the monitors?"

Douglas replied "Yep. We're on it. If we see anything suspicious we'll send an alert text."

"Cool, but that reminds me, we need to make sure all of our phones are on silent."

"Mitch, have you got the safe combination?"

"Memorized"

"Awesome, but I'm emailing you an enhanced clip from the video feed now, so that you'll have it while we're in there just in case. There's no telling what nerves will do to your memory."

"Good idea, thanks."

JJ turned to Jules- "Jules, your guy still on Holloway?"

"Yeah, I just talked to him an hour ago."

"Cool. I think we're ready."

"They're coming in." Monica pointed to monitor one.

The view from the smoke detector camera showed thirty girls being filed into the conference room at The Office. The scene was similar to what the group had witnessed two weeks ago, and just as disturbing. These girls were so young, and so scared.

As she watched the girls stand for inspection, Jules began to cry.

"SO WHAT do you think?" Chloe came out of her close in the most amazing outfit Claire had ever seen.

"Where did you get that?" Claire was envious.

"Mom took me to the mall yesterday. I told her I needed a new outfit for school pictures."

Claire looked in the mirror, at her old shoes, her mother's clothes, and felt awful.

"Hey, try this." Chloe handed Claire a khaki green camisole and a brown leather belt. Claire put on the camisole and layered the open button down shirt over top, and Chloe helped her get the shirt cinched just right under the belt. Then she went to her jewelry box and picked out a beaded necklace and a pair of feather dangles and handed them to Claire. As Claire put on the jewelry, Chloe went to her closet and retrieved the perfect pair of scrunch boots.

"If we tuck your jeans into your socks like this, they fit just like skinnies. Look," Chloe turned Claire to the mirror "perfect!"

Claire was amazed at the transformation. Her mood brightened instantly, she looked fantastic.

"You are a genius!" Claire hugged her friend and then started on her make-up.

Claire couldn't wait to see Shawn Jamison. She had been thinking about him for a week now. She had decided it was time to bite the bullet and make the first move. Dooley's party would be the perfect opportunity.

At 10:30 pm Chloe walked down the dark hall to her mother's room and knocked on the door.

"C'm in."

"Hey mom, I just wanted to say goodnight." Chloe peaked in the doorway, enough for her mother to see a silhouette of her face.

"'Night girls. I'll probably be gone for work when you wake up tomorrow, so you're on your own."

"Ok, 'night mom." Chloe closed the door and walked down the hall to her room. She shut the door loudly, and then she and Claire tiptoed towards the kitchen and out the back door.

Chloe had arranged to have Sarah Walker's sister pick them up at the end of the block. Jack Dooley lived just a mile away, but Chloe wanted to arrive in a car. It made her feel grown up. This was going to be the first high school party she and Claire had attended, and the first time she'd ever gotten drunk.

Chloe had been practicing at home, sneaking a beer from the refrigerator now and then. She couldn't stand the taste, and wasn't sure she was going to be able to fake it. She had practiced over and over in front of the mirror, but every time the beer touched her tongue her face made an involuntary smirk.

"Here, take this- it will help." Sarah Walker's sister handed each of the girls a cup and poured it full of red liquid.

"What is this?" Claire asked. She wasn't in the habit of going along just because.

"Punch and grain alcohol. You won't taste the alcohol, but it will give you a good head start on a buzz."

Sarah demonstrated by taking the first sip. And the other girls followed. Claire thought it didn't taste half bad. Perhaps she could get used to this drinking thing.

The party was huge. Jack Dooley lived at the end of a long private road. His family was rich, really rich. Even for this part of town. His driveway was a half-mile long. That made it a great party house, because there were no nosy neighbors close by to call the police. His house was surrounded by woods, with lots of places to sneak off and make out. Claire eyed the woods as they traveled down the driveway, imagining taking Shawn Jamison to one of those spots. The grain alcohol was beginning to work, and her confidence was building.

TONY RAMANO'S first stop was his garage. He parked the black 1988 El Camino and hung the keys on his key rack. He picked up a second set of keys off the rack and went to the other car in the garage.   He removed the car cover from his vintage silver 280 Z, climbed in and started the engine.

Tony caught up with the gps signal on interstate 40, headed east. It was 11:00 pm, and traffic was light. The screen on his phone indicated that the car was traveling one half mile ahead of him. He kept a safe distance so as not to be seen. The change in cars was a good start, but he wouldn't risk getting caught a second time.

The signal traveled several miles before exiting interstate 40. Tony followed the signal to the Nashville Airport exit.

'Just what are you up to, Holloway?' Tony thought as he followed the signal up to the departing flights deck. Then the signal stopped.

Slowly Tony approached the gps signal but could not see the Mercedes SUV. His monitor assured him he was approaching the device, but the Mercedes was nowhere to be found. Tony pulled forward until his monitor indicated he was right next to the transmitter. On his right, parked in the departing flight lane was a large cream colored SUV.

Tony saw it was an Escalade. He sat for a few minutes, blocking traffic, staring at the man pulling luggage out of the back of the car for his wife. He watched in shock as the man kissed his wife good-by and returned to his car. Tony Ramano cursed himself when he realized what Holloway had done.

TIM SAT at the bar and remembered that first night. He remembered the anger and frustration. It had been a year since being discharged from the army the night the soldier had showed up. What would his life had been if he hadn't met the soldier? Would he still be working at Torres' bar? Had he really been better off working for Richard Sampson all these years? Tim contemplated his life choices over tequila.

Perhaps he would have gone to college. He was a bright kid. Maybe he would have studied computers, created his own dot com business and made it rich. Or maybe he would open a gym, like that dickhead Ramano. He knew more about weightlifting than that quido wop, and could lift circles around that bitch trainer Jules.

How Tim hated working out with her. He had spent his life in the gym and knew more about dead lifts and cleans than she ever would. But each week, he showed up for his appointments and let her think she was teaching him something. Each week he listened to her patronize him, as he feigned ignorance. Each week he took his orders from Richard Sampson and let that bitch act like she was better than him, like he needed her help.

Tim reached for his fifth shot. He was starting to see the light, and had convinced himself. Yes, Tim Holloway would have been better off if he had never met Richard Sampson. And now was his chance to take back everything that had been taken from him.

At 10:30 pm, Tim Holloway paid his bill, climbed into his SUV, and headed for Franklin.

"OH MY GOD there he is!!" Chloe grabbed Claire's arm so tight Claire winced.

Shawn Jamison was playing pool with two other ninth grade boys. He was drinking from a red plastic cup and laughing at the lousy shot his friend had just made. Claire thought he looked incredible.

"You want to go get a drink?" She asked Chloe- the punch was kicking in and she wanted more.

"Yeah." Chloe said, not taking her eyes off of Shawn Jamison.

Chloe and Claire made there way to the famous Dooley kitchen. The Dooley kitchen was a legend for its fully stocked bar. Tonight it displayed an array of liquors, cocktail mixers, and two full kegs. The kitchen table had been turned into an all-you-can-drink, make-your-own cocktail bar. Claire found just what she wanted, more punch and grain.

Claire was regretting the choice the minute it hit her lips, and her mother's white shirt.

"Oh my god I'm soooooooooo sorry!" A ditsy blond in a miniskirt was apologizing and laughing at the same time. She wiped at Claire with a napkin, trying to remove the red punch she had just spilled, but then lost her balance and clung to Claire's arm to recover herself.

"I can't believe I did that. Oh - my - god. Oh my god, I'm so sorry!" The drunken girl kept wiping at Claire with her right hand, while spilling her beer on Claire's borrowed boots with her left. Claire tried to push her away but the girl kept coming.

"It's ok, really. I'll just go clean up in the bathroom." Claire finally pulled the blond girl's hand off her chest and pushed her aside. She looked up for Chloe but didn't see her. 'Really?'

She thought to herself. Chloe had left her there covered in punch. 'Real cool.' Claire was beginning to rethink her evening plans.

Claire went searching for a bathroom. She walked down a long hall that led to the Dooley family bedrooms. Claire found the bathroom at the end of the hall. She opened the door and surprised herself to find a girl sitting on the toilet.

"Oh! I'm sorry..." Claire started to turn and walk out when the girl stood, wiped, and flushed.

"Hey, don't worry about it. Nothing anyone else hasn't seen." The girl talked loudly and used her hands as she spoke. Claire thought she must be drunk.

She was very thin, and her blond hair looked like straw. Her eyes looked as if they were going to bulge out of their sockets. But still, Claire could see she had probably been pretty once. The girl washed her hands and checked herself out in the mirror. Claire recognized the look of sadness in her eyes.

The girl caught Claire looking at her and her eyes got wider. She turned around to face Claire so suddenly it made Claire jump. She laughed nervously and said to Claire,

"Don't be so jumpy. There are worse things in life, ya know?"

Then suddenly the door to the bathroom opened and a very good looking older boy stuck his head in the door.

"Stephanie- it's time to go!"

Claire thought she saw Stephanie wince, and then she turned to Claire.

"They're all pigs, you know." This time there was no expression in her eyes.

And then Stephanie was gone.

'That was odd' Claire thought to herself. Her first high school party was turning out to be a real winner.

Claire locked the door and unbuttoned her mother's shirt. The red punch had spilled down the entire front, and would stain if she didn't get it out fast. She filled the sink with cold water, submerged the shirt, and began washing it with hand soap.

There was a knock at the door.

"Shit!" to herself, and then a little louder " Just a minute!"

Fortunately the red stain was starting to fade and was hardly visible. But the shirt was soaking wet. Claire wrung as much of the water out that she could. She found a trash bag under the sink, folded the shirt into a tiny wad, put it into the bag, and placed the bag in her purse. She would have to go without it. Claire checked herself out in the mirror and thought she looked pretty hot in Chloe's camisole and her mother's jeans. She was proud of her adaptability. Time to look for Shawn.

The knock on the door came louder and faster this time.

Claire opened the door to see two ninth grade girls waiting for the bathroom. They looked extremely pissed off.

"Chill. It's all yours!" Claire stood a little taller.

Then she saw them. Heading into one of the bedrooms down the hall. Shawn Jamison was leading Chloe by the hand. Chloe was laughing. The door shut behind them.

Claire stopped in her tracks. This wasn't happening. She was supposed to be the one going into that room with Shawn Jamison. How could Chloe do this? All this time. All this effort-she had finally gotten the courage and now her best friend goes behind her back?

Claire walked directly to the room with every intent to burst in and confront her friend. She turned the handle but the door was locked.

"Go away!" It was Shawn's voice. Chloe was laughing.

Claire's heart sank. She turned and walked down the hall to the living room, to the front door, and out to the driveway. It was freezing, but Claire didn't care. She walked the half mile down the dark driveway, then the three blocks to her own street. She didn't even notice the lights as they approached.

IT WAS 11:15 PM when Tim Holloway entered the west Franklin subdivision. He was afraid he was too late. He shouldn't have stayed for that last shot of tequila. He was scolding himself when he saw her. Some girl, walking down the street in freezing cold weather wearing nothing but a tank top and blue jeans. Idiot teenagers! Tim thought.

As he came upon her Tim slowed to a stop. He leaned out his window to ask if she was ok. That's when he recognized her. She had been crying, and she was shivering.

"You're Claire, right?" Tim spoke clearly and pleasantly.

The recognition surprised Claire, and she was instantly suspicious. She stepped away from the car.

"It's ok, I'm Tim. I'm a friend of your mom's. A client actually, from the gym. She's shown me your pictures quite a bit, she's real proud of you. I just left your house. Your parents had me over for dinner and I had left, but I realized I left my cell phone so I'm heading back. Why don't you hop in?"

"No, thanks."

"It's ok, really. I'm not a maniac, I swear. Besides, you look like you're freezing! It's warm in here."

Claire was freezing. And she wanted to sit down. She just wanted to be back in her own room, under the covers by herself.

"Ok, thanks." And Claire climbed in.

Tim Holloway rolled up the window, locked the doors, and headed back down the road. As they approached the Spalding house, Claire heard his cell phone ring from inside his jacket pocket.

Thirty Five

THE TEAM spent two hours watching another auction. They sat motionless, watching the computer monitor as, one by one, the girls were inspected, questioned, and ultimately purchased to be used by the purchaser. Tonight though, was different. Two of the customers were women.

"I can't even believe that there are women traffickers. These women are probably going to take the girls to a brothel. They'll make a hundred times the purchase price of each girl the first year, more if the girl's a virgin." Jules shared with the group more of what she had learned from the ESTN website.

"They tell these girls they have to work off their debt for bringing them here, and then they'll be allowed to leave. Then they have to work off the cost of their food, clothing, medical care, which is a sham. The madams barely spend a dime on these girls, keeping them underfed and living in completely unacceptable conditions. The girls "work" eighteen hours a day in the brothel, but never see a dime. After a just a few years, they become too old, and too sick to continue working and the madam drops them out on the street to die."

"I don't get it." Monica was disturbed. "How can anyone ignore humanity that way? How can any human being treat another that way without any remorse, any feeling?"

"Slavery and oppression are as old as time, Mon." Douglas took Monica's hand in his. "The only thing that changes is the demographic of the victim. The truth is, we're all animals, all capable of devouring another for our own gain. It's our nature."

"No, I don't agree at all." Jules stood up. "I refuse to believe that point of view. We are *not* born that way."

Mitch jumped in this time. "Jules, face it, evil does exist. We're looking at it right in front of us."

"I know what I see, and it makes me sick. But if we are all born with evil in us, we must be born with good in us as well. If we are capable of good or evil, then we have a choice, and we should always have the opportunity to make a new choice."

"I'd love to find out you're right someday, Jules." Douglas put his hand on her shoulder, then looked at the computer monitor.

"I think it's time for you to go."

It was 2:15 am and The Office was empty.

AT MIDNIGHT, Tony Ramano sat outside The Office. He had parked across the street, behind an old van, and watched through the windows. He had seen some awful things in his career, but mostly men hurting bad men. It always seemed justifiable when the target was an adult with a bad history. There should be an unwritten rule that when it comes to evil, children should be off limits.

Holloway never showed up. That surprised Tony. He thought he would catch him here and resume his surveillance. Perhaps he was staying home tonight, laying low. Tony texted a friend who owed him a favor, gave him Holloway's address and asked him to check it out.

A few hours later Tony received a text. "not home"

By this time clients were beginning to leave with their packages. Tony was filled with rage as he watched the girls leave. Through binoculars he could see their tiny, young faces. Some actually looked hopeful.

By 2:10 am Tony watched as Richard Sampson and his colleagues left The Office. Tony pulled out his keys and started his engine, but left the lights off. Keeping a safe distance, Tony followed Sampson to the Transport Express garage. He parked about 300 yards across the street from the side of the building where he had a wide angle view. He could see every entrance form his vantage point. Here it was quiet.

Richard Sampson was the only one here at this hour. He entered the building through the back entrance at the loading dock, was inside for ten minutes, then returned to his car and left.

Tony stayed and waited.

TIM HOLLOWAY pulled into the Spalding driveway which took him to the back of the house. The house was dark. It was 11:20 pm. Tim looked at Claire and pulled his jacket back to expose his weapon. He said, "Come with me."

The two got out of the car and walked to the garage windows. Tim shined his flashlight into the garage. It was empty.

With his hand on Claire's arm Tim led her back to the SUV. He walked to the drivers' side and climbed in.

"What are you going to do with me?" Claire had sobered up fast. Her eyes scanned the interior of the vehicle for some way out. But he had a gun.

"Shut up." Tim wouldn't look at her.

"It doesn't matter."

"I said shut up."

"I don't care what you say. It doesn't matter."

"If you don't shut up I'm going to put this thing down your throat and pull the trigger." Tim Holloway waved the gun in front of her face.

"Go ahead, I don't care anymore." And Claire meant it. She turned to face the window and began to cry.

JULES, MITCH, AND JJ gathered together in JJ's new car. It was a beater, an old black Ford Explorer. He had traded in his Taurus for anonymity. They traveled down Charlotte Pike heading to Transport Express. When they arrived, Sampson's car was still in the parking lot. JJ parked across the street from the back entrance, in an alley, his car hidden by a large building that housed a food processing company. They had a full view of the rear of the building.

The three watched as Sampson left Transport Express, got into his car, and leave the parking lot. They sat in silence as they waited five more minutes. Finally Mitch spoke.

"Ready J?"

"As I'll ever be."

Mitch kissed Jules. "Be quick." She told him.

JJ handed Jules his laptop, connected to the internet through her mobile hot spot phone, and she placed it on the passenger seat. JJ had created a split screen so that Jules could monitor both cameras at once.

"Ok, you know what to do, right?"

"Got it, now lets get this done."

Jules would stay in the car, monitoring the cameras. She was also in charge of monitoring the parking lot and alerting JJ and Mitch if anyone were to show up unexpectedly. In all of the hours of video the team had watched, neither Sampson nor his men had ever returned to the Transport Express offices after he dropped his money in the safe. But there was always a first. And Jules was ready.

Mitch and JJ walked to the rear entrance of the building. JJ had hacked into the Transport Express security feed and created a continuous loop of inactivity. If anyone were watching, JJ and Mitch would not be seen entering the building via surveillance tonight.

JJ tried his master key on Sampson's office door. It still worked. JJ was prepared to pick the lock, or even remove the handle from the door, but Richard Sampson had been arrogant enough to think that he'd never be challenged.

Once inside the office, Mitch put on a pair of latex cleaning gloves and walked directly to the safe. He removed the picture from the wall and began putting in the combination.

33-43-56-14. Nothing happened. He tried it again, and again, and it didn't work.

"Shit!" Mitch exclaimed.

"Ok, don't panic, let's check the video." JJ reminded Mitch about the video he had sent to Mitch's email.

Mitch pulled out his phone, opened up his email and watched the video. JJ had been right, Mitch had confused the numbers. He returned to the safe and used the correct combination and this time it worked.

FOR TWO HOURS, Tim Holloway just drove. He drove through the streets of Franklin, through the projects where he shouted insults to the men on the streets. Then through the shopping district of Cool Springs, where the lights from the stores made orange and green glows on Clair's fair skin.

At first Claire wasn't scared. She was still pissed at Chloe, and she didn't care what happened. But now she realized this was

248

for real. She wasn't sure what this man had intended to do to her. He said he was her mother's client, that her mom had shown him her picture. Had he planned this all along? Had he been stalking her? Was he going to rape her? Claire began to panic.

"Where are you taking me?"

"I thought you didn't care."

Claire tried to act cool, so she wouldn't let on her fear. Her father always told her that animals sense fear, that fear can trigger an attack.

"I don't," her voice was shaky " I'm just trying to make conversation. We've been driving around for like, hours."

"Yeah, well you just shut up. I'll worry about where we're going."

Claire decided to stay quiet. Better to not piss him off. She closed her eyes and rested her head on the closed window, trying to pretend she was asleep, but she couldn't rest in his car.

Eventually the car slowed, and then it stopped. Claire looked up and saw that they were in a parking lot in front of a large building. The sign above the front door read "Transport Express Office Entrance".

Tim turned to Claire and said "Let's go."

Claire unbuckled her seatbelt and got out of the car slowly. By this time she was terrified.

TONY RAMANO watched as JJ and Mitch entered the building from the rear entrance. He looked from where they came and could see a shadow from JJ's car in the alley between two buildings. He was relieved to see the two, and assumed Jules was safe in the car waiting for then as planned. He checked his watch. It was 2:42 am.

At 2:47 am, Tony watched as a large SUV slowly moved down the street in front of him. He slid down his seat so he wouldn't be noticed in the old car. As the car passed Tony saw it was Holloway, and there was someone in the passenger seat. The SUV traveled to the front parking lot, and stopped. Once the lights were turned off, Tony sat up and watched as Tim Holloway led Claire Spalding into the Transport Express building through the front door.

Tony pulled out his phone.

Thirty Six

JULES' TEXT alert made her jump.

"Oh God" She couldn't imagine what had gone wrong. What she saw horrified her.

'holloway has claire going into te now'

'what????'

'tim has claire and he is taking her into te- im going in'

Tim Holloway has Claire? Tony must be mistaken; Claire was with a friend tonight. He must be with one of the girls from earlier.

Claire dismissed Tony's mistake, but still couldn't relax. She had to warn Mitch that Tim Holloway was inside the building.

MITCH HAD JUST closed the safe when his text alert went off.

'tim holloway in building'

"Shit!"

JJ had removed the button cam from the computer speaker on Sampson's desk, and the listening device from the phone. He looked up at Mitch.

"What is it?"

Mitch whispered as he replaced the painting on the wall covering the safe.

"Holloway is in the ...."

"Dad!"

Mitch and JJ turned to see Claire standing in the doorway, followed by Tim Holloway. Tim's left forearm was around Claire's neck, and his right hand held a gun, pointed at her head.

THE VIDEO FEED from the camera on Sampson's desk went to static, and Jules knew JJ and Mitch were almost finished. Removing the surveillance equipment was the last thing to do before leaving Sampson's office.

Jules didn't know what to do. She wanted to go in to help them, but she had been instructed to stay in the car and be ready in case the two had to leave quickly. If she went inside, what could she do? She was no match for Tim Holloway. She prayed Mitch received her text in time to hide or leave before Tim found them.

But before she had a chance to consider any other option, she watched in shock and horror as the feed from the button cam on the back of Sampson's desk convinced her that Tony had not been mistaken about Claire.

BACK AT JJ'S apartment, Monica and Douglas watched helplessly as their friends were in trouble.

"Something's wrong, we need to call the police." Monica was already picking up the phone.

"And say what, Mon? JJ and Mitch are breaking and entering private property."

"Someone else is in there! Who are they talking to?"

"I don't know, but there's nothing we can do right now, anyways."

"Maybe I could call the office telephone, distract them, maybe it could give ......" Monica's rambling was interrupted by what she saw unfolding on the computer monitor before them.

"TIM, LET HER GO. She's a kid. This is between us and Richard Sampson." Mitch was trying to be diplomatic.

Tim stroked Claire's hair. "Don't you think she'd make a nice addition to our selection?"

Mitch bolted after Tim, but he held the gun up close to Claire's temple. "I'd stay right there if I were you."

"What do you want?" JJ asked.

"I want what's mine. What you have in that bag. This office. The entire operation. I've earned it. It's my turn." Keeping the gun close to Claire's temple, Holloway used his left hand to pull a flask from his jacket pocket, and take a drink.

Mitch thought he had an opportunity. Holloway was drunk, and irrational.

"Here, take it. Just let Claire go." Mitch held out the duffel filled with the contents of the safe. He was trying to draw Holloway away from Claire. Tim was bigger and stronger than Mitch, but he was reckless and drunk. Mitch thought he could outwit him.

"It's not that easy Mitch. You see, I'm owed something. I've put my life into this operation. I've given up my entire future to help Richard Sampson succeed. I'm done helping everyone else. Now it's your turn to help me."

"So how do we do that, Tim?"

"By giving me your daughter, of course. White girls cost extra. They'll look kindly on me for bringing her to them. When they get here tomorrow and find that Richard's taken all of the money and flown the coup, they'll be happy to find a loyal replacement, someone that can get them quality girls." Tim pulled Claire close and kissed her on the head.

Tim raised the gun towards Mitch. "I'm very sorry to have to do this Mitch, you seem like a nice guy...."

The sound was much louder than he expected. Tony Ramano had never actually used a tire iron on another person's head, but he had witnessed the affects one had had on a colleague. If Tim Holloway survived, he might not ever be the same.

IT HAPPENED so fast Jules wasn't sure she could trust her eyes, but she had heard the shot. She couldn't stay in the car any longer. She wasn't using her brain, she told herself she should be quiet, avoid notice, but her feet weren't listening. Before she realized what she was doing she was in the office looking at the mess.

"DAD!" Claire ran to Mitch, who was on the floor. The bullet had just grazed his shoulder.

"Dad, I'm so sorry! If I hadn't snuck out..."

Mitch put his hand on Claire's cheek. "It's ok, Claire. I'm ok. Help me up."

Claire helped her father up and the two hugged. Jules could not believe the scene in front of her. She ran to her husband and daughter and joined them.

Tony was the first to speak.

"Jules, you need to take Claire home."

"Is he dead?" Jules was looking at Tim Holloway.

Tony bent down and placed a finger on Holloway's carotid artery to check for a pulse.

"No, but he'll be out for a while."

"Good. What are we going to do with him?"

"Don't worry about that, I've got an idea. You take Claire home and I'll make sure Mitch and JJ get home safe as well, understand?" Tony was holding Jules by the shoulders.

Jules looked up at Mitch.

"It's ok, go." Mitch hugged his wife and daughter and sent them out.

When Jules returned to the car she found her cell phone vibrating on the seat. She had forgotten about Monica and Douglas. They were at JJ's apartment watching the monitors. They must have been terrified.

Jules answered Monica's call and filled them in on what had happened. She decided she preferred being with her friends to going home to an empty house, so she took Claire to JJ's.

When they arrived Monica had hot chocolate waiting for Claire. The sleep aid she had mixed with the cocoa took effect quickly. Jules tucked Claire into the air bed and sat with her until she was completely asleep.

AFTER JJ DROVE the SUV into the Transport Express garage, it took all three of them to hoist Tim Holloway into the back. Mitch retrieved Tim's wallet from his jacket pocket. When the others gave him questioning looks, Mitch explained, "I have an idea of my own."

JJ covered Tim Holloway with a moving blanket from the garage, locked the doors, and the three of them went back inside the office.

JJ removed the remaining video cameras while Mitch re-opened the safe. He removed all of the cash and placed it in the duffel with the log books and folders. Tony found the bullet that had scraped Mitch's arm and pulled it out of the wall with a pair of pliers JJ had retrieved from the garage.

JJ used a wet mechanic's towel to wipe a few drops of Mitch's blood from the wall. Sampson's choice of flooring, a red oriental rug, was the perfect disguise for the drops of blood, both from Mitch's arm and Holloway's head. Tony smudged them with his foot to blend in with the pattern on the rug, then wrapped the tire iron in the towel. The three surveyed the room, everything looked in order.

Mitch took Tim's wallet and dropped it on the floor below the wall safe.

"Wait, let me see that." JJ asked for the wallet.

Mitch handed JJ the wallet and JJ removed the driver's license. He took the license to the copier and made color copies of the front and back, returned the license to the wallet and dropped it below the safe.

JJ looked at Mitch, "I think your idea just got brilliant."

The three left the office and locked the door. Tony handed Mitch the keys to his 280 Z and held up the keys to Tim's Mercedes.

"I've got this. Close the garage door behind me. You two take my car to your apartment JJ, and I'll meet up with you there in an about an hour." Tony climbed into the SUV and drove off. He picked up his cell phone and dialed a number.

"Pete, sorry to wake you. I need one more favor."

Thirty Seven

TONY RAMANO arrived at JJ's apartment at 4:45 am Thursday morning to find the team sitting on the floor around piles of papers. Monica was dictating and Jules was typing on JJ's laptop.

Each of them stopped and waited for Tony to speak.

"It seems that Tim Holloway is gone. He's broken into Richard Sampson's office, stolen the contents of his safe, and disappeared. When Sampson opens the safe tonight for his friends they will find the safe empty, Holloway's wallet on the floor, and assume Tim Holloway ripped them off. It's a sick gift, my friends, but I'll take it. How's the report for TBI coming Jules?"

"Done." Jules handed Tony a thick folder.

"Done? That was fast."

"Open it." Jules nodded to Tony.

Tony sat down on the floor next to Jules and opened the folder. The first page was dated June 15, 2009, and titled "Espiranza and Muniz". It listed the names of two Chilean ex-soldiers, their personal biographies, career history, addresses, and contact numbers. The next two pages were 8X10 photos of the men.

"What is this?" Tony was confused.

Mitch explained. "Richard Sampson created that folder. It details the entire trafficking operation, including his Chilean contacts, names of girls transported through The Office doors, and the name and contact information of brothel owners, pimps, and even some private Johns." Mitch handed Tony a business card with the name of TBI Agent Robert Aguirre.

"He was going turn them in?"

"Looks like it. He kept detailed notes of every auction in these logbooks. He played it real smart."

JJ added "And better yet, he kept pictures of all the girls. On the back of many of the girls' photos he named the pimps who purchased them. It's possible these girls can be found and recovered."

"I'm going through the log books now and compiling the information from tonight's auction. I'm just about done." Jules smiled at Tony.

"Son of a bitch! He was going to rat out the entire operation? He wanted out?" Tony was trying to take it all in.

"I don't think he ever wanted in." Monica handed Tony another folder. This one was marked 'CD'.

Tony opened the folder and entered another world. The first document was a clip from The Washington Herald, dated June 12, 2010.

Paul Schafer- 1921-2010

Paul Schafer was a Nazi. He was born in Troisdorf, Germany in 1921. He joined the Hitler Youth movement as a young boy, became a Corporal in the German army, and served as a Medic during World War II. After the war, Paul Schafer became an evangelical preacher, created a home for children, and a Lutheran ministry. Following sexual abuse charges, Schafer fled Germany. In 1961, Schafer moved to Chile, and established the Dignidad Beneficent society outside of Parral. The cult-like compound was eventually called Colonia Dignidad.

Situated on over 70 square miles of Chile's central valley, four hours from Santiago, Colonia Dignidad was arranged like a Bavarian village. Residents tended livestock, managed their own bakery, dairy, and several mills that provided resources for much of Chile. The utopian society was widely accepted and appreciated by their Chilean neighbors, as they provided free medical care to some of the nations poorest children. Few outsiders, however, ever saw the insides of the compound.

The unbelievable truth kept from the public was that Schafer's utopian village was in reality, a house of torture. Investigations into life at Colonia Dignidad reveal evidence of child molestation, forced labor, money laundering, weapons trafficking, kidnapping, torture and murder. The majority of abuses occurred against residents of Colonia Dignidad, as a means of maintaining mental control and order among his followers.

Children born inside Colonia Dignidad were taken from their parents and raised separately. Women and men were kept apart, and sexual relations were forbidden. Women and men were drugged to keep them in line and reduce their sexual desires. Members of Colonial Dignidad were not allowed personal possessions. They were to refer to their leader, Paul Schafer as "Uncle", and were under the constant fear of God's punishment for their sins. Paul Schaffer had a regular routine of asking his followers to reveal other members of the congregation who had sinned. These members were then expected to confess their sins publicly, and would often be tortured as penance.

Schafer had a select group of boys he called his "sprinters". These boys held a special status among the compound and were considered Schafer's favorites. Schafer would rely on his sprinters to communicate messages for him and carry out menial tasks on a regular basis. Recent evidence has revealed that

Schaffer had a habit of using narcotics to drug these boys and abuse them sexually.

In 1974, following the coup d'etat of the socialist president Salvador Allende, junta leader Augusto Pinochet created the National Intelligence Directorate, or DINA, in an effort to control possible political opponents. DINA was run by Colonel Manuel Contreras, and was responsible for rounding up political opponents and delivering them to interrogation centers where they were tortured and often killed. Colonia Dignidad was one of those centers.

Colonia Dignidad boasted state of the art laboratories, where biological weapons, including sarin gas were manufactured and stockpiled. Underground cellars throughout the compound served as torture chambers, separated from the peaceful daily life of Colonia Dignidad. 'Uncle' Paul Schafer cooperated with Contreras and DINA and aided in mass executions and disappearances.

Early attempts to investigate Colonia Dignidad were met with resistance by Schafer's supporters within the compound. In 1982, the German Government, with the help of Amnesty International, requested permission from the Pinochet Government to cooperate with an investigation into allegations of CD, but it was denied, along with requests in 1985, and 1988.

In 1996, Paul Schafer was charged with child abuse by a Chilean judge. Chilean police made over thirty attempts to apprehend Schafer by raiding the compound, but to no avail. It is suspected Schafer hid in any one of the multiple hidden tunnels and passageways among the compound. Schafer left the compound sometime in the late 1990's, but no one knows the exact date.

Paul Schafer was tried in his absence for the sexual abuse of 26 Chilean minors, and found guilty in a Chilean court. He was finally found, in a suburb of Argentina in 2005 and sent back to Chile to serve his time and face more charges of the disappearances of several political activists, human rights abuses, and more child rape charges. Paul Schafer died in prison on April 24, 2010, of heart failure. He was 88 years old.

TONY FINISHED reading the article and was more confused than ever. He looked up at Mitch.

"Look at these." Behind the article, Mitch pulled out an envelope full of photographs. On the front of the envelope were the words "Richard Sampson - 1975-1979". Tony looked at them one by one.

The first photograph was of a young Richard Sampson, wearing a lab coat and safety glasses. He was in a science lab, holding up a beaker and smiling at the camera. In the background there was writing on a chalkboard, it looked like German.

The second photograph was taken in the same lab. Richard Sampson was wearing the same lab coat, but no glasses. He was standing next to a small man with a receding hair line and bifocals. The man had his arm around Sampson. At the bottom right of the photo was the inscription- "Yours always- Uncle"

The next photo was disturbing. The room was dark and dingy, but Tony could make out the image of Sampson having sex with a young girl. The girl had been bent over a table, and Sampson had entered her from behind. Her face was turned towards the camera. Her eyes were blank, and a tear fell down her cheek. There were other men in the room, Chilean men, drinking beer, and smiling. Tony put the photos down in disgust.

"Keep going." Mitch handed him the next one.

This one was a picture of young Richard Sampson in army fatigues holding a gun to a man's head. The man was tied to a chair, with a black canvas sack over his head. The final picture revealed the shackled man's head slumped over, and Richard Sampson's hand at his side.

Tony put the pictures back into the envelope, and continued to sort through the file. There was another envelope. This one was labeled, "Sophia Sampson". All of the photos in this envelope were of a pretty red headed teenager. Judging by her style of clothing, they looked to have been taken in the mid to late 1980's. Each picture was of the same girl, in a different setting. In one picture the girl was with an older man.

Tony continued to leaf through the folder and found a document dated September 24, 1979. It was an official letter from President Augusto Pinochet.

Señor Richard Sampson,

This is to recognize your honorable duty to our government, and recognize your years of service. Our deepest thanks for your cooperation with our efforts to promote prosperity in Chile. I know you have made your grandfather proud, and we thank him for bringing you to us. May you prosper all the rest of your days.

Sincerely,
President Augusto Pinochet.

The letter had been signed by the president himself.

Sampson's discharge documents from the army were in the file. Richard Sampson was given an honorable discharge from the United States Army on August 15, 1979.

There were more newspaper articles, about Pinochet, the coup d'etat, Colonia Dignidad, and American support of DINA. Tony read them all in silence.

The last item in the folder was a letter. It had been inside an envelope addressed to Jennifer Sampson, but there was no postage or postmark. It had never been sent. The letter was dated December 1, 1976.

Dear Jenny,

I can't tell you how much I miss you. I hate this place. I hate everything about it. The people are horrible and the things they make me do are disgusting. I have come to hate the army and everything about it.

Jenny I can't wait to see you and Sophia. Papa has sent me photographs, she has your beautiful hair! I pray for a day where she never has to see the things I've seen.

I love you always,
Ricky

"He was just a kid." Tony looked at the others.

"From what we can tell, Sampson was sent to Chile as a teenager, by his grandfather." Mitch filled Tony in.

"We were able to find out more about him on the web. His name is Victor Diaz, he was a colonel in the Chilean army, and served with General Augusto Pinochet in the 50's and 60's. He retired to America in 1969. He lives in Nashville."

"These are blackmail photos. Richard Sampson was forced into trafficking these girls." Tony looked at Mitch.

"What I can't figure out is what he is waiting for. He's been keeping diligent notes for years, why hasn't he gone to the feds yet? There must be something in it for him?" Jules poured herself more coffee.

"He has a ten year old granddaughter." JJ pulled up Sophia Sampson Reynolds's Facebook page. Her daughter, Sammie looked just like her grandfather.

Thirty Eight

THE TEAM continued to work through the morning, and by 5:30 am, Jules needed a break. She closed her eyes briefly. When she opened them, it was 7:30 am.

Jules found Monica bleaching Douglas' hair in the bathroom, Mitch on the computer, and JJ cutting and pasting.

Claire was sitting on the floor, looking at pictures. Jules watched her daughter in the morning light. Claire was so beautiful. The image of her being lined up with the other girls at the auction made Jules want to vomit. She refocused her attention on the photos Claire was holding, the 8X10 headshots of the abducted girls.

"I know this girl, Mom." Claire was holding a photo of a pretty blond girl, who looked about Claire's age.

"You know her? How?"

"She was at the party last night. Only she doesn't look so pretty anymore. Her name is Stephanie."

"I don't understand, she was at the party, freely?" This didn't fit Jules' understanding of how the operation worked. Perhaps this girl had escaped.

"I don't think so, some guy called her away and she went with him. She looked miserable."

Jules flipped the picture over and saw the words 'Baker Brothers' on the back of photo. Jules picked up the list Sampson had created of Johns and found the name Baker on the list. There were two Bakers. Tony and Randall. The address was in Franklin, TN, and the two were listed as 'independent'. What did that mean?

When Jules went into the kitchen, Claire pulled Stephanie's picture from the pile, folded it, and put it into her purse.

"HOW DO I LOOK?" Douglas emerged from the bathroom a new man. His formerly dark brown, wavy hair had been transformed to a light golden blond, short, military style crop. He looked taller, and broader, and was wearing a t-shirt and dark blue mechanics' coveralls. He looked, oddly enough, like Tim Holloway.

"Perfect, now stand right here." JJ positioned Douglas by the window in front of a blue sheet, then aimed and shot the perfect passport photo. Within minutes he had the photo printed, copied and pasted into an old passport containing the personal information of Tim Holloway. He packaged the passport together with phony drivers' license, business documents, banking referrals, and residential affidavit.

"OK, you know what to do?" Tony directed his questions to Monica and Douglas.

"Sure do, Boss. We're ready." Douglas did his best to seem at ease, but he was nervous, Jules could tell.

"Good- text me when it's done." Tony gave Douglas a hand shake and a pat on the back. Douglas nodded back.

Monica hugged her friends good-by and the two headed out the door with a duffel full of cash.

"OK, so Mitch, are we on schedule for plan B?" JJ asked.

"Yes, I've got Sampson's statement here. When he arrives at Transport Express I'll be waiting."

"And Jules, you're clear?"

"Perfectly."

"Good. And Tony, can you handle one more day on stakeout?"

"Absolutely. Looking forward to it." Tony Ramano rubbed the side of his neck.

"Ok, then. Remember, this is command central, any pertinent information comes to me, and I'll alert the appropriate ones. Now, let's go."

Jules, Claire, Mitch, and Tony left JJ's apartment together. In the parking lot Jules pulled Tony aside.

"Tony I can't tell you how much I appreciate your help. I can't even believe I've gotten you mixed up in all of this. But thank you. You saved Claire's life." Jules hugged her boss, and tears fell down her face.

Tony Ramano took Jules by the face and looked directly into her eyes.

"Jules, you are a brave woman. I'm honored to be a part of what you've started. Thank you for sharing this with me." Tony kissed Jules on the cheek, waved good-by to Mitch and Claire, and left to find Richard Sampson.

AT 8 AM, JJ called Jason at Transport Express.

"Jason, it's JJ."

"J, what's up? Heard you gave up the fight bro? I have to say I was a little disappointed. I was hoping you'd be back someday."

"I have a feeling we'll see each other again soon, Jason. Maybe you can help with that."

"Anything, what?" Jason really liked JJ, and trusted him implicitly.

"Can you cancel Sampson's appointments today, and keep him out of the office for a few hours?"

"Hmmm. I guess. What's going on?"

"I'll explain later, Jason, I promise. If you could keep him away until about 3:00 pm, that would be great."

"Any suggestions on how I should do that, J?"

"I know you can think of something, thanks man, I'm counting on you." JJ hung up the phone.

"YOU WERE LATE last night. I missed you." From her bed, Jennifer Sampson watched her husband put on his tie.

"Jen, you know I'm always late on poker nights." Richard Sampson walked to the bed and sat down on the edge.

Jennifer looked deep into her husband's eyes. She felt like she hadn't really seen him in years. He was distracted. Constantly distracted.

"I know. I just miss you. Maybe we should start a poker night of our own."

"That sounds like a good idea." Richard Sampson kissed his wife just as his cell phone began to ring.

"Boss, I had to cancel your morning appointments with Stillman and Reagents, and your noon appointment with Gerry Atman. "

"What? What's going on?"

"Gas leak. Smelled it the minute I came in. I called the gas company and they're here now. They have evacuated the whole building. They think they've found the problem, but estimate it will be after 2:00 pm before they'll have it fixed. In the mean time they're not letting anyone in the building."

"That's ridiculous. I have to get in to my office. I'll just come by to get my papers and do my work somewhere else."

Jason was starting to get nervous. He had never had to lie to his boss before, and Richard Sampson was not the type you'd want to get caught lying to.

"You can try, but I'm telling you, it's like dealing with the National Guard. They won't even let me go back in to get my breakfast. I think one of them is armed!"

"Jesus Christ. Where are they working?"

"In the utility closet."

"Ok, just keep them out of my office, and call me when it's all clear to come back."

"Sure thing sir."

Sampson hung up and Jason sighed with relief. JJ better have a good plan because when Richard Sampson found out the truth, Jason was going to be out of a job.

Richard Sampson put down his phone and began taking off his tie, then his shirt.

"What are you doing?" Jennifer asked.

"I just got the morning off!" Richard Sampson continued to undress and climbed back into the bed with his wife.

BY 8:15 AM, Tony Ramano was parked across the street from Richard Sampson's Nashville home. It was a nice home, in a nice neighborhood, but not the ostentatious show-off that Tony was expecting. The two story brick colonial had black shutters and a white front door. Hydrangeas decorated the home in traditional southern style.

Richard Sampson's car was still in the driveway. Good. Tony would stay alert this time. He would not repeat the same mistake twice.

JULES LISTENED to her daughter explain the events of the previous night. Considering the drama her daughter had been through she could not find it in herself to punish Claire for sneaking out and drinking.

"Chloe must have been worried when she couldn't find you at the party. When did you finally respond to her text?"

"This morning. I wanted her to freak out. She deserves it."

"Are you sure that's fair? Did she know you liked Shawn?"

Claire was silent for a long time.

"Well, no. I guess you're right. I never told her. It doesn't matter anymore. I can't stop thinking about Stephanie. About the other girls."

"Neither can I, that's why we're doing what we're doing. Hopefully after tonight, those girls in the pictures will be free to go home."

When they arrived home, Jules filled a hot bath and sent Claire to bed. Jules gave herself three hours to nap. She placed her cell phone by the bed, connected it to the charger, and fell asleep instantly. When she awoke she found Claire snuggled up with Carolyn on the living room sofa, watching a movie. Jules phoned Stella and checked on her boys, made a pot of strong coffee, and than began gathering her things.

In her backpack she placed the written statement, copies of all of Sampson's log books, copies of the photographs of the girls, the complete list of pimps, and the dossiers of Sampson's Chilean partners. She also included copies of the video surveillance from JJ's cameras, and the video from Brian Fielding's SD card.

When she felt she had everything ready to go, Jules took a break to snuggle with her daughter and mother-in-law.

MONICA AND DOUGLAS arrived at Owen Roberts International Airport at 12:10 pm Thursday afternoon with two overnight bags. It took them 20 minutes by cab to get to the Grand Cayman Hotel, where they checked in as Mr. and Mrs. Tim Holloway.

At 1:15 pm, Tim Holloway exited the Grand Cayman Hotel. With briefcase in hand, Mr. Holloway walked across the street and entered the Grand Cayman International Bank.

At 2:00 pm, Douglas sent a text to Mitch.
'done'

Then Douglas texted a series of numbers to JJ, along with the password 'redeemed'.

JJ AND MITCH arrived at Transport Express at 2:15 pm. Jason was at the front desk.

"JJ! Are you ready to tell me what's going on?"

"Not yet, but it's almost over. You can let Sampson know he can come back now. We'll be in his office."

"You're not going to hurt him are you J?"

JJ laughed. On the contrary, he almost felt sorry for Richard Sampson. He was about to deliver some very bad news.

Sampson arrived at his office at 2:45 pm.

"I'm sorry about this morning, Sir, there was nothing I could do...."

Sampson cut Jason off with his hand in the air.

"It's ok, Jason. I needed the morning off anyways."

Richard Sampson actually smiled at Jason. Jason was overwhelmed. He had never seen Sampson smile.

"What the hell is going on?" Sampson walked into his open office to find JJ in his desk chair, and Mitch sitting across from him. The smile had left his face.

Mitch stood and offered the chair.

"Take a seat, Dick."

"I will not, what are you two up to? How did you get in here?" Sampson was incredulous.

"Take a seat, Dick." Mitch spoke with authority, and handed Richard Sampson his statement. He walked around to the side of the desk and sat up on the corner.

Sampson looked down at the paper in his hands, then back up at JJ and Mitch. JJ would later describe the look on Richard Sampson's face as a combination of disbelief, sorrow, and relief. The letter read:

December 19, 2012
Agent Aguirre,

I am ready to pursue our agreement. Enclosed you will find documentation of the entire operation, my Chilean contacts, a complete list of all individuals involved with contact information, a record of many of the girls who have passed through my doors, and video surveillance evidence.

I am requesting protection for my family, including my daughter and her family, immediately upon delivery of this evidence. Details of the next money exchange are enclosed in this package. Thank you for your help in this matter.

Richard Sampson

Sampson looked at the pile on his desk and recognized his log books and files. He finally sat.

"It's over, Dick." Mitch said. "At 4:00 pm this letter will be delivered to agent Robert Aguirre, along with all pertinent documentation. We've kept these out for you." Mitch handed Sampson a folder containing all of the documents, letters, and photos tying Richard Sampson to Colonia Dignidad, and his service in the army.

"I'm sorry. Truly sorry. I can't say that I understand, or even like you, but I am sorry for the circumstances of your life. Tomorrow, an article will appear in the Nashville Journal outlining the overnight arrest of Richard Sampson, his colleagues, and two Chilean men for operating a human trafficking ring. Eventually, police will be looking for Tim Holloway for the theft of the operation's proceeds, as well as the contents of your Cayman Island account. They will never find him."

JJ continued. "You will be safe, with your family. You will be granted a new life, in a new place. And according to the rest of the world, Richard Sampson will be living in a Tennessee prison for the next twenty five years."

Mitch finished. "Ownership of The Office and Transport Express will be returned to me and JJ respectively, as outlined in the original ownership documents the police will find when they examine your hard drive."

Sampson was speechless. He stared at the ground for a long time, then finally looked up at the two men before him.

"I should go home, and talk to my wife." Richard Sampson took his files, and left. It was the last time either Mitch or JJ saw their old business partner.

Thirty Nine

JULES DROPPED the backpack off to Agent Robert Aguirre, Thursday afternoon, at 4:00 pm sharp.

"This is everything you told me about?"

"Yes, you'll find everything you need in that pack. The money exchange is tonight at midnight."

"Well, if I find what I think I'm going to find in here," Aguirre tapped on the backpack, "then we'll have the police waiting for them."

Agent Aguirre gave Jules his card and she left for home. There was nothing to do now but wait, again.

"JULES, COME HERE quick!" Mitch called Jules into the family room, where he was watching news anchor Lauren Murphy, standing outside Transport Express, on Channel Two News. It was 7:00 am Monday morning.

"Following a two year long TBI investigation, Metro Police arrested a local business man, two of his co-workers, and two South American men early Friday morning, in a large scale human trafficking ring." Murphy reported.

Images on the screen showed police placing Richard Sampson and the two Chileans into police cars. The next image was a headshot of Mayor Schoals.

"Implicated in the scandalous crime is our own Mayor Tom Schoals, who police allege was seen at a private auction in which foreign teenage girls were sold as sexual slaves. Officials at the Mayor's Nashville office have no comment at this time."

"Acting on information gathered by TBI, Metro Police and FBI agents are working together on this complicated case. So far, FBI agents have raided sixty five homes, and four brothels throughout all of Tennessee, Georgia, and Alabama, and recovered over fifty women and girls between the ages of twelve to twenty-five."

A TBI spokesperson was facing the camera. "This is one of the largest human trafficking operations we've uncovered in the country. We hope to be able to return each of these girls to their families. The unfortunate truth however, is that some of these girls come from environments that make it too risky to return. Poverty, ignorance, and certain cultural climates actually encourage the practice of trafficking. We will have to carefully evaluate each case individually before re-uniting these girls with their families."

Lauren Murphy returned to the screen.

"We will continue to update you with breaking news on these shocking events as they come in. Reporting live from Nashville, this is Lauren Murphy, Channel 2 News."

Jules looked at Mitch. "It's over."

"It's over." Mitch said back to Jules.

AT 9 AM Friday, December 20, Tim Holloway made a wire transfer in the amount of five million dollars from his Cayman Island account, to Devin Trousdale's Tennessee Bank and Credit Union account. The following Monday, Devin Trousdale arrived at the credit union and asked to speak to Shirley.

"I would like to purchase several cashier's checks." Trousdale handed Shirley a piece of paper with the account number.

After a few clicks of her mouse, Shirley looked at Mr. Trousdale with one raised eyebrow. "I'm sorry sir, deposits this large are held for a minimum of five to seven business days. Those funds won't be available until next week."

Devin Trousdale leaned in close to whisper to Shirley.

"Think of this as one last favor for Richard Sampson."

Devin thought he saw Shirley wince, before turning her attention to her computer monitor.

Devin Trousdale purchased four cashier's checks, each in the amount of one million dollars, addressed to End Slavery Tennessee, and withdrew the remaining one million in cash. Devin placed each cashier's check in an envelope, and drove to the ESTN office.

Devin peeked his head in the door as he knocked.

"May I help you?" The woman at the desk smiled at the stranger.

"I just wanted to drop these off."

Devin Trousdale placed four million dollars on the desk, smiled, and walked out of the office.

278

The Nashville Journal
Justin Toomey- writer
December 23, 2012

Acting on information from TBI, Metro Police arrested local businessman Richard Sampson over the weekend, for his involvement in a scandal that has rocked this Nashville community.

For over ten years, Richard Sampson has operated a human trafficking ring that spans two continents. TBI, in conjunction with the FBI and local law enforcement, has been investigating the operation for the past two years, and on Friday, conducted a sting operation which resulted in the arrest of Richard Sampson and two Chilean men , Alejandro Espiranza and Frances Muniz, on three hundred counts of human trafficking.

TBI spokesperson Laurel Hayes reports, "This isn't even a drop in the bucket compared to the extent of this operation. We estimate that Richard Sampson is responsible for the exploitation of over 1,000 individuals over the past decade. We are very fortunate to have very strong evidence and feel certain we will be able to achieve a conviction on at least 150 counts."

The victims in this case include mostly young women up to twenty-three years old, and young girls between the ages of twelve and eighteen. Approximately two percent of the individuals we've been able to identify, however, have been boys aged eight to sixteen.

Law enforcement officers have been able to identify over forty five pimps and fifteen brothel owners from Tennessee, Alabama, and Georgia. At this point, twenty five arrests have been made.

Human trafficking has many faces, and this investigation has revealed a surprising fact. A small percentage of the victims identified in the Sampson Ring, as it's being called, are local teenage girls, living at home with their parents.

According to Hayes, "There is a growing trend to force local girls into prostitution. These girls are tricked into participating by someone they trust. The pimp will then threaten them into continued quiet submission. We've identified over fifteen teen girls across the state who are currently living at home, going to school and living out a 'normal' life on the outside, but living a very secret life as a prostitute at night."

It is estimated that the sale of humans for sexual exploitation and forced labor generates over thirty million dollars a year, making it the second largest criminal enterprise in the world. It is also the fastest growing criminal enterprise in the world. Investigators from the Netherlands reported that a single sex slave could earn her pimp over $250,000 per year.

At this moment, twenty seven million people are in slavery, thirteen million of those are children. There are more slaves in the world today than ever in history. Human trafficking occurs in over one hundred and thirty countries, including the United States. Over one hundred thousand young American women and children are sexually exploited every year.

The Sampson Ring (SR) dealt to individual pimps, brothel owners, and private high end clients, called johns.

According to Nashville Journal sources, several prominent Nashville citizens are among SR log books, including Mayor Tom Schoals. It has been alleged that our Mayor has been a long time client of SR, and maintains an apartment in Brentwood where he keeps a young girl. Attempts to speak with the Mayor, or his representative have been denied.

Sandra Wallace, with the Tennessee Department of Children's Services' Human trafficking division explains the difficulty in handling victim rescue following discoveries of this nature.

"Treacherous conditions, disease, and neglect take a large toll on these victims, and often, after a few years these children become sick, and often die. Pimps and brothel owners will care for children as long as they are generating an income. Once the child becomes an expense, they are discarded. Many trafficked children end up on the street, or dead. A large percentage of these children will never be found."

Women and girls who have been trafficked for sexual exploitation often suffer from sexually transmitted diseases, including HIV, and permanent reproductive damage.

Ms. Wallace stated, "Our goal is to place all recovered victims back at home with their families. But the reality is that some home situations are not suitable for return. Poverty puts a family at grave risk for falling into trafficking. It's hard to believe, but some parents actually sell their children in order to survive."

She continues "Some of the victims we recover come from cultures in which sexual exploitation is so prevalent, we would be putting the child at risk by sending them back to their communities. In places like Cambodia, for instance, folk wisdom teaches that having sexual intercourse with a child will bring youth and vitality, or even cure disease like HIV. We will work diligently to find a permanent, safe home for each child we are unable to return to their homeland."

Much of the Nashville business community is in shock following Friday's revelation. Richard Sampson has been an outstanding member of the Nashville business community since the 1980's. He is the founder of Pathways, a managed care company, and more recently the CEO of two small businesses, Transport Express trucking company, and The Office, a small business incubator in North Nashville. He is a member of the Better Business Bureau, the Nashville Small Business Association, and the Entrepreneurship Center. Richard Sampson is currently in custody at the Nashville State Penitentiary, awaiting arraignment.

Police are also looking for Richard Sampson's assistant, Tim Holloway, for questioning in the Sampson Ring investigation. Tim Holloway has not been seen since Wednesday, December 18, 2012.

The Nashville Journal will continue to publish updates on this incredible case.

JJ'S PHONE alerted him at 2:00 pm Monday, December 30. Mitch was texting.

'need to talk. can u meet here at 3'

'yep'

JJ walked into the reception at The Office at 2:58. It was odd to walk into this place, in broad daylight.

"I have an appointment with Mitch Spalding"

"You can go right in, he's expecting you." Celia smiled sweetly at JJ.

Mitch greeted JJ with a hug and motioned for him to sit down on Richard Sampson's large leather chair. Mitch sat behind the grand mahogany desk. Mitch had only been back in The

Office for one day, the place had been taken over by police and forensic investigators until today.

"How are you, boss?" Mitch smiled big at JJ

"Good, real good. Just in the process of unpacking right now. You seem to be settling in well. I didn't take you for an uptown guy."

Mitch laughed. "Ha, I don't see myself in this much longer. I have a meeting with a decorator next week."

"Decorator? Why Mitch Spalding, have you come into some money?" JJ winked.

"I've looked at these documents over and over to the point where I feel like I've memorized every line. For some reason, this page keeps grabbing my attention." Mitch handed JJ a copy of the dossier of Frances Muniz.

"This impression at the bottom caught my attention, and Ive become a little obsessed over it. I think I've finally figured it out." Mitch retrieved the paper from JJ, and turned it over. On the back, JJ saw pencil marking over the area. The pencil revealed the reverse of an imprint. It was a series of numbers.

"Do these numbers mean anything to you?" Mitch asked JJ.

JJ looked at the numbers, then looked up at Mitch with wide eyes. Very slowly he spoke.

"They look like numbers to an anonymous account."

"That's what I thought. Do you think you can look into this?" Mitch handed JJ a sticky note with the numbers written in ink.

"I'll see what I can find out." JJ smiled at Mitch, took the paper and left.

Forty

Kissimmee Reporter
Howard Sheraton- reporter
January 3, 2013

*Fisherman Bobby Mullins caught a big one yesterday out on
Johns Lake. At 12:30 pm, Mr. Mullins was fishing with his son
when his line snagged on something. As Mr. Mullins worked to
free his line, he was surprised to pull up a windshield wiper. After
a closer look, Mr. Mullins saw a car, about two feet under the
surface.*

*Police were called in to investigate, and eventually drug a 2010
tan Mercedes G class SUV from the lake. No license plates were
found on the vehicle, and the vehicle identification number has
been etched off. Police are asking for help identifying the vehicle.
If you have any information that could help, please call the
Florida State Police Crimestoppers Hotline at (888) 555-5486.*

      AGENT AGUIRE hung up his phone and called Jules into
his office.

"Good to see you, Jules, thanks for coming in."

"Is everything ok? Your assistant said it was urgent." The call Jules received earlier that day disturbed her. For the past week, she had felt relief, and was beginning to relax. The urgent call from the TBI office made her uneasy.

"Everything's fine. I'm sorry Sally worried you. I've called you in to give you an update, I thought you deserved one, considering the help you've been to our investigation."

"Oh, ok." Jules took a deep breath and sat down.

Agent Aguirre placed a stack of photos on the desk and slid them over to Jules.

"The following people have been arrested and are awaiting trial. They have been charged with trafficking of humans in the Tennessee court. The DA feels certain he has enough to gain convictions on all of them."

Jules flipped through the pictures- close to fifty in all, men and women who had purchased another human being for profit. It made her sick. One of the photos struck her. It was of a very handsome young man. He looked so young. Jules thought he could have been a teen himself. She lingered on the photograph.

"That's Tony Baker. He and his brother were independent contractors in Franklin, TN."

"What does that mean?" Jules remembered seeing the Baker Brothers' name on the back of the photo of the girl Claire recognized.

"Well they weren't truly independent. Much like the prostitutes themselves, these guys owe some kind of debt to the traffickers, a drug debt most likely. Traffickers use drugs to lure in "clients". The Baker Brothers owed Sampson for the drugs, so they would prostitute young girls and pay a percentage back to Sampson. This would go on until the debt is paid. Sampson gains control by keeping the contractors and their girls dependent on the drugs. As long as they keep coming back for the drugs, their debt is never paid."

"So now what? What happens to those girls who worked for the independent contractors?"

"They're free. For now anyways. We've located almost 20 of the girls. Sampson kept good records. But conviction of trafficking of humans still carries short sentences, sometimes as little as six years. Hopefully, in that time, these girls will grow up, move, and never have to worry about their captors again. The Baker Brothers, however, have prior convictions for drugs and breaking and entering. This is their third strike, they will likely see life in prison."

"When will we know for sure?"

"It could be six months to a year before these bastards go to trial. But you can rest assured they will not see outside before then. None have been granted bail."

"Good. And Richard Sampson?"

"You will never see him again."

"Good." Jules stood up to leave.

"Jules..."

Jules turned and looked to Agent Aguirre. "Yes?"

"Don't let your guard down just yet. We still haven't located Tim Holloway. I'd be careful if I were you."

"Sure, thanks." Jules turned quickly and walked out the door.

"GOOD MORNING Celia!" Mitch Spalding walked into The Office on Friday, January 3, 2013 in a great mood. A chapter in his life was over, and life was beginning to feel exciting again. Fitting for the beginning of the year.

"Good morning Mitch." Celia smiled at Mitch. She liked him. For the past year she had heard many things about Mitch Spalding, most of them from Richard Sampson, and most of them untrue. She was seeing the real Mitch Spalding for the first time, and she was grateful he was her boss.

Mitch's cell phone alerted him as he entered his office.

'meet in an hour over here' It was JJ.

'see you then'.

Mitch arrived at Transport Express at 10:00 am.

"What's up, boss?" Mitch knocked on the open door to JJ's office. He walked in and sat down in the chair across the desk from JJ. JJ's classic toy 18-wheeler sat on his desk, next to a framed photograph of a young blond woman.

"Who's this? I don't recall hearing about her?" The girl in the picture was pretty.

"That's Penny. It's a long story. Lets' just say she's re-entered my life recently." JJ's smile revealed he was extremely happy with this.

"So.....I'm assuming you've found something out?"

"Yeah, those numbers are account numbers, just as you suspected. They're Swiss, and they belong to the Chileans."

"How can you be sure?"

"Well, the fact that they were written on the Chilean's dossier was a good clue. But I was able to get into the account and view the transactions. The money flows from several different South American banks into this account, and then there are periodic withdrawals. Currently the balance is $9.3 million, but over the past five years, over $150 million has traveled through this account."

"Holy Shit!" Mitch could not believe what he was hearing. "Can you do something with that money?"

"Your wish is my command, boss."

JULES DROVE CLAIRE to the address she found in the school directory. The Miller's house was a two story, whitewashed brick, cottage style home, with window boxes that were empty this time of year. Jules stayed in the car as Claire walked up the walk to the front door.

Susan Miller answered the door. "Can I help you?"

"Hi, my name is Claire, and I go to school with Stephanie. I was wondering if I could see her for a minute?"

Since moving to Tennessee, Susan Miller had never met another girl who wanted to hang out with her daughter. Claire was pretty and clean cut, and Susan Miller was thrilled.

"Sure, Claire. Come on in and have a seat. Let me go get her for you."

Claire sat down on a sofa in the living room and waited.

Stephanie was surprised when she walked out into the living room. She recognized the girl on her sofa, but could not remember how she'd known her.

"Hi." Claire stood up when she saw Stephanie entering the room. She wasn't sure how she would be received.

"Do I know you?" Stephanie was inherently suspicious of everyone.

"We met, briefly, at Dooley's party."

"Oh." Stephanie could not remember.

"Look, I don't want to bother you, I just came to give you this." Claire handed Stephanie a newspaper clipping. Stephanie looked at Claire with a surprised look.

Before she left, Claire approached Stephanie and pulled her close. Claire whispered in Stephanie's ear, "you're free", then left the Millers' home.

Williamson Herald
Jackson Harris
January 25, 2013

Three Williamson County men were arrested on several counts of trafficking of humans yesterday, in a Williamson County court. Two of the men, brothers Tony and Randall Baker, have been operating a prostitution ring in Williamson County for the past five years. They have been charged with forcing over twenty young girls into prostitution. All of the victims in this case are minors, with the youngest only twelve years old.

The Baker Brothers, as they are known to law enforcement, are no stranger to the courts. Previous convictions for drug distribution and breaking and entering make this current arrest their third strike. Both brothers will be facing life in prison.

The third man, Oliver Sparks, worked as a guidance counselor at West Franklin High School. He has been arrested for solicitation. Mr. Sparks has been fired from his position with the high school, and has lost his teaching license.

The Washington Post
Justin Toomey- staff writer
January 31, 2013

For the past two weeks, Metro Police and the FBI have been looking for a person of interest in the Sampson Ring, as it is being called in Nashville, TN.

The Sampson Ring is one of the largest human trafficking operations uncovered in the United States to date, and was run by

Nashville entrepreneur, Richard Sampson. Currently, over one hundred and twenty five individuals have been charged in connection with the trafficking operation.

Police are now looking for Richard Sampson's assistant, Tim Holloway. Holloway is wanted for questioning regarding his involvement in the Sampson Ring. Police have been unable to locate Tim Holloway, and sources say that until yesterday, there has been no trace of the Nashville native.

Sources close to this case have informed this writer of suspicious funds transfers made into accounts owned by Tim Holloway over the past several weeks. First, on December 19, 2012, a wire transfer in the amount of five million dollars was made from Richard Sampson's offshore account in the Cayman Islands, to a Cayman Island account owned by Tim Holloway.

Then, on January 4, 2013, over nine million dollars was transferred from a numbered account in Switzerland, to Tim Holloway's offshore account in the Cayman Islands. Our sources allege that the funds originated from an account operated by Richard Sampson's Chilean partners, Frances Muniz and Alejandro Espiranza. These men are currently in a Tennessee State Prison, awaiting trial for their involvement in the Sampson Ring.

Police investigators have declined to comment on these allegations, and have stated that they are 'looking into it'. Bank secrecy laws have made it difficult for state police investigators to access Holloway's account information. The FBI has opened an official investigation of Tim Holloway, but has declined to comment.

Holloway's role in the Sampson Ring is unclear, and police are reluctant to speculate publicly. But sources tell this writer that

Tim Holloway had been a long-time assistant to Richard Sampson, and had held a grudge towards his employer. Tennessee State Police are asking anyone who may recognize the photo below, to please call their hotline at (888) 555-4592.

THE SOUND OF a loud voice woke him, and the moment he opened his eyes, the pounding pierced his skull. Closing his eyes, he brought his hands to his face and slowly massaged his head until he found the spot. One touch and he remembered.

Tim Holloway opened his eyes once more and forced them to adjust to the light. He wasn't sure where he was, but he heard voices. The bright morning light filtered in through louvered windows that let in a cool breeze and the smell of fresh, salty air. He was in a small light room, on a cot outfitted with fine, soft sheets and a thin blanket.

Standing on shaky legs, Holloway made his way out of the bedroom and into a wide hallway. He followed the sound of the voice to an open room, lined with glass windows. Outside he saw the sea.

"He's alive! Hey Ace, I'll call ya back later." A tall, broad shouldered man put down his phone and approached Tim with his hand extended. "Jim O'Connell, your captain." He spoke with a New York Italian accent.

Holloway stood stunned. The last thing he remembered was dragging that little Spalding bitch into Sampson's office, ready to get paybacks and claim his share of the operation. He remembered feeling hot pain on the back of the head, then nothing, until now.

"What?.............."

"Shhhh, sit. Tony told me you had a rough spill. Rest for a minute." O'Connell led Holloway to an oversized soft leather chair.

"Tony?.............."

"You don't remember anything do you? Sorry pal, that's gotta hurt." O'Connell gestured to his head.

"You don't remember coming to Ramano looking for help?"

"Ramano!"

"Yeah, my cousin Tony. Well sorta, it's a long story. Anyways, he calls me and says he's got this friend who's in a bit of trouble, needs to get out of town and start new, if you know what I mean. And I owes it to Tony, on account of...., well, I just owes it to 'im. So here ya go. These are your new digs, not too shabby eh?"

"Where am I?"

"Alghera, the most beautiful beaches in all of Sardinia. Right over there's the port. I'll take you there tomorrow and show you around. We'll head out on Monday."

"Head out? What are you talking about? Italy? I need to get home."

O'Connell handed Holloway an envelope. "Man, you sure don't remember anything. That bump on your head must have really done you in. I'll give you a few minutes. When you're ready, I've got breakfast cooking in the kitchen, down the hall on your right. You've never tasted coffee like they do it here in Sardinia!"

As O'Connell left the room, Tim Holloway opened the envelope to find several items. A passport, in the name of Jeremy Stutts, from Boise, Idaho. A six month work visa, drivers' license, 2,000 Euros, and a photo copy of an article from the Nashville Journal, dated January 31, 2013.

Holloway read about the bust, the stolen money, and the country-wide search for Richard Sampson's assistant, and understood.   Ramano had given him a second chance. He closed his eyes and breathed in the briny air. Jeremy Stutts smiled contently, and went for his coffee.

JENNIFER JONES SAMPSON finished reading the article and put the paper down on the table beside her. The salt air stung her sunburnt face, and her nose was still sore from the surgery. She was still suffering from the shock and anger of learning of her husband's deceit. But she understood now, it wasn't his choice. Had they ended up in Michigan, or Iowa, or South Texas, Jennifer may not have been as forgiving. But here, on the beach, Jennifer Sampson felt she could get used to her new life.

She watched her granddaughter play in the sand, and saw the smiles on her daughter's face. And she saw the teenaged boy she once knew, 40 years ago, smile and laugh. Yes, life could be good. She was sure of that today.

Nashville Reporter
February 3, 2013
Staff Writer- Obituary

Victor Diaz   - January 31, 2013

Colonel Victor Diaz died last week, of a heart attack. Colonel Diaz was born in Chile and served in the Chilean Army for forty five years. He is survived by his daughter Francisca Sampson, Grandson Richard Sampson, and Great Granddaughter Sophia Sampson Reynolds. Services will be held at Forrest Hills Funeral Home February 5, 2013 at 1:00 pm.

ELIANA SAT IN her bed and looked through the windows. There were no bars this time, only white blinds against a sterile white wall. It felt so good to be clean. The sheets felt like heaven against her skin, and her hair smelled of strawberries and vanilla. The ladies who checked on her were good to her. They smiled at her and kissed her forehead. Eliana was confused by the contradictory feelings.

The virus growing inside her would take her life. The doctors had told her so. Her malnourished state had made Eliana more susceptible, and vulnerable to the fast growing mutation. Eliana could not go home. Her family could not take care of her, and they could not afford to come to her. She had a new home now. They called it Hospice, and she would remain there for the rest of her life.

At night, the vines from her iron garden would come calling. How wonderful, she thought, that they had found her once again. She spent more and more time in the garden, with her father now. He assured her that soon, very soon, she would be with him forever.

Epilogue

SUSAN MILLER opened the door at 4:00 pm, extended her hand, and welcomed her guest.

"Stephanie..." her mother called down the hall. "Suzi is here."

Stephanie slowly emerged from her bedroom, peered down the hall, took a long deep breath and dragged her feet all the way into the living room. She was not sure she could do this. Funny, after everything she had been through, all the pain, the fear, and the horror of her life with Tony paled in comparison to these days. It was easier hiding her troubles, easier pretending it was all a dream. But now, her secret was out. Stephanie felt like the whole world knew. And she was expected to 'heal', to become 'restored', and return to a normal life.

What was normal? How the hell did she know? How do you become normal after something like this? Stephanie didn't think she could ever feel normal. She was damaged and broken. She was a cheap slut, a worthless whore. There was no way she would ever be normal again. And now she has an advocate, an Intervention Specialist, ha! Now she was a charity case, a poster child.

Stephanie had done her research on End Slavery Tennessee. According to the website, their mission is to create a slave-free Tennessee and holistically restore survivors of human trafficking.

'Whatever.' Stephanie thought. All this talk about abolishing slavery and restoring survivors sounded like nonsense to her. No one could ever understand what she went through. No one could stop the evil that flows through the men she encountered. They would always be out there, and she would always be a victim. There was no hope for her.

Stephanie thought the woman coming to visit her that afternoon was a do-gooder. A missionary out to make herself feel better by being nice to the downtrodden. But she knew the truth. There were no guardian angels working on her side. This was not a wonderful life. Suzi White was an arrogant fool to think she could come in here and magically resurrect the old Stephanie Miller. A complete and arrogant fool.

Stephanie made her way into the living room and flopped into the sofa across from Suzi.

"Hi Stephanie, I'm Suzi White, with End Slavery Tennessee. I will be your Intervention Specialist." Suzi White smiled politely and refused to take offense when Stephanie looked the other way.

"I think I'll let you two talk." Mrs. Miller smiled at Suzi and walked out of the room.

Stephanie was conscious of Suzi's gaze, which never left her face. When Stephanie finally gave in and looked her in the eye, Suzi stepped in.

"I was in the life too. Six years. When I got out I never thought I'd ever feel right again." Suzi bent down to meet Stephanie's eyes. "It does get better, I promise. The work is hard, and sometimes you want to just give up and die. But it gets better."

Stephanie turned away again. She didn't want to talk to Suzi White.

STEPHANIE LOOKED AT herself in the mirror for the fifteenth time. Her hair was starting to grow in again. Her face was filling out, but her mouth still hurt from the root canals. The dentist her ESTN case manager took her to was nice, but Stephanie would always associate her with the smell of antiseptic and rotten teeth.

They say full recovery from meth can take years. Stephanie wasn't sure she could make it, although she knew she was different from the others in rehab. The other girls had been smoking for years, and it hurt Stephanie to look at their pockmarked faces and rotting teeth. Stephanie knew that in that place, she was the lucky one, the one that would get away much easier than the rest. But she didn't feel lucky. The pain, insomnia, and the despair constantly beckoned her back to the drugs.

Suzi came to visit her when permitted, at Sunset Rehabilitation Center in Waverly, TN. And eventually, Stephanie began to wake up to the sun, the horses, and the fresh country air. She discovered she liked riding horses as much as she enjoyed tending to them. The powerful, yet peaceful creatures taught Stephanie a great deal, and she actually missed them when she returned to her home in Franklin.

Today, Stephanie was going to meet her new horse, at least her new horse for the time being. For the next three months, Stephanie would spend 12 hours a week learning to ride and care for a mare named Chelsea. Chelsea works for Temple Farms, a non-profit organization that provides equine therapy for young girls and women recovering from drug addiction and abuse. Stephanie thinks Chelsea will be much smarter than Dr. Dragon.

Dr. Dragon is Stephanie's nickname for the counselor her mother had taken her to months ago, before she knew Stephanie was a whore. No, not a whore, 'sexually exploited'. Tony had drilled the word whore so deep into her brain; Stephanie had to work overtime to replace it with the truth.

Dr. Dragon was so nicknamed because of the therapist's open addiction to cigarettes. It made Stephanie sick, physically and mentally. The smell was a constant reminder of dark basements and tiny bedrooms, and Stephanie wondered how a person can claim to 'heal' you of your troubles while continuing to indulge her own. The thoughts distracted her during her sessions.

"Stephanie, you're not paying attention. How are we going to make this work if you won't listen?" Susan Miller nags throughout each session.

Stephanie rolls her eyes, and her father storms out. "This is a waste of time!"

And it was.

Thankfully, End Slavery Tennessee connected the Miller family with Temple Farms. Instead of hashing out past resentments about moving to Tennessee, the family would ride together, learn how to groom the horses, and even master a few tricks and jumps. They actually joked together in the car on the way to the farm. And for the first time, Stephanie felt a glimmer of hope.

MRS. KLIPPINGER arrived every day at 9 am. She was Stephanie's tutor. Stephanie had always thought homeschooling was for religious freaks, retards and social misfits, until it was time for her to return to high school. After eight months of detox, rehabilitation, and counseling, Stephanie was not ready to face the other students of West Franklin High School. It didn't matter that the names of the victims of Sampson's Ring were never released to the public. Stephanie would always feel as if everyone knew. And she sure as hell wasn't willing to start over again as a freshman.

Mrs. Klippinger's eyes danced and smiled as she greeted her. "You must be Stephanie!"

Mrs. Klippinger spent the first day getting to know Stephanie. Or rather, she spent the first day telling her about herself, about her two kittens, Rascal and Tate, about her grandchildren who lived in New Mexico, and about her husband, who was killed in the Vietnam War.

Mrs. Klippinger was gentle, sweet, and patient. She was a spiritual woman, who had known many difficulties and hardships in her life. She was respectful and candid, and treated Stephanie like she was an equal. It was a trick, Stephanie thought, and decided she would not let this woman into her life.

There were others, too. Mrs. Herrera came to the house on Tuesday afternoons to teach Spanish. And after the first six months, on Wednesdays, Stephanie went to the university school for English and science lessons.

It was hard work, but in a little less than a year, Stephanie had almost mastered the ninth and tenth grade. She would be ready to begin her junior year of high school with the rest of the public school crowd. Academically at least. This afternoon, they were studying math; Algebra two.

"Do you mind if I watch?" Susan Miller walked tentatively into the room.

Stephanie glared at her mom. Despite her stubborn attempts to build a wall around herself, she found that she really liked Mrs. Klippinger, and eventually came to look forward to her tutoring sessions. There was no pressure to discuss her feelings, relive her past, or play any bonding games. The focus was her mind, which she discovered was one great big sponge, ready to absorb everything in its midst. Stephanie loved learning. As her mind opened to new information it was like emerging into a whole new world, all within the safety of Mrs. Klippinger's smiling eyes. And now her mom was intruding.

"Moooom....." Stephanie began to protest.

"I'll stay out of the way, I promise, but I could really use a little help myself. I have no idea why I need to understand quadratic equations for nursing school, but if I don't figure it out, I won't pass the entrance exams. Let me just glean a little from your lessons?" Susan Miller smiled at her daughter like a toddler begging for ice cream.

"Fine," Stephanie sighed, and turned back to her problem. She tried to ignore the fact that her overbearing mother was watching over her shoulder.

Overbearing was an understatement. Since the day her mother learned that Stephanie had been trafficked, she kept a protective watch over her daughter. At first Stephanie didn't notice. She didn't notice much of anything, tucked away in rehab, and then in her room for days on end. But as she began to emerge from her trauma induced seclusion, as she began to heal (she never thought she use that word), Stephanie felt the need for some independence. And that's when her mother's obsessive watchfulness began to drive her crazy.

Despite the apologies, the forgiveness exercises, and the intense family therapy sessions, Stephanie still struggled to let go of the anger and resentment she held towards her parents, who had turned their backs on her when she really needed help. Had they listened to her that very first day, her life may have turned out differently. No, they didn't put the meth in her hands, or hand her over to her traffickers, but her parents refused to see the signs of her victimization. Instead, they assumed she was a rebellious, reckless, vindictive teenager. And that hurt more than any cigarette burn or human bite ever would.

Susan Miller didn't stay out of the way at all. She asked question after question. Stephanie's agitation grew, until her mother asked a question that was so asinine, Stephanie had to laugh.

"Are you laughing at me Stephanie?" Susan Miller was a little offended by her daughter's arrogance, but felt simultaneously happy to hear her daughter laugh.

"Mom, are you serious? This is the easiest part....."
Stephanie took over the lesson, and began to show her mother
how to factor the equation and solve for x, while Mrs. Klippinger
sat back and watched. Susan asked more questions, and Stephanie
answered them. She was patient, and when Susan finally got it,
Stephanie jumped up and clapped with such exaggeration she fell
back over her chair, and onto the floor.

Susan Miller couldn't contain herself. Her laughing began
as a snicker, and erupted into full snorts in a matter of seconds. At
first, Stephanie looked at her mother in disgusted surprise. But as
she struggled to right herself and stand up she slipped and landed
back on her rear again. Stephanie looked up and saw her mother
trying hard to stifle another laugh, and finally let go. There was
no fighting it. She had not laughed in almost two years, and if felt
good. Susan Miller got down on the floor, placed her arms around
her daughter, and the two sat and laughed until they cried. Mrs.
Klippinger excused herself, but no one was listening.

"HOW LONG did it take?" Stephanie asked Suzi, during
one of her many middle of the night phone calls. She couldn't
sleep again.

Suzi didn't need to ask. She knew exactly what Stephanie
wanted to know, what Stephanie was agonizing over.

"I have to be honest, Steph, it has been a long road. But
you and I are different, ya know? I didn't have a mom and dad,
anyone to come home to."

"What happened to them?" For the first time, Stephanie
realized she knew very little about Suzi. She felt selfish for not
getting to know this person who had been her closest friend and
ally for the past year.

"It don't matter. They're just gone. When I got out, I lived with the Terrell's for almost a year. There were four other kids there, and one of 'em was mean. " Suzi paused for several minutes before continuing.

"Bobby Terrell teased me something fierce. He used to get real close to my face and say 'you sure is a pretty little nigger.....' If it weren't for Miss Judy I would've gone back to the life, or ended up in jail, or worse."

"What happened?"

"She got me a phone." Suzi began to laugh. "And boy, you should have seen how afraid of that phone Bobby Terrell was." Her laughs were hearty and full, real.

"I told that bully if he even looked me in the eye again I'd cry rape and send him to juvy. The first time I pulled out that phone and pretended to dial 911 he started to cry. 'I'm sorry, I'm sorry' he says." Suzi laughed so hard she had tears in her eyes.

"I carried that cell phone with me all the time, and if he even looked at me I would pull it out and wave it in his face. He never bothered me again. Miss Judy used to tell me, 'self-defense starts up here.'" Suzi tapped at her temple. "She was right."

"Miss Judy was your case manager from End Slavery Tennessee?" Stephanie asked.

"She was my case manager, mentor, and only friend. I wouldn't be alive without her. I won't lie to you; it's been hard, so hard that there were a lot of times I thought going back to the life would be easier. When I came out I didn't even know my real name. I had been in the life so long I didn't know how to read or write, I didn't have an ID, or know my social security number, things most people don't even think about. Miss Judy stuck with me, got me educated."

Suzi paused for a minute, while Stephanie let the words soak in.

"When I was 18 years old I got to leave the Terrell's house, but I had no job, no skills, and was reading at a fifth grade level. I'd had so many prostitution charges on my record, even

McDonald's wouldn't hire me. Miss Judy brought me to a woman's home- for people like me, and woman running from abuse, or just getting out of jail. She paid for my stay for the first few months, bought me clothes and food, and helped me find a job at the grocery store across the street. The manager there was nice enough to give me a chance."

"It never leaves you though. I'm sorry to tell you that, but it's true. What I'm doing now, right now with you, that's what keeps me going. I'm happy now. I never knew what that felt like, but now I do. I am learning to trust people, learning to trust men, and live and have fun. And being able to help girls like me gives me hope. That's something I've never experienced in my life."

THE NEXT FIVE years would continue to challenge Stephanie Miller, a human trafficking survivor. At sixteen years old, she would have to muster up the courage to challenge her trafficker in court, and relive the worst five months of her life. Stephanie would spend years in counseling, working through feelings of worthlessness, self-loathing, fear of intimacy, and anger. While her relationship with her parents improved over time, Stephanie wondered if she would ever feel the true forgiveness she read about.

She would not return to public high school. She couldn't bear it. Stephanie did not feel strong enough to return to the school she associated with boys that tricked girls, girls that judged girls, and authority figures that abused their power and exploited girls.

Stephanie would finish the eleventh and twelfth grades at Carlton Academy, an expensive private school in south Franklin for kids who have struggled with traumatic events. Her tuition would be subsidized by the donations of private citizens who recognize the tremendous needs of trafficking victims.

These citizens would support Stephanie Miller for the rest of her life. They would fund research and training efforts designed to prevent the exploitation of others. They would fund counseling centers and rehabilitation services that helped survivors with the most basic needs of physical and emotional rehabilitation from abuse, neglect, torture, and rape. They would purchase clothes and food for women who had nothing, shelter and transportation to go to work. These citizens provided agencies like End Slavery Tennessee the funding needed to abolish slavery in Tennessee and America, and holistically restore survivors of human trafficking.

"NORMAL IS SUBJECTIVE." Stephanie tells Mandy, a fourteen-year-old Hispanic girl sitting next to her in the waiting room. "You will probably never feel normal again, at least not the way you used to think of normal. You will always imagine that other girls are judging you, that the boys want to eat you alive, and that the cops want to condemn you."

Mandy was referred to End Slavery Tennessee by the Tennessee Victim's Specialist of the FBI. She was released from the hospital three weeks ago, after being rescued from a guerrilla pimp in Murfreesboro, TN. Stephanie accompanies her to her first appointment with her new counselor. She looks over at the scared little girl sitting beside her, who is withdrawn and refuses to look at her.

"I know it sounds like a cliché, but you will find a 'new normal'. It does get better."

The circumstance and characters in this story are fictional, and the sole creation of this authors' mind. However, the events are based on true stories.

Paul Schafer was a Nazi who started Colonia Dignidad, molested young boys, and aided the Pinochet government in the torture, murder, and disappearances of tens of thousands of individuals.

Human trafficking is very real, and the stories of Stephanie Miller and Eliana are based on real life stories of girls who have suffered horrible abuses at the hands of traffickers, brothel owners, pimps, and johns.

Human trafficking is a real problem in Nashville, TN.

The events surrounding the investigation, exposure, and arrests of individuals involved in Sampson's Ring have been dramatized for the sake of fiction, but in reality, good men and women of the Tennessee Bureau of Investigation, the Federal Bureau of Investigation, and state and local police authorities work tirelessly every day to stop the horrific practice of trafficking human beings for forced labor and sexual exploitation. And agencies like End Slavery Tennessee work around the clock to stop human trafficking, and support survivors of this terrible crime.

A portion of the proceeds of your purchase have gone to aid in the fight against human trafficking. Thank You!

Statistics on Human Trafficking

Slavery is simply involuntary servitude, but the law defines Human Trafficking, or Trafficking in Persons (TIP), like this:

An act or attempted act of recruiting, transporting, transferring, harboring or receiving a person by means of force, abduction, fraud, coercion, purchase, sale, threats, abuse of power for the purpose of exploitation.

Child/Human Trafficking is one of the fastest growing crimes in the world. Child/ human trafficking is the world's second largest criminal enterprise, after drugs. *U.S. State Department*

300,000 Children in the US are at risk for commercial sexual exploitation
US Department of Justice

Approximately 80% of human trafficking victims are women and girls and up to 50% are minors. *U.S. State Department*

Worldwide

27 million: number of slaves in the world, more than at any time in history

$90: Average cost of a slave

$32 billion dollar industry

2 children are trafficked every minute

In the US

12-14: Average age of entry into prostitution

7 years: Average life of a commercial sex slave, once trafficked

83% of victims in confirmed sex-trafficking incidents were identified as U.S. citizens

33% of all runaways will be sexually exploited within 48 hours

90% of all runaways will eventually end up in the commercial sex trade

In Tennessee

85: Counties reported at least 1 case of human trafficking in 2011

4: Counties reported over 100 cases of human trafficking in 2011

1,000: Number of the reported minor runaways taken by traffickers each year; these are just the ones reported.

In Nashville

Over 100: Cases of minor sex trafficking reported in Davidson County in 2011

Over 100: Cases of adult sex trafficking in Davidson County in 2011

For more information on how you can get involved....

End Slavery Tennessee:
http://www.endslaverytn.org

Homeland Security
http://www.dhs.gov/topic/human-trafficking

United Nations Office on Drugs and Crime:
http://www.unodc.org/unodc/en/human-trafficking/what-is-human-trafficking.html

FBI
http://www.fbi.gov/about-us/investigate/civilrights/human_trafficking

Polaris Project
http://www.polarisproject.org/

www.sampsonsring.com